THE
STALIN
STAIN

W. H. MEFFORD

Fulton Books, Inc.
Meadville, PA

Published by Fulton Books 2021

ISBN 978-1-63710-379-1 (paperback)
ISBN 978-1-63710-380-7 (digital)

Printed in the United States of America

This work is dedicated to my family and friends; the sun, the moon, and the stars; and those out there still fightin' the good fight. And Alice.

It didn't do you any harm. That's why you turned out so well.

> —Said to Stalin by his mother Keke right before her death when the dictator asked the old woman why, in his youth, she beat him so hard.

You'd have done better to have become a priest.

> —Stalin's mother, Keke, to her mass-murdering son when he told her he was like a Russian Tsar.

There was blood, always a great deal of blood wherever the small dark man turned up.

> —Trotsky speaking about Stalin

But one must sometimes correct history.

> —Stalin

Death solves all problems. No man, no problem.

> —Stalin

Every crime was possible for Stalin, and there was not one he had not committed. Whatever standards we use to take his measure, he has the glory of being the greatest criminal in history and, let us hope, for all time to come.

—Milovan Dijilas, Yugoslavian Dissident.

When small men begin to cast big shadows, it means that the sun is about to set.

—Lin Yutang, Writer and Translator

Let him rot.

—An eighteen-year-old Soviet high school student upon learning of Stalin's death.

Lenin left us a great inheritance and we, his heirs, have fucked it all up.

—Stalin to his inner circle of minions

When Stalin says, "Dance," a wise man dances.

—Khrushchev

I am guarding the gold, the gold
I am burying the gold, burying the gold
Guess where, pure damsel with your golden hair.

—One of Stalin's favorite songs to sing

PROLOGUE

Joseph Stalin was not his real name.

As the homicidal dictator of the Soviet Empire for nearly three decades, he ruled the largest country in the world, covering one-seventh of the earth's land surface, an area so vast it nearly exceeded the land surface of the planet Pluto. And yet, this leader of the Soviet Empire did not have a drop of true Slavic Russian blood coursing through his veins.

His birth name was not Stalin but Joseph Vissarionovich Dzhugashvili, and his heritage was not Slavic Russian but Georgian, which meant his blood ran closer to Persian than ethnic Russian. Many Slavic Russians considered Georgians to be an inferior culture.

He had almost oriental eyes that flashed a wolf's yellow when he was angry. His skin was swarthy and horribly pitted. He was diminutive in stature, who Truman would disrespect by calling him "the little squirt." He walked in a quirky, pigeon-toed nearly sideways gait as a result of an accident to his legs in his youth. He spoke the Russian language with a prominent, discordant, and almost comical Georgian accent, which he never lost.

Behind his back, those brave or imprudent or foolish enough would mimic the odd way he walked and talked. And yet, shamefully, the ignorant, feudal Russian peasants would allow this non-Slavic, non-Russian "foreigner," a Georgian cobbler's son, to command their country as a demigod while he indiscriminately slaughtered twenty-five million, perhaps millions more, of their fellow countrymen. They would soon learn that, to Stalin the Great, human life was irrelevant. His all-consuming drive for power had little need for a sense of morality. Joseph Dzhugashvili was personally unencumbered by empathy and reality, and his strategy was to use murder as an instrument of political power while he allowed the ideal of Bolshevism to degenerate into the reality of Fascism. He likely killed millions more than Hitler ever did. He once said, "Death is the solution to all problems—no man, no problem."

Prior to Stalin becoming the godlike tyrant of the Soviet Empire, he was many other things. He was a choirboy with an angel's voice singing vespers in white surplices, a seminarian studying to be a bishop, who, after a single year, became an atheist, a romantic poet, an underground revolutionary, a political manipulator, a secret double agent who reported on his own people, and a violent gangster, bank robber, protection racketeer, extortionist, kidnapper, pirate, and arsonist. He also procreated many illegitimate children across the face of Russia.

Joseph Dzhugashvili was born dirt poor in the little, far away Caucasian town of Gori at the mouth of the Kura River in the raucous independent Kingdom of Georgia. The tumultuous town was geographically closer to Baghdad than it was to the then Russian Tsarist capital of St. Petersburg. Georgians were decidedly not Russian as they had their own language, traditions, food, culture, and independent spirit. It was whispered that the baby boy Joseph was born with six toes, but, more accurately, his foot deformity was that the second and third toes were fused together. Such deformities in superstitious Georgia were thought to be the sign of intervention by diabolical forces. Some whispered that he wore a devil's hoof inside his shoe.

His father, called Beso, was a morose, illiterate cobbler and a raging drunkard who routinely and savagely beat his wife and young son. There were those who said that his father actually had Ossetian roots and that Stalin later would sometimes speak some Ossetian. Ossetians were an Iranic-speaking people of the Caucasus. They were looked down upon, and for a long time, they were pagans. Behind Stalin's back, his minions at times would refer to him simply and with disdain as "the Osset."

Stalin's mother, called Keke, was a washerwoman and seamstress of speculative loose morals who, when not doting on him, also liked to give her young son, who they called Soso, severe thrashings. At one point, Keke kicked the drunkard father out of their home, and young Soso rarely saw him again.

There were rumors that, years later, Stalin had his father murdered Trotsky-style with an ax to the back of the head. Stalin's father thought that his son was not his, that he was a *nabichuari*, a bastard, and being a bastard child in Georgia was a mark of disgrace.

Some thought that Stalin's real father was the Gori priest, Charkviani, who had officiated at Beso and Keke's wedding. The priest would later be found murdered in his home, and speculation was that the boy, Joseph, had arranged it. Town gossip also proposed that the boy's real father was a prosperous Gori wine merchant, Yakov Egnatashvili, or Gori's police chief, Damaian Davrichewy, or Maurice Ephrussi, a relative of French oil magnate Baron Alphonse de Rothschild who owned oil fields in the Caucasus. Perhaps it was famed Central Asian explorer Nikolai Przhevalsky or even future emperor Alexander III. In later life, Stalin would, perhaps deservedly, refer to his mother as "the prostitute" while some Georgians referred to her simply as "the old whore."

Stalin's mother wished her son to become a priest, and, thus, he attended the hometown Gori Church School and later a seminary in Tiflis, the Georgian capital a thousand miles away from the Russian Tsar's capital of St. Petersburg. Russia's future mass murderer began as a choirboy who possessed a beautiful singing voice and was studying for the priesthood and who also liked to write self-styled romantic poetry.

Things changed. While attending the seminary in Tiflis, young Soso caught the fire of Marxism and revolution and began dangerously agitating these concepts to his fellow seminarians. He became infatuated with a rising revolutionary leader, Vladimir Ulyanov, who would call himself Lenin, and his cause of overthrowing the repressive and uncaring ruling Tsar, dethroning the empire's three-hundred-year rule of the Romanov royal family. For his revolutionary enthusiasm, young Soso was expelled from the seminary only to become a professional underground provocateur. He then acquired the revolutionary name of "Koba" after a fictional, dashing Caucasian outlaw he admired.

Over the years, Koba Dzhugashvili's bold criminal underground activities caught the attention of Lenin. Lenin's new Bolshevik Party continually needed an infusion of money to discharge their revolutionary cause. Lenin quickly realized that he could use the cruel and sinisterly criminal talents of this young revolutionary from the Caucasus now calling himself Koba, who apparently knew how to raise money by any means necessary through numerous terrorists' acts including bombings, bloody stagecoach heists, bank stickups, murder, arson, blackmail, robbing people's homes, protection rackets, and bold hijackings of money transports on land and at sea. Lenin would at first come to affectionately call Koba "my wonderful Georgian," only in later years come to dislike and distrust him. Speculation was that Lenin would likely have dispatched his "wonderful Georgian" had Lenin not fortuitously died of a stroke in 1924.

Others were also noticing this troublemaker and young revolutionary Koba, namely the Tsar's despised secret police called the Okhrana. Over the years, Koba was captured and exiled to the unforgiving Siberia gulags multiple times, but he always somehow managed to escape to continue his revolutionary activities anew. Few knew, but some suspected, that Stalin was, in fact, an Okhrana spy playing both sides. He was helping fuel the underground revolution while at the same time tattling to the Tsar's secret police about his revolutionary comrades' activities. He was a traitor to the cause; in more modern parlance, a snitch, a rat.

Stalin would have two wives, each dying during their marriage to him.

His first wife was a dark-eyed Georgian dressmaker named Ekaterina Svanidze, known as Kato, who was from a cultured Bolshevik family. The couple lived in a hut near the Baku oil fields though the young revolutionary Koba was rarely home. Together they had a child, a son they called Yakov. Not long afterward, Kato, at age twenty-two, died of typhus, colitis, and peritoneal TB, and the baby boy was put into the care of her family to raise. Koba, foreshadowing, said, "She died, and with her died my last warm feelings for people." Stalin rarely saw his son, Yakov, at one point going ten years between visits. During the Great Patriotic War, Yakov joined the Soviet military, was captured by the Germans, and held in a Nazi prisoner of war camp. He was shot by a guard and died there against the camp's razor wire in an escape attempt rather than revealing any secrets about the Russian Red Army.

Eleven years after his first wife died, Stalin remarried. This time, he married a sixteen-year-old schoolgirl with flashing gypsy eyes named Nadezhda Alliluyeva, who was called Nadya. She was the daughter of one of Stalin's Georgian revolutionary friends. Rumors abounded that Stalin had had a sexual relationship with the half-gypsy Olga Alliluyeva, the wife of his Bolshevik comrade, and the result of this tryst was the birth of a baby girl, Nadya, meaning that when Stalin would later marry her, he was, in fact, marrying his own daughter. Whether true or not, it was a certainty that Stalin had a lover's affair with Olga Alliluyeva, which means, at the least, he was bedding his future mother-in-law. He also had an affair with the sister of his dead wife.

Joseph and Nadya would have two children— Vasily, who became an outrageous drunkard, and a daughter, Svetlana, who was the apple of her father's eye until in her teens she unwisely took up with a Jew, who Stalin banished to hard labor. Svetlana would marry four times and eventually defect to the United States. Stalin and Nadya also adopted a son, Artyom.

After years of tempestuous rows, Stalin's wife, Nadya, age thirty-one, committed suicide on November 9, 1932, shooting herself in the chest with a Mauser pistol in her bedroom at the Stalin's flat in the Kremlin's Poteshny Palace. Inexplicably, colored bruises and blood were found on her face and neck. Rumors persisted that Stalin had had her killed or did the deed himself. The world was told she died of appendicitis.

In 1913, Joseph Vissarionovich Dzhugashvili, once called Sosa then Koba, changed his revolutionary name to Stalin, meaning "man of steel." It was by this Bolshevik name that he would unleash his uncontrollable wrath, and the world would come to know him as the ruthless dictator Stalin, an indifferent serial killer of millions of his own countrymen, liquidating his enemies, real and imagined, his cohorts, old Bolsheviks comrades, party bureaucrats, military officers, members of his security organs, Jews, an entire peasant class, former friends, and members of his own family.

Stalin had grown to dislike and not trust his countrymen, the clannish Georgians. They knew too much about his real early years, not the version he portrayed in Russian history books. They liked to gossip too much, about his birth deformities, his drunken father and whoremongering mother, his childhood beatings, his being an illegitimate bastard child, his eviction from the seminary, and his being a double agent for the Tsar's secret police.

When he became the new Russian Tsar following Lenin's death, Stalin had all the history books rewritten to make it appear that he was an authentic hero of the revolution and of the subsequent Civil War. "One must sometimes correct history," he once said. He was not an active hero of the revolution. Some called him a "gray blur" during those world-changing times, merely dancing in the shadows of these great events. Trotsky called him "the man who missed the revolution." What Stalin *did* do was oversee the destruction of the Bolsheviks' promise of revolution to deliver instead a murderous and repressive totalitarianism rule.

He fancied himself a superior leader during the Great Patriotic War and suffered from the delusion that he had a gift for military command. And yet, when his army generals and his German spies, like Victor Sorge, told him that the Germans were going to invade the Soviet Union, he thought them to be idiots. He refused to believe that Hitler would take such action. There was even a German soldier who changed sides to fight along with Stalin's Red Army. He warned that the German invasion was imminent, giving Stalin the exact date of the invasion and the German code name for the attack, Operation Barbarossa. Stalin refused to believe him and had him shot for spreading rumors. Even while German bombers were relentlessly strafing Kiev, Riga, and Sebastopol, Stalin was asleep at his Kuntsevo *dacha*, and those who answered the urgent telephone calls from the generals to report the invasion refused to awaken the boss. Later, when he did learn of the invasion and of Hitler's betrayal of Germany and Russia's friendship pact, Stalin could not cope with it. He had a nervous breakdown and in deep depression isolated himself for nearly a week while foreigners invaded his country.

After the Great War, Stalin's always precarious health took a turn for the worse. He suffered from high blood pressure and fainting spells, and it was rumored that he had had several strokes or heart attacks in 1945 and again in 1947. Physically, Stalin, throughout his life, had abundant physical limitations and tormenting maladies. His many body defects included a disturbingly pitted face from smallpox, a withered left arm, a foot with two fused toes, and a listing limp as a result of his legs being run over by a runaway carriage when he was twelve years old. He had painful, yellow, rotting teeth, and later bothersome dentures. He had debilitating headaches, painfully inflamed rheumatism, maddening psoriasis, and flaring tonsillitis, especially under stress. As he aged, Stalin's health and mental faculties, which were already badly damaged, precipitously deteriorated to disturbing levels, including possibly heart surgery in 1951. He was a lifelong chain-smoker until just before his death, and there was speculation that he had throat cancer. Often, he needed help standing. His body painfully limped along. His once full head of hair had thinned, his face had shrunken, his already slight stature had diminished. He moved his withered arm with great difficulty, and his mind, weakened with cerebral arteriosclerosis, wandered without focus, and he became abstracted, forgetful, and extremely volatile. The doctors who performed his autopsy found his liver so enlarged that it poked through his ribs.

He was seventy-three years old when he sucked his last breath, proving that the Great Stalin was, alas, a mere mortal and not an indestructible demigod.

He died an agonizing and lonely death at his country *dacha* near Kuntsevo, surrounded by his dwindling inner circle of colleagues posing as friends but who actually feared and despised him. In the end, the supreme master of human misery died alone, morose, unhappy, and paranoid, having managed to destroy all those who he had loved or befriended.

The official version, of course, was that the Great Stalin died March 5, 1953, of a stroke while working tirelessly at his office in the Kremlin. Not surprisingly, this was a lie. He died not in Kremlin at all, but rather, he died at his country home from where, in reality, he spent his last days ruling his massive empire. And, yes, he did suffer a massive stroke, but he was likely also poisoned by conspirators.

In the end, he was a neurotic with an uncontrollable Georgian temper and a murderous schizophrenic with at once a Messiah complex and at the same time an inferiority complex wide as the Caspian Sea about his small physique with his pocked-marked face, shortened arm, and webbed toes.

Right before his death, Stalin began executing Soviet physicians because many of them were Jewish. The infamous Doctors' Plot. But he spared the life of the Jewish doctor Lina Shtern. Why? Because she was doing research on extending human life, and Stalin wanted to extend his life span, perhaps wishing to add the position of immortal to round off his resumé.

Khrushchev called him a *litsedei*, a man of many faces. Those faces were on the cover of *Time* magazine in America ten times. He was also named *Time* magazine Man of the Year twice in 1939 and 1942. Despite killing millions of people, Stalin was twice nominated for the Nobel Peace Prize.

He was a man who, ruling by terror, transformed his backward, peasant nation into a superpower, but at what cost in human life?

Stalin spent a lifetime glorifying his past while concealing his dark secrets. Few knew the truth: Stalin was likely murdered, leaving behind a secret stash of hidden treasures of an untold fortune.

Stalin once mused about history, "I know that after my death, a pile of rubbish will be heaped on my grave, but the wind of history will sooner or later sweep it away without mercy."

Maybe, maybe not…

CHAPTER 1

'Twas brillig, and the slithy toves did gyre and gimble in the wabe.

"The devil's uncle," Moscow investigator Illya Podipenko muttered to himself. He thought that in his past year of living in America, he had adopted the English language passingly well, but this...this seemed like a different language altogether! Perhaps an ancient tongue?

Illya slanted back against the park bench, shook his head amusingly, closed his eyes. A contented mid-life man contemplating an exciting journey. He was a smallish, roundish, spare man with thinning hair on top and an amiable but resolute bearing. He walked with a modest gait, sometimes, when deep in thought, with his hands interlocked across his lower back like a professor meandering a campus somewhere along the Ivy Leagues of America. He had entered Central Park from the east side, off East Seventy-Sixth Street. He sat shifting his weight on a shaded bench near the Conservatory Water. In the distance sat the model boathouse.

Like a flower straining for nourishing shafts of early summer light, the Moscow militiaman tilted his pale face toward the sun's warmth. *Ah, New York City in the first days of June*, he breathed in serenely. Budding cherry blossoms. Light, perfumed air. Wonderful blue skies. Swooping hawks. Drifting clouds. *And Moscow this time of year?* he pondered. Well, the stifling heat and the traditional summer peat fires around the city that burned the eyes and choked the throat were only weeks away. He wouldn't miss them.

He listened to the sounds of Central Park. In front of him, grown men shouted, and young sons gleefully echoed in delight as they tacked their wind-powered, white-sailed sloops and motored-powered toy boats over the Conservatory Water. Birds called out from Lebanon cedars, willows, and pine trees. Behind him, sirens wailed toward Lenox Hill Hospital.

'Twas brillig, and the slithy toves did gyre and gimble in the wabe.

He appreciated the quote from a work called *The Jabberwocky*. He was just uncertain what the confounding words meant. The quote was depicted in bronze on the northern end of the Conservatory Water, engraved in a granite circle around a fanciful sculpture of the famous characters from *Alice's Adventures in Wonderland*, one of the Moscow investigator's favorite books. Grouped around Alice on her mushroom were the invitees to an outlandish tea party: the Mad Hatter, the March Hare, the Cheshire

Cat, the White Rabbit, Alice's Cat Dinah, and, of course, the bashful Dormouse.

It occurred to Illya Podipenko that this sculpture could have symbolized the past of his very own Mother Russia, perhaps a meeting at Stalin's near *dacha* during the old Soviet days, with the great leader Stalin's ever-nervous entourage forcibly drinking until they puked and compulsorily dancing with one another to records spun on Stalin's prized American gramophone.

Contemplating the sculpture, Illya Podipenko smiled to himself. Yes, there was sadistic, child-raping Beria and Molotov and Malenkov. There was Ukrainian peasant Khrushchev, too, and bearded Kalinin and Bulganin. And, of course, the centerpiece of the sculpture, the Mad Hatter himself, Stalin, with his shriveled left arm, broken, yellow teeth and pock-marked face, no doubt devising the day's list of who of his fellow Soviet countrymen should be packed off to the slave camps or who, more simply, should be made to just disappear.

Illya sighed deeply. Where in America should he visit on his vacation? He had a month between his just-ended lecture series at Columbia University and the July beginning of his lecture series for new recruits at the New York office of the FBI. New Orleans? Las Vegas? The Grand Canyon? New York's Finger Lakes area? Visit all them in a single, outrageous thirty-day swing across the United States?

He was contemplating these thoughts, eyes contentedly lidded, when suddenly he felt a peculiar change in the air currents around him. A faint, wonderful scent tantalized his nostrils. Then he thought he felt a slight weight shift on the bench next to him.

A youthful woman's voice whispered in Russian, "You must help me, Investigator. They killed my grandfather. And they may be coming after me."

"Pardon?"

Illya Podipenko wasn't certain the voice was real or imagined. Had he dreamt it? Perhaps he had momentarily dozed off beneath the early summer's genial sunshine.

A single eyelid slid open. He, unsure, glanced sideways. Seated next to him was a vision, a young woman, a girl really, not much older than…what? Eighteen? Nineteen? His brow furrowed in befuddlement. *The girl looked oddly familiar,* he thought to himself.

"Did you say something, miss?" he asked, embarrassed. He shifted about uncomfortably.

The girl leaned closer to him. She was lovely. Sunlight and water shimmered like fiery gemstones in her large, blue-green, slightly slanted eyes. Her light olive skin was smooth as butter. "I think people may be after me," she whispered, more into the man's shoulder than his bent ear. "I need your help."

"People? What people?" Illya blinked around him. "I don't see any people," he responded stupidly, considering in front of him were at least three dozen people encircling the Conservatory Water park.

"No, no, please, understand. I wasn't followed."

"Ah, yes, yes… I see, well…that's good…isn't it?" The man rubbed his face with both hands. "You are Russian?" he asked her, confused.

"No. American."

"But…but you speak fluent Russian?" An incredulous look buffed his eyes.

"Why shouldn't I? I was born here, in Brighton Beach, you know, Little Odessa. I speak Georgian, too, and French and German." Suddenly, the girl shrugged her shoulders as if at once exasperated. She tugged at one of his arms. "*Please*, Investigator Podipenko, can we walk?"

Investigator Podipenko? "You know my name?" His words were addled.

"Of course. I will explain everything on the way." Gently, she nudged the man to his feet.

"On the way…on the way *where*?"

"Well, as they say, the devil is in the details."

"Details? What details? We don't have any details."

The girl said, "I know, right? Isn't it wonderful! We're free to make it up as we go along." Excitedly, she stood up on her toes, pointing vaguely eastward, across the water. "There," she said enthusiastically, "the Boathouse Restaurant. Let's eat. I'm *starving!* But you'll have to pay. I have no money." With one hand, she grasped a canvas valise on the bench next to her then leaned her shoulder into the curve of the man's back, pushing his body grindingly forward one step at a time as if she were pushing a broken-down jalopy out of the mud.

*****

"Come on, Professor. Where is your American can-do spirit!"

Illya responded, "I am not an American. Nor a professor for that fact."

Their table was on the red bricked, copper-roofed boathouse's open-air veranda. The view was spectacular. kayaks, rowboats, and the occasional gondola went skimming across the water like rain on glass. In the distance beyond lay the gothic, sandstone Bethesda Terrace.

Across the linen tablecloth from Illya Podipenko emanated slurps and sucking noises so unashamedly socially dysfunctional and profound they could have been coming from a cannibal feasting on a wayward missionary.

"Are you going to finish that?" the girl suddenly asked Illya Podipenko.

The question was so startlingly unexpected it made the man jump. He regarded glumly and longingly the remaining half of his perfectly prepared mutton sandwich.

"Well… I…oh, go ahead…you have it." He pushed his china plate around a depthless bowl the Caesar salad for two that the girl had finished unencumbered by colleagues. Her BLT and French fries had disappeared like logs in a wood chipper.

"When did you last eat?" Illya alarmingly inquired, slack-jawed. "I read about the Donner party, but I thought it was urban myth."

"You're funny." The words barely leaked around a voracious mouthful of his precious mutton sandwich.

Illya took a hurried sip at his cup of tea before she could claim that as well.

"Hmm." She paused, considering. "Noon. Lunch. That's the last time I ate." She shrugged gaily. "I'm always hungry. My stars, am I glad I caught up with you. I didn't know exactly where my next meal was coming from. I'm on the run after all. I figured I either have to forage the wilds for food or be forced to go curb shopping or dumpster diving." She shrugged her shoulders. "Just sayin'."

"What…what?" the man uttered. "I don't think I understand—"

The girl's lips caught the end of a straw attached to a thick vanilla milkshake, followed by a sucking sound like a vacuum cleaner searching for dirt in a crevice. A moment later, she sloped back in her chair, grinning. She was magnificent in her youth. Her face was broad, cheeks sharp as stones. Her skin in the afternoon sunlight glistened beneath hair cut tight across her forehead. Afternoon light played in her eyes, turning them the color of fresh plums.

"I heard some sound advice the other day," the man said to the young girl. "'*Never eat more than you can lift.*'"

"Who said that?" The girl laughed.

"Miss Piggy."

"Dude, you watch the *Muppets*!" she howled out so loudly that her words plunked across the pond water, causing floating geese to flap their wings in alarm.

The Moscow policeman's face reddened. He glanced at the tables around him. "Well…it is a good way for me to learn English, you see…"

"I know, right? The great Moscow police investigator Illya Podipenko watches the *Muppets*. That's awesome!"

The man put the napkin to his lips, speaking in a low timbre. "How do you know my name?" he inquired.

"You don't remember me?" Her full lips fell to a playful pout.

"I admit it, you do look vaguely familiar." It was the best he could come up with on short notice.

"Vaguely? You certainly know how to play to a woman's vanity."

Illya's neck darkened beneath his collar. "I meant…well, I meet a lot of people…"

The comment caused the girl to guffaw so that nearby diners turned their heads. "I'm teasing you, Professor. I was a student of yours at Columbia. Last quarter, *The Romanov Dynasty, the Rasputin Murders, and the Fabergé Eggs*. You were fascinating, exquisite. Most interesting course I've ever taken."

"Thank you…but I'm not really a professor, I mean…in the strictest sense. I am merely a guest lecturer."

"Whatever. I know the real you, a famous Russian police investigator from the Moscow Militia. You solved that Fabergé Egg case some years ago. Became a hero not only in the Russian Federation but around the world. That's why Columbia University's Russian Institute offered you a lecture chair for two years to teach students about how you solved all those murders of the Rasputin descendants and how you recovered those five unknown priceless Fabergé eggs."

"I suppose I am old enough and fortunate enough to have acquired certain skill sets," said Illya. "Besides, it wasn't just me. I had a lot of help…"

The girl offered a frown. "Are you always so modest?"

"Modest? I… I'm not sure…" His throat became dry. He played with the napkin in his lap, glanced across the table, then squinted his eyes skyward in thought. "Katya… Katya… Tevoradze!" he at last blurted triumphantly.

"I knew it. You *do* remember my name!"

Illya Podipenko straightened. "At times I have a passable memory," he offered, weakly. "Besides, you are not so easy to forget, if I may say so. An 'A' student as I recall, top of the class. And…well…"

"What?"

His eyes fell to his hands on the table. "I was going to also say you are quite…outgoing, so to speak. And beautiful, very beautiful."

"Wait, what? You think I'm *beautiful?*" The girl's eyes lit like beacons at sea. At once she was on her feet. With her hands, she slapped at the sides of the khaki shorts she was wearing. "This is going to be great!" she shouted. "A dream come true!"

"Pardon?" Illya gaped up at the woman.

"Tonight. I've dreamed about it for a year!"

Illya looked blank. "Tonight? What about it?"

The girl's eyebrows scuttled across her smooth forehead, and she gave Illya Podipenko a look that could have said, *Exactly how thick are you, anyway?*

"Tonight," she emphasized the word distinctly as if now teaching a slow child, "is *the* night. I at last get to make mad, beautiful love to you, to go totally heels up."

The man in mid-sip inhaled hot tea straight down his gullet and hawked it back onto the front of his shirt.

*****

"Professor, wait up!"

Illya Podipenko's short legs were stamping straight and stiff as if on motorized stilts. "I'm not a professor, I am a *lecturer*," he called mindfully over his shoulder, the words carried in the late afternoon breeze.

"Investigator then." Directly behind the man, as if she were a cloak he was wearing, matching him step for step, was the girl. Her valise dangled in one of her hands. "Was it something I said? All right, I apologize then. Perhaps I was too forward."

"*Perhaps?*" Suddenly, Illya wheeled about. He didn't know how to respond. His chest was visibly pumping, his face colored. Exasperatedly, he slapped his hands against the sides of his thin jacket. "You just can't go around saying such things, Katya Tevoradze. It's not...well, *proper.*"

"But it's the truth. I always tell the truth to the people I love."

"*WHAT?*" The investigator's head pivoted atop his shoulders. "That doesn't make any sense, young lady!"

"Does love really ever make sense?" Her smile was so sweet and innocent and subtle it could have been an angel's.

"How many people have you been in love with?" He didn't even know why he had asked such a half-witted question.

"Five."

"Five?"

"Yes. My mother, Lyuda. My father, Giorgi. My grandfather, Sandro. My uncle, Grisha. And now... you. That's five!"

"*The devil's uncle!*" He was on the move again, lengthening his strides. "It's quite possible, my dear Katya Tevoradze, that you are insane as Stalin, or mad as...*him!*" He levered a shaking finger toward the bronze statue of the Mad Hatter.

"Oh, I *love* him!" the girl shrieked. Like a vapor, she had disappeared from the man's side. She now was standing in front of the bronze storybook figures, her eyes lit like candles, mouth smiling agape. She danced on her toes as if incontinent.

"What? Who?" asked the man.

"The Mad Hatter!"

"That could explain a lot." Illya pulled up then added, "So that makes six, it seems."

"Pardon?"

"Six people you now love. Six, including a statue of the Mad Hatter."

"Illya, don't be silly," she scornfully chided him. "The Mad Hatter isn't human."

"Congratulations for understanding the subtlety of reality, my dear," Illya replied. "Come, Katya Tevoradze, sit." On a bench not far from the Alice in Wonderland caricatures, Illya Podipenko patted a calming hand on a seat next to him.

The girl happily obeyed. When she sat, she did so with her legs and shoulders softly up against the man next to her. She felt so warm and fresh it made Illya Podipenko's toes crimp inside his shoes. "Now, listen, Katya," he began, much like an enduring uncle, "you simply must tell me exactly what is going on here. You accost me in Central Park, you allege wild tales of your grandfather being murdered and people who may or may not be following you—"

"And I said that I was in love with you," she interjected as a reminder, "don't forget that!"

"Ah, yes, well, of course…that too."

"I understand that you think it is the ravings of a demented girl, but I don't care. It is what it is."

Illya's eyes patiently scanned the blue of the sky. He exhaled air deeply through his lips. "Katya, don't get me wrong. I am flattered, very flattered, *extremely* flattered, that someone as young and beautiful as you would even give a rumpled, old, near-pensioner like me even a second look. Let's face it, I am old, round, and dumpy."

"So that's what I love," she responded. "It is the imperfections I find attractive. I think you are handsome. Like a movie star."

"A movie star, eh? Like Shrunk?"

"And funny too." Katya howled. "I believe his correct name is Shrek."

"Yes, well…" Illya's voice haltingly trailed off. He shuffled his feet, gathering himself. "You see, Katya, I think what you could be experiencing some sort of transference."

"Is that a thing?" The woman pulled her lips askew.

"What I'm trying to say is that it happens often that a student, for whatever reasons, develops a deep feeling for their professors—"

"Not a professor, remember? A lecturer. And Moscow's most famous investigator."

Illya nodded addedly. "Well, I don't know if what you say is accurate. But it's possible that the same phenomenon holds true for *lecturers* and investigators. Anyway, the point is, Katya, the professor or lecturer or investigator is an authority figure, perhaps a father figure. That can be very alluring to a young mind. Students frequently transfer what they mistakenly feel is love onto such a person. It usually doesn't last long, however, once the student learns that the professor or lecturer or investigator is just as human as everyone else, with all the foibles and idiosyncrasies available to anyone struggling through the human drama. More, perhaps, than even the average person."

The girl momentarily rested the tip of her tongue on her teeth. "Perhaps it is the idiosyncrasies I love. Did you ever consider that? Like when you are deep in thought, you squint your eyes, tilt your head, and roll your tongue around your mouth."

Illya vastly considered the point, eyes squinted, head tilted, tongue flapping across his lips like a hooked carp.

"There it is," the girl leaned in, whispering into the collar of his shirt.

"Is it?" Illya seemed surprised. His face inadvertently hued.

"See, that's what I love about you, Professor. Whoops! I forgot! You aren't a professor, and I am not supposed to be in love with you." She smiled then had a thought. "Obsessed! That's the word. I am *obsessed* with you." She seemed genuinely pleased by the current discovery.

"That's a very nice word," Illya weakly agreed, nodding, happy to have moved off the uncomfortable concept of love. He was quiet a moment then turned toward the girl. He could see the reflection of his own wrinkled face in the shining irises of her eyes. When he spoke, his words were soft.

"You must tell me, Katya, what this is all about. Tell me about your grandfather's supposed murder. Tell me about the people who may or may not be chasing you and why."

Against his better judgment, suddenly he took one of the girl's hands in his, like a father would to a daughter. He gestured toward the fanciful statue in the distance. "Do you know what the King said to Alice? *'Begin at the beginning and go on till you come to the end then stop.'*"

She was born in 1997, Katya Tevoradze began her story, in Little Odessa. Her parents were named Giorgi and Lyuda. Giorgi was a tough man, a longshoreman on the New York docks who drank heavily and would stumble home at night to occasionally beat his wife. He died of a heart attack in 2001. Three years later, Lyuda died of ovarian cancer, and Katya, then aged seven, moved in with her grandfather, Sandro Tevoradze, and his younger brother, Grisha. Sandro was a fine old man, a great, proud Georgian who at one time was a bootmaker, a factory worker, a cook for the Red Army, and, at last his dream, the owner of a small restaurant in America's Little Odessa neighborhood selling imported Russian foods and spirits and fresh flowers. He and his brother retired five years ago, selling their small restaurant, to spend their remaining days drinking vodka and playing dominoes. They spent most hours of the day in a small Russian dive called The Dubenka Club off Brighton Second Street. At night, Sandro and Grisha liked to drink still more vodka and reminisce about their days as youths in Mother Russia. But two days ago, Sandro Tevoradze was found at the bottom of a steep, black stairwell of the small house he owned with his brother, Grisha, apparently having accidentally tumbled to his death. He was eighty-two years old.

"So you believe it was not an accident but that your grandfather was murdered?" inquired Illya Podipenko, sitting back straight against the wooden bench.

The girl's eyes searched his. "I have no doubt," she uttered at last. "Grandpa Sandro never took that back stairway, *never!* The steps were too steep for him, the light too dim, and an old, rickety handrail was virtually useless. In fact, my grandfather frequently begged me never to use the back stairway. Always the front, he ordered me."

"I see," breathed out Illya. He watched a young family approach the Alice sculptures. A young boy, perhaps four years old, screeched in joy as he ran his hand against the patina of the Mad Hatter's coat sleeve, worn smooth by four decades of hands stroking it "And what about the police?" the man asked at length.

"What about the police?"

"You filed a report, surely."

"Of course," responded the girl

"And?"

"And they said they would look into it. But I don't think they believed me. They were pretty much convinced it was a case of an old man losing his balance and tumbling to his death. They said it happens all the time."

"Hmm." Illya was sitting hunched, elbow on his knees. With the tips of his fingers, he gave his face a vigorous rub then sat back hard. "And so," he began, "now you, a young girl in New York, a college student, now you live alone in your grandfather's house…"

"Not any longer, now that I'm with you." At once, he felt the girl's arm thread itself through his. Her head softly found Illya's shoulder, and she sighed contentedly. "So here's the thing," she cooed softly. "Much of what I own is in my valise here. I apologize for not having room for pajamas or nighties. I may have to sleep in the nude. I hope you don't mind."

"*The devil's uncle,*" Illya sputtered.

They had strolled Central Park's east side for what seemed like miles, following East Drive past Cedar Hill and The Glade and the obelisk and the reservoir. The sun was disappearing behind tall trees and stately buildings. A breeze whiffled the green grass. Illya's feet were beginning to screech at him while the girl seemed to dance gaily beside him as if practicing incessant ballroom turns. As he often did when lost in contemplation, the Moscow investigator ambled along with a single arm crooked behind his back.

"Why would anyone want to murder your grandfather?" he finally asked, turning toward the girl.

"I think he and his brother, Grisha, knew a secret."

Illya stopped short. "A secret? What kind of secret?"

"Don't know, dude. That's why they call them secrets. Something to do with Stalin, I think, something from their past. Perhaps the information was valuable."

"What? Stalin? He's been dead sixty years!"

"I understand this," the girl ceded the point. "I am just telling you what I know. Grandpa Sandro several times said he wanted to pass along a secret to me, an *immense* secret, he called it, someday before he died." Katya seemed to experience a rare moment of quietness then added, "He never got the chance."

"I see..." Illya paused. "Did your grandfather and his brother know Stalin personally?"

Katya nodded her head. "Yes, they did. Back in the day, Grandpa Sandro and Uncle Grisha were soldiers in the Red Army. They were cooks. At some point, apparently, they were appointed to Stalin's personal staff. Kitchen help and waiters at one of his *dachas* outside of Moscow. Apparently one day, Stalin asked them, well, ordered them, to do a personal favor."

"A personal favor? For Stalin? That's impressive."

"Perhaps not," corrected the girl. "I think it went badly."

"Why do you say that?"

Katya pitched her arms against the curve of her hips. "Because that's why Grandpa Sandro and Uncle

Grisha turned up in the United States. They escaped their own Russian homeland under the darkness of night. Perhaps Stalin had put them on one of his famous death lists of people to be taken out in the forest and shot in the back of the head."

"Goodness." Illya surveyed the distance. "So they fled their Russian homeland to live here in the United States?"

Katya nodded yes. Illya Podipenko was silent for a moment then asked, "You say your grandfather and uncle played dominoes every day at the Dubenka Club in Little Odessa?"

The girl's lips spread. "You remembered what I said," she replied, "I thought you might."

"I try to pay attention," the investigator whispered, smiling. "So does your Uncle Grisha also know this secret from the times of Joseph Stalin?"

"Yes. But that may have been the problem."

"Explain, please."

"Uncle Grisha began drinking way too much, particularly in his old age, this past year or so. It worried my grandfather Sandro terribly and scared him, I can tell you that. Grandpa would keep warning Uncle Grisha to quiet down, to be careful about guarding the dangerous secret they shared. But Uncle Grisha couldn't help himself. When he drank, he liked to talk loudly about the old days in Russia."

Illya Podipenko sat in silence then said, almost to himself, "So it is possible that someone else, through Uncle Grisha's drunken talk, could have learned of this dark Stalin secret? And this event could have cost your grandfather his life?"

The girl nodded affirmatively.

"It seems to me," Illya added calmly, "that possessing this curious secret is a liability. Your uncle Grisha may be in a great deal of danger himself."

"I knew you would understand," the girl said. She reached over, taking her valise in one of her hands. She stood, waiting. "So now we go, yes?" she asked.

"What?" Illya peered up at her, perplexed.

"To visit Uncle Grisha. That was going to be your next move, right?"

"Visit Uncle Grisha, right, right," Illya responded hesitantly, his fingers scratching thoughtfully at the top of his scalp. "That would make sense, I suppose."

A moment later, he found himself absently shuffling behind the girl, who was pulling him tolerantly along by his arm as if he were a Thorazine patient at a home.

CHAPTER 2

Passing over the East River on the Manhattan Bridge, they eventually disembarked the Q-line train at the Surf Avenue-Ocean Parkway station at Brooklyn's Brighton Beach. During the entire forty-five-minute ride, with twenty stops, Katya Tevoradze had sat up close to the Moscow militiaman, vigorously chattering away about her youth, her parents' unfortunate deaths, her dance classes, movies, her choir practice, books she liked and didn't like, her soccer games, pet tricks she admired, possibly something about knockwurst, her language classes at Columbia, her dream of working in international business, and, oddly, the moon and its effect on tides. Illya couldn't fathom how the girl managed it. She talked so fast, and her subject matter changed direction so precipitously her words seemed to escape her lips in a discursive clang of unrelated syllables. Illya was consumedly depleted. Crowding his mind were itchy questions. *What was he doing there? Who was this pretty, highly charged girl who operated on a voltage more appropriate to a radioactive isotope than a standard gauge human being? And what was this sordid business about a grandfather, this*

*Sandro Tevoradze, who the girl claimed had been mur-
dered? And now someone could be following her? And
what about this furtive Stalin secret that may have cost
Sandro his life? And what about Uncle Grisha? Did any
of it make any sense?*

Mere hours ago, Illya Podipenko had been
blissfully contemplating vacation destinations. But
now... The Moscow investigator was wrestling with
these and other imponderables as they made their
way west along the Boardwalk toward Luna Park,
where, in the background, riders of the old Cyclone
wooden roller coaster could be heard screaming in
delight.

"You've been to Little Odessa, I suppose," he
thought he heard Katya ask. Beside him, she skipped
determinedly.

"Many times," responded Illya in short bursts
of breath. "Weekends mostly. To shop at the M&I."

"I *love* the M&I!" the girl shrieked so loud it
made Illya flinch. "Blini! Meat pastries! Smoked
salmon! *Harcho!* Real Georgian food! Flatbread filled
with cheese!"

Illya labored keeping pace. He found himself
following irresistibly in the girl's wake as they hurried past ornamental building fronts primped in
spray-can graffiti, trendy beach shops, and other
assorted small businesses ardently prosecuting the
commerce of the day. At some point, they looped
back toward Brighton Beach. Energetic Rollerbladers
skidded by. Dark-skinned street vendors hawked foreign cigarettes. Wild-haired Rasta boys were dealing

sweet-smelling ganja on street corners. Bright-colored cyclists bent over their handlebars as they snaked between leisurely people walking dogs. In the old Russian manner, elderly ladies in peroxided hair, red pomade, fur coats, and odd hats huddled together on benches gossiping in their native language.

As afternoon was fading to evening, Illya saw the sun sitting low, balancing like a swollen orange on the edge of the ocean, rays like blades slicing across the waters of the Atlantic. Seagulls screeched out to one another. A turn onto Brighton Beach Avenue had the Moscow investigator and the college girl passing ethnic restaurants, crowded kiosks, and modish boutiques, all situated beneath the clatter of the elevated train running overhead. At some point, they stopped so the girl could buy a strawberry Turkish Taffy bar at a candy store.

Soon after, they braked to a stop in front of the wooden dive called The Dubenka Club, which loosely translated meant *The Truncheon*. Red letters in Georgian peeled from the grease-smudged glass of the front door.

"Don't expect much." Katya smiled, pushing open the door. "It's pretty grotty, a gangsters' hangout. The owner is a Georgian thug named Dato Matrabazi along with his three brothers. They use the tavern as a front for their underworld activities, drug trafficking, extortion rackets, money laundering, murder, even sweatshops in the Mariana Islands. At night, this turns into a sleazy nightclub with foreign karaoke, Russian pole dancers, and hookers with chlamydia. Truth is, the Matrabazi brothers are a bunch of ass clowns."

"Charming, well-spoken," uttered Illya, following the girl who marched straight-shouldered into a room black and rank as a mountain cave. Illya attempted to blink light into his vision and once done saw a dozen pairs of white eyes pivoting speculatively toward him and the girl, glinting in the half-light more in menace than in good fellowship. Illya calculated that his chances of being randomly disemboweled by a tape-handled shank ranked from good to excellent.

The room grew abruptly quiet. A sodden wooden bar that ran along a side wall reeked of spilled vodka, crushed-out cigars, dreams scattered to the four winds, and empty bags of pork scratching. On the wall behind the bar, Illya saw the red-and-white flag of Georgia featuring the large Saint George's Cross and four smaller crosses. From somewhere, Illya heard mournful songs of the Gulag that Vysotsky sang.

Disconcertingly, the girl stomped without intimidation past shadowy, big-shouldered men in leather jackets and gold chains as if she were the Queen of England come for a royal visit. At the end of the bar, an alarmingly colossus of a man with a massive chest and prehensile jaw stood threateningly. Perhaps a murderous giant from Russian folklore, Illya gulped to himself, or maybe an unfortunate Chernobyl regress. His face was wan and blank as if free from a lifetime of contemplation. As he passed by the man, Illya could have sworn he had heard an unnerving beast's growl slither up from deep within the man's chest, and he thought it a possibility that, when called upon, the giant could shoot flames from his nostrils. He noticed that the man's knuckles were chinked and scabbed over, perhaps from fighting, perhaps from scraping the ground when walking. "Somewhere, Darwin weeps," Illya muttered under his breath. The giant possessed unequivocally the largest cranium Illya had ever seen, a cinderblock three times the size of a normal man's head, every inch of it thewed with gristle. "Sotos Syndrome," Illya unexpectantly whispered into the back of Katya's neck. He was clinging so close to her he could have been a mobile shadow. "Also known as cerebral gigantism," he decided to add, "a rare genetic disorder."

"Good to know," the girl responded, fearlessly strutting straight ahead. "Thanks for sharing."

They passed through the bar area into a small back room done up in red velvet. In a corner, a CD player was playing the song "Apareka" by the popular Georgian group Trio Mandili. There were perhaps twenty tables, all but one unoccupied. They approached the man from the rear. Illya could see that the back of the man's head was meaty and hairless as a stone. His head was tilted down from his neck as if sleeping, or perhaps newly dead.

"Uncle Grisha," the girl called out, approaching, "I've brought a friend." There was no response. "*Uncle Grisha!*" she repeated louder, this time tapping the man on one of his shoulders, which caused the man's body to suddenly fly erect, a grunt of confusion rumbling from deep in his throat. The sudden movement and roaring sound startled Illya so much a big toe nearly sprung through one of his socks.

"Uncle Grisha, it's me, Katya. I've brought someone for you to meet." With one hand, the girl gently patted the man's shoulder while with the other she seized Illya's jacket sleeve, dragging him along behind her as if he were a late-walking toddler.

The man's head turned slowly, his deep-set, bloodshot eyes blinking to gain focus. His face was raddled with chinks and crevices, cheekbones high and angular, nose large as a Ukrainian potato. What could have been a vodka drool leaked from the corner of his mouth. For a long moment, he gawked stupefyingly into the girl's face then grinned and uttered her name with such fondness she could have been appearing to him in a dream. "My darling niece, Katya. What are you doing here, my little dove? This is no place for a beautiful child."

"I've brought a new friend, Uncle Grisha," she softly repeated directly into one of the man's ears. "Someone for you to meet."

"Eh, what's that you say? A new friend?" With that, the old man's questioning gaze fell squarely against the pale, blank face of Illya Podipenko.

"The serpent's tail!" the man cried out. His feet under the small table were seeking traction. His body crashed sideways in an effort to leap out of his chair. "It's a ghost," he screeched, "what kind of devil's trickery is this?"

"What? No, no, Uncle Grisha. This is the professor from Columbia University I was telling you about. He is from Moscow. He is not a ghost. He is our *friend*, Uncle Grisha. He has come to help us."

"Help us…" The old man's voice trailed off. He propped an elbow on the table in front of him, tilting his forehead into one of his thick, callused hands. His head shook side to side like a loosed igneous rock. "But it is the famous marshal. Back from the grave. I'd know him anywhere."

All of a sudden, the mist cleared for Illya Podipenko, and he saw lucidly what was happening here. He took a step forward, his tone moderate. "The marshal was my father, sir. Marshal Konstantin Podipenko. I am the marshal's son, Illya Konstantinovich Podipenko."

The man's head rose sharply. "What's that you say? The marshal's son? Here, boy, let's have a look at you." From his shirt pocket, the man removed wire spectacles, placing the end pieces behind his ears, then moved his squinted face so close to his visitor's that Illya could smell the beet soup Uncle Grisha had had for lunch.

"My god," the man wheezed, "a duplicate if I've ever seen one!" With that, the old man stumbled from his chair, his powerful arms circling Illya like a steel cinch. He crushed Illya to his chest so vigorously Illya thought he heard his spine snap. "The living, breathing son of the great marshal, who would believe it! I knew you as an infant."

"Eee-shh." Illya tried to respond but could only manage the hiss of a leaky air hose, all expendable air having been ventilated from his lungs. His nose seemed crushed uncompromisingly and quite painfully directly into Uncle Grisha's stubbled chin.

"Come, boychick, sit, sit," demanded the old man. "We must commemorate this special occasion! Silva!" he suddenly roared over his shoulder to the young bartender, "a fresh bottle of peppered vodka, three clean-wiped glasses, and a plate of cucumbers! And don't dally, man! We have much to celebrate!" The pensioner shoved Illya into a chair across the table with such force Illya thought it possible the chair's wooden legs would snap like twigs. Then Uncle Grisha at once became all exaggeratedly formal, skirting the table and maître d'-like gently pulling out a chair in which Katya Tevoradze was to sit. He kissed the young woman commandingly on top of her head then fell into his own chair like a sack of Russian turnips.

"I knew your father well, boychick," the man wagged a finger. "Your father, Konstantin, was a brave, fearless soldier. A sniper, a deadly assassin. Stalingrad. Six months of hell. Bloodiest battle in human history. Nearly two million killed. Hitler thought he would blow through Stalingrad on his way to the oil fields of the Caucasus, in the end, of course, the Red Army smashed Von Paulus's entire German Sixth Army. Even back then, you could tell your father, Konstantin, was destined for greatness. He won many hero medals, personally decorated by Stalin himself. And, of course, my older brother, Sandro, may God protect his dear departed soul, and I reported to Konstantin Alexandrivich a few years later at Stalin's *dacha* in Kuntsevo. We were part of your father's attachment, kitchen staff, cooks, at times waiters for Stalin's intolerable late-night dinners with his *siloviki*, his inner circle of bootlickers and backscratchers. It was your blessed father who made it possible for my brother and me to realize our childhood dream. I don't know why, but we always wanted to live in America. And look, here I am! It was your father who made it all happen!"

The man named Silva appeared gaunt-faced and indifferent. He carelessly plunked a tray with the vodka and glasses and a plate of pickled garlic on the table between the three people. Silva was one of the Matrabazi brothers. He was a shockingly thin, pale man with sunken eyes and wet-looking dark hair hard-combed back from his forehead. His open-front shirt revealed the formidable neck tattoos of a Georgian mobster. A yellowed toothpick poked from the side of his mouth, and he wore the perpetual leer of a sodomite.

"*Spasibo*, Silva!" Grisha roared.

"No pra-a-a-blem," he responded with the socialness of a mollusk. He had the bleating hack of a pack-a-day man. Without another word, he spun around and departed. Illya noticed that, once behind the long bar, Silva lit a cigarette and discreetly picked up a mobile phone, speaking furtively into it, all the while peering over his shoulder toward Illya and his companions. Illya's heartbeat paced in his chest.

Grisha noticed. He said, "Silva is one of the Matrabazi brothers. He's an idiot. Don't fret about him. You can trust him to always do something stupid."

"Who is the recessive gene at the end of the bar?" inquired Illya Podipenko.

"That would be Carza Matrabazi, the youngest of the four Matrabazi brothers. We call him Carza the Creature. Behind his back, of course. I have seen him take three men in his arms and squeeze them to death at one time." At the memory of it, Uncle Grisha let out a roar of laughter as if it had been all in good fun. "There was a rumor that Stalin had one of his scientists attempt to crossbreed apes with humans to produce a man-ape, a hybrid super warrior for his Red Army. Sometimes, when I look at Carza, I think that perhaps the experiment succeeded. Or perhaps failed. In any case, the giant is the Matrabazi organization's enforcer."

"Yes, I can see that," offered the investigator from Moscow.

Uncle Grisha poured unsparingly. "To my dear brother Sandro, to my lovely, beautiful niece Katya, and to my new friend Illya Konstantinovich," he shouted, raising his glass in the air. "*Na Zdorovie!*"

They drank, Katya choking in fitful spasms, gasping for air as the white-hot liquid torched the tissue at the back of her throat. Uncle Grisha smiled and re-poured.

"I was, of course, saddened when I heard the news that your great father had died," he said suddenly morose. "I followed the news in our Russian-language papers here. Putin appropriately gave the marshal a hero's state funeral, buried his ashes in the Kremlin wall. I am glad for that. The marshal deserved it." The old man's body was beginning to precariously tilt, and Illya wondered exactly how many liters of vodka dear Uncle Grisha had already swilled that afternoon. The old man squinted a blurry eye in Illya's general direction. "You were close to the marshal?"

"I believe so," Illya nodded, "particularly toward the end. I admit, my father at first was a bit put off by me not continuing in the Red Army after my compulsory two years' service. After all, our family's military tree stretched back to the seventeen hundreds when my great-great-grandfather was a general in the Russian Army battling the Ottoman Empire. But eventually, my father forgave my indiscretion. In the end, he confided to me that I made the right choice in joining the Moscow militia instead of choosing the Red Army."

"I understand." Uncle Grisha nodded. "And you have become a hero in your own right, no? Solving that nasty business surrounding the deaths of Rasputin's descendants and recovering the priceless imperial Fabergé eggs that no one even knew existed. Oh, yes, I read all about it. I can't help feeling your noble papa would have been extremely proud of you, Illya Konstantinovich."

"Thank you, Uncle Grisha," modestly replied the man from Moscow, not entirely certain why he had called him "uncle." "My great sadness is that the marshal did not hold on long enough to witness the outcome of that case." Illya fidgeted for a cigarette. He was typically uncomfortable talking about himself. He deftly changed the subject. "So," he began, "my pretty little student Katya tells me she believes her grandfather's unfortunate tumble down some dark stairs three days ago was not an accident. Do you concur?"

"Of course," Uncle Grisha grumbled, narrowing his eyes while the girl smiled sweetly and added an enthusiastically knowing look toward Illya as if to say, *See, I told you so.*

"Who would want to murder your brother, Sandro Tevoradze?" Illya asked simply.

To this, Uncle Grisha angled across the table, his craggy head beckoning the Moscow militiaman forward. Illya leaned in. "Look around, boychick. Do you know where we are?"

"The Dubenka?" answered Illya Podipenko.

"That is correct. My dear brother, Sandro, and I have been coming here for decades. Every day. Playing dominoes in the afternoon, right here at this table. You know who happens to operate this fine establishment?"

Illya thought back. "Katya said it was a gangster by the name of Dato Matrabazi."

"Right again. Dato Matrabazi. A greedy Georgian, absolutely ruthless. He runs the family operations here in America for his older brother in Moscow, Zaza Matrabazi. Zaza is head of the entire Matrabazi international operation, drugs, prostitution, extortion, money laundering. If possible, Zaza is even greedier and crazier than Dato."

For a moment, Illya sat wordlessly. He lifted his head to blow a gray tendril of cigarette smoke toward the ceiling and an out-of-order paddle fan. He noticed that the "no smoking" sign above the doorway fortuitously had seven bullet holes in it. At last, he said, "I still don't see what this has to do with the death of your brother, Sandro."

Uncle Grisha pitched even closer. "Gold," he whispered, "and rubles and priceless jewels, emeralds, and diamonds. Worth billions, *billions*! All remaining from the time of the Great Devil Stalin."

"I-I don't understand," Illya mumbled. "What gold, what rubles, what jewel—"

"Shhh," came the reply in form of a vodka spray. The old Georgian hurriedly shot a glance over his shoulder while, simultaneously, shoving an index finger the size of a kielbasa against Illya's lips. "It's a secret. I am the last living person to know about it. Stalin hid gold and diamonds and other treasures, you understand? They have never been found. No one knows they even exist. But they have learned about it."

"They?" Who they?" hopelessly inquired the Moscow militiaman.

"*They*." Uncle Grisha disconcertedly shushed directly into Illya's chin. Across the table, the old man's head rocked in the general direction of the next room, at last providing Illya Podipenko needed enlightenment.

"Ah, the Matrabazi brothers—" Illya managed to squeak out before Uncle Grisha once again slammed a silencing finger hard against the man's lips.

"Yes, the Matrabazi brothers. Sandro and I had the unfortunate habit of drinking to excess while playing dominoes. I fear at times we talked too carelessly about Stalin's hidden treasures. Mostly me, really. People overheard, you understand?"

Illya Podipenko's brain threatened overload. Facts, images flashed so brilliantly behind his eyes his mind had trouble absorbing them. He was about to ask a stupidly random question when Uncle Grisha noticed that the bartender, Silva, was approaching the table. At once, he grasped Illya's forearm with such force that Illya could feel capillaries crushing beneath his skin.

"They want information. My brother, Sandro, wouldn't give them any, and they killed him," the old man mouthed. Illya detected a sadness in his eyes. "They may try to kill me. Then they will come after young Katya here…unless you protect her. Do you know what I am saying, Illya Konstantinovich? Protect her with your life!"

"But—"

"Another round, old man?" inquired Silva around the stained toothpick sucked deep into his lips.

"Ah, alas, no, Silva, my good man," Uncle Grisha chortled expansively, waving his hands in the air. "It is time for this old man to wander home for a nap then a bit of dinner. But thank you all the same, my friend Silva." Uncle Grisha slipped a sideway wink to Illya and Katya.

The bartender dipped his shoulders listlessly, and when he turned his back, Uncle Grisha leaned forward and placed both hands on the table. He rose unsteadily from his chair and wobbled toward the doorway. He paused for a moment and turned to whisper under his breath to his niece, Katya.

"Our place. Eight o'clock tonight. Bring your new friend. I'll explain everything. It is time you knew the truth."

CHAPTER 3

They had discarded their shoes and socks near the Grimaldo's Chair lifeguard station and were squeezing the sands of Brighton Beach between their toes. Illya's feet barked from all the walking. The young girl had managed to wear him out. Presently, she was happily finishing off a waffle cone with vanilla ice cream and sprinkles on top that they had bought for her at Luna Park. The waters of the Atlantic lapped the shore, causing small whitecaps to foam, and a breeze floated over them. Big, hairy men in bright Speedos sat in the sand not far away with their cups of warm beers next to them. Out on the horizon, the evening sun was fading, and the sky appeared lazy and shaded. Night was approaching, and in the distance, they watched dark trawlers seining out on the water with gulls cawing and sweeping by. Further out, heat lightning snapped and popped between fretful clouds. Behind the couple, the thousand running lights of the giant Deno's Wonder Wheel glittered like a marvelous beacon. Somewhere in the expanse, Illya thought he heard the stirring, mellow sound of

Berber pipes sensually floating on the late afternoon breeze and men playing accordions and panduris.

The girl earnestly studied Illya Podipenko. She liked the fact that he had a sincere bearing about him. No airs. A worker bee. Unharried by professional aspirations. A man who, when he shared a confidence with you, you could believe it. She admired all the chinks and crevices in his face. An intrinsic look in his eye made him seem worthy of your trust.

Following the perplexing meeting with the girl's Uncle Grisha, Illya Podipenko and his young companion had strolled the streets of Little Odessa and its environs, scouring Russian bookstores and gazing in the windows of quaint shops with painted Russian nesting dolls and beautiful hand-painted black lacquered papier-mâché boxes from Palekh. Along the way, they passed the Muslim mosque at Brighton Seventh Street and Neptune Avenue where they paused to watch Muslims from Pakistan and Bangladesh pray. They walked the two blocks of Brighton Beach Avenue under the elevated train and saw street vendors hawking all manner of Russian goods and food. They bought sweets at a Korean market and a fresh loaf of caraway bread from a Russian bakery. They sauntered along the Riegelmann Boardwalk past the aquarium all the way to the Steeplechase Pier, and at a nearby playground, they paused to watch Russian pensioners playing chess. They passed teens huddled chummily, shouting and laughing and puffing on their flavored Juul vapes. They took selfies in front of a stadium where minor league baseball was played.

They stopped to watch giant cranes and powerful bulldozers determinedly making tall, modern condos where smaller bungalows had existed for decades. The girl had inhaled two loaded hot dogs and cheese fries from Nathan's on Surf Avenue, and then, against Illya's better judgment, they took in a carnival side-show where they gawked at a snake charmer, a contortionist, and a performer billed as Dr. Claw who put fish hooks in his eyelids and then, inexplicably, picked up a clock with them.

It was quite possible, Illya Podipenko became aware, that the young girl, who had been blissfully skipping beside him, had been chatting away in hypersonic speed virtually nonstop, the entire time, apparently unencumbered by the need to pause for oxygen; but she also was so open and full of life. He was glad that they decided to sit in the cool sand for a spell.

"I love Brighton Beach," the girl was now saying. "This area, from Sheepshead Bay to Sea Gate was purchased from Native Americans in 1645 for a gun, a blanket, and a kettle."

"What kind of kettle?" asked Illya Podipenko.

"Seriously?" the girl frowned. "Does it matter?"

Illya shrugged his shoulders. "I don't know. It must have been a pretty special kettle for the Native Americans to be willing to accept it in trade for Little Odessa."

The girl swatted at Illya's shoulder. "Who knows, maybe it was a special kettle. Maybe it was filled with bundles of money."

"Then not so different from today's politicians," Illya said.

Katya was quiet a moment, squinting her eyes in the distance. "So what did you think of Uncle Grisha?" at last she asked Illya Podipenko.

For the past twenty minutes, Illya had serenely listened as the young girl told him about the lives of her grandfather, Sandro Tevoradze, and his younger brother, Grisha, who, she had said, were born in the mid-1930s in a mud hut in the village of Khashuri on the Kura River in Soviet Georgia, the once proud independent republic that unpopular native son, Joseph Stalin, as soon as he could, would strip the country of its autonomy and forcibly suck it back into the Russian empire, an act of betrayal many Georgians to this day would not forget.

When Katya's grandfather and uncle were mere infants, the girl explained to the Moscow investigator, their peasant family, as part of Stalin's brutal scheme to exterminate Russia's entire Kulak peasant class, was uprooted and sent to one of the forced labor camps in distant Kazakhstan. Both parents died in the Gulag in the 1930s, as did millions of other kulaks, and the young orphaned boys, Sandro and Grisha, were shuttled from one prisoner hut in a collective farm to another until at last they were sent off to an orphanage in faraway Moscow.

It was a startlingly dreadful place: unkempt and vermin-infested, with daily beatings, sodomizations, and older bullies pummeling frightened weaklings on a scheduled basis. It was during these hard times that Sandro and Grisha truly became inseparable as brothers by necessity guarding each other's back. They were growing strong and tough and smart, and as early teenagers, they agreed they had had enough of being guests of the Russian state and ran off to live on the streets of the inner city of Moscow. They soon joined one of the many gangs of abandoned children who begged, stole, and even murdered in order to survive. They slept in abandoned warehouses, stairways, and in corridors. But youthful gangs were becoming such a problem that the now-in-charge potentate, the Great and All-Powerful Joseph Stalin, passed a law that anyone over age twelve caught in a crime would be shot immediately. This decree encouraged the boys to abandoned their free-roaming criminal ways in favor of alternative romantic pursuits. Thus, lying about their ages; in 1949, they decided to join the proud Russian Army that had defeated the hated Germans in the Great Patriotic War. They were assigned as Army cooks and became somewhat well-known for their preparing imaginative Georgian meals for their fellow soldiers.

One fateful day in January 1952, they got a call that changed their lives forever. The Generalissimo, the Great Stalin himself, surprisingly requested a meeting with the two young Georgian soldiers in person. The courageous lads would gladly and bravely and without so much as a flinch stand nose-to-nose with any enemy of the motherland. But this was something decidedly different. This was being summoned to appear before the *Vozhd*, the leader, the immortal deity Stalin. The boys had heard all the stories, the harrowing whispered tales of citizens who, having been personally summoned by Stalin, afterward seemed to have awkwardly and inexplicably vanished from the planet.

Sandro and Grisha were taken by private car through the Kremlin's Spassky Gate just as the clock tower was fatefully tolling above them. They were ushered into the triangular Yellow Palace, which was built for Catherine the Great and was the old Senate building. An elevator shuttled them to the second floor to the infamous room known as the Little Corner, Stalin's office. They were kept waiting in an anteroom by stern-faced guards for a half hour on a bench outside the hallowed office, thirty minutes that seemed to stretch agonizingly into a week. In his nervousness, Sandro had sweated completely through his army uniform; Grisha had gnawed the inside of a cheek to blood. When at last a guard appeared in front of them saying "The boss will you see you," the men had jumped like startled quail and had to help each other up from the wooden bench. Right before pushing open the heavy door, the guard muttered to the army soldiers, "Look him directly in the eyes. He doesn't trust people whose eyes fade away. He thinks they are hiding something."

The boys entered the room on bloodless legs, helping one another in an attempt to stand straight as ramparts. The room was long and rectangular and was underlit. A lengthy table was scattered with papers and dirty ashtrays. There was wood paneling,

extended windows with heavy red velvet drapes, polished floors, and red-and-green carpets. Portraits of
Lenin and Marx decorated the walls. A large desk
stood in the right rear corner.

Behind the desk sat a surprisingly undersized,
swarthy man in a wrinkled party tunic. He had a
thick, broad mustache and a disturbingly pitted face.
Purple smoke billowed from the bowl of a pipe he
had wedged between yellow teeth. A small desk lamp
with a crooked shade and thinly watted bulb disconcertingly cast his face in shadows.

He paid the boys no attention, continuing to
studiously work over long lists he appeared to be
marking with a red crayon. He looked as if he was
crossing out names then adding new names to the
lists. The boys had heard all the tales of Stalin and
his death lists. The older of the boys, Sandro, gulped
audibly while the younger, Grisha, considered turning and bolting straight through the closed door
behind them.

"You are Georgians?" Sandro thought he heard
a voice ask, speaking in his Georgian accent.

The boys became mute statues, unable to call
upon a single word.

"You are Georgians?" the man shouted, slap-
ping a hand on his desk. "I demand an answer!"

"Yes, proud Georgians, Comrade Stalin!"
Sandro's congealed vocal chords managed to squeak
out. Clearly, Stalin was no Yorick, decided Sandro,
a so-called fellow of infinite jest as Shakespeare had
once written.

"Where?"

"Where, Comrade Stalin?"

"Where, idiot! Do not toy with me! Where were you born, what village?"

"Khashuri, Comrade Stalin," Sandro answered raggedly while his brother, Grisha, contemplated sprinting all the way to Lenin's Tomb.

"Khashuri," the man chuffed out of the side of his mouth around the stem of his pipe. It was uttered as if Khashuri and all those unfortunate enough to be born there were to be truly pitied. "I was born in Gori," he suddenly announced and for a moment stopped working on his lists. He seemed briefly lost in his own thought. The two brothers stood wordless, unsure if a response was required. There wasn't a schoolboy in all the Soviet Union who didn't know that their beloved *Vozhd* was born in Gori.

"You prepare Georgian dishes?" the man abruptly asked.

"Pardon?" replied Sandro Tevoradze.

Stalin clapped the desk once more. His face darkened, uncovering blue engorged veins around his temples. He still hadn't looked up from the lists in front of him. "If I have to repeat myself one more time, you, boys, might find yourselves a head shorter by tomorrow morning. Tell me Georgian dishes you prepare!"

Sandro began his answer in an inadvertently formal tone that quavered in the air between his lips and the desk where the boss was sitting. "Well, I'd like to think, Comrade, we prepare our cuisine in the best Georgian tradition, using influences from throughout the Caucasus and Eastern Europe while adding some Middle Eastern culinary. We incorporate a broad interplay of gastronomic concepts carried along the old Silk Road trade route by merchants and travelers alike—" Without warning, Sandro cried out as his young brother Grisha gave him a crushing boot kick to his ankle.

"Fucking imbecile," he whispered. "You are playing with our lives here!"

"Next!" screamed the leader.

"What my older brother was trying to say," Grisha jumped in to fill the void, "is that we do not limit ourselves to a single style of cuisine. We borrow the best recipes from the entire region. Georgian *Mtsvadi* kababs and corn porridge, Siberian *pelmeni*, pepper skins stuffed with walnut sauce called *Apyrphlchara* from Abkhazia. Very delicious. *Satsvi* from Guria, Khinkall dumplings, thick *lavashi* bread, a nice *shchi* of cabbage soup and veal, Mingrelian *Khachapuri...*"

"No!" Stalin shrieked.

"Pardon, Comrade?"

"Nothing Mingrelian, ever! I have grown weary of Mingrelians," he chortled quietly to himself then circled a name on his list. The two young boys goggled at each other wide-eyed, unsure if they should buy Stalin's Mingrelian henchman Lavrenti Berea a going-away gift.

"You, young men, come highly recommended," the leader called out. His tone indicated that perhaps he was contemplating that the recommendation had been in error.

"Thank you, Comrade," Sandro quickly replied. "May we inquire who was kind enough to recommend us?"

Stalin paused. For the first time, he lifted his eyes from the lists in front of him. His head slowly turned toward the boys. His eyes glared yellow at the two young man as if they were slow learners. "If I wanted you to know that information, do you not think that I would have already shared it with you?" Stalin desolately shook his head and went back to his lists.

"Yes, Generalissimo, of course, Generalissimo," Grisha replied in a chatter. Next to him, his older brother nudged Grisha with his shoulder. He nodded to a dark shadow against the curtains behind and off to the side of the leader's desk. There, the boys noticed a single shoe on the carpeting, a polished Army boot. Then another boot appeared, and before long in the half light, a body moved silently forward. The young men recognized the Army officer immediately. It was the famed young Stalingrad assassin, Konstantin Podipenko. The face of the man expansively smiled at them, and his eye gave them a good-natured wink. Then his body silently receded back into the shadows as quickly as it had appeared.

Presently, thoughtfully, Konstantin Podipenko's son, Illya, leaned his arms and hands backward, supporting his body in the Brighton Beach sand.

He said to the young girl next to him, "So you ask me what do I think of Uncle Grisha? Well, I suppose I would say *curiouser and curiouser*, to quote our fabled friend, Alice," the man replied. "A rather adventurous and mysterious life, if I may say so. And now your uncle Grisha speaks of hidden Stalin treasures. Nasty Georgian underworld thugs. An apparent murder of his brother, your grandfather…" He trailed off, shrugging his shoulders. "What's not to like about Uncle Grisha?"

"Be serious, won't you, Illya?" scolded the young girl. She brushed back her black hair and put a pink clip in it. She was wearing cutoff jeans and a tie-dyed T-shirt. "You forgot to mention that you swore your oath to Uncle Grisha you would protect me."

"My oath…?" The militiaman suddenly stroked his throbbing forearm that at the Dubenka Club Uncle Grisha had clenched in such earnestness that a sweltering purple ring now garnished it. "Not many options were offered," he reminded the girl, his tone unfortunately edged harder than he had intended. He could feel the girl gazing at him.

"Oh, I see." At once, her lovely smile had faded. The edges of her young face turned somber, and her tone became more formal. "I apologize, then, Investigator Illya Podipenko, that I troubled you this afternoon in Central Park. Quite obviously, I have made a mess of your life, your planned vacation. Perhaps it is better that after dinner we shall go our separate ways."

"Pardon? Oh, no, no, Katya," Illya replied hurriedly, softly. He could see what looked like a single tear forming at the corner of the girl's eyes. His chest involuntarily gave a single thump. Slowly, he reached out, folding one of Katya's hands warmly in his own. "I'm afraid you must get used to my dry wit, such as it is, my new, little friend…that is…if we are going to be working together."

"Wait, what?" The girl raised her chin hopefully.

"Of course, Katya. What did you think? I was going to leave an unspeakably beautiful, young woman all alone to fight Georgian hoodlums? We are in this together now, Katya, together, for good or bad."

Her wondrous eyes sparked in approval, and she smiled sweetly. "Do you really think so, Illya?" she whispered excitedly.

"Think what? For good or bad?"

"No, the other part."

"There was another part?"

Katya's large eyes blinked. "You called me an unspeakably beautiful, young woman."

The man flinched. A line of perspiration inadvertently formed itself across his forehead. Illya forced a smile. "Did I? Why, yes…yes, of course. I think you are an unspeakably beautiful, young woman. Well, perhaps not *unspeakably* beautiful because, obviously, I just spoke about it, but—"

"There's your dry wit again!" the woman shouted so loudly that two concerned joggers paused to see if she needed help. "I love it, Illya!"

The man tilted his head at her. Then, quite unplanned, he leaned over, kissing the top of one of her hands. "You will stay with me tonight. I must protect you now."

At once, Katya's eyes glowed like burning embers. "Dude, I like where your head is right now. I'm all in! But suddenly, I'm famished. Let's eat!"

*****

Across the table, her young, wide eyes sparkled in the candlelight. Illya thought he could detect incandescent and strangely sensual specks of jade in the irises of her eyes. At their second meal of the day, they were sipping sweet Georgian white wine and eating stuffed eggplant and chicken in a walnut-curry sauce and brown bread at the comfortable little Vilka's restaurant off Brighton Second Street near the playground. Tchaikovsky's "Waltz of the Flowers" gently played in the background.

Illya Podipenko could feel the flesh of his belly shamefully thrusting against the waistband of his trousers. The promise of future heartburn flirted with him. Illya was thankful that Columbia University had paid him an unconscionable sum of money as a special lecturer, for he realized that, once more, he would be paying for the current repast.

For twenty-five minutes, the young girl had sat across from him chattering unabated, each syllable chirped out in such an excited, bewildering rush; Illya at times found it challenging to follow the flow of conversation. It seemed that sometimes she spoke in English then just as quickly switched to Russian, then threw on top of it some arcane Georgian phraseology that kept his mind spiraling around like a sucking eddy.

Still, Illya admitted to himself, he rather enjoyed sitting there stirring cherry jam into his cup of tea, listening to her talk, her conversation so open, so earnest and genuine and at times quite amusing.

Thoughtfully, he leaned against the back of his chair. He dabbed a napkin at the corner of his mouth, sighing. He thought it was all going nicely, right up to the moment Katya Tevoradze asked one of her patented out-of-nowhere questions, asking it with such uncomplicated innocence, she could have been merely a child inquiring what makes pepper hot. The question so surprised her dinner partner that a tender wedge of chicken had gotten inhaled directly into his throat, and he took to hacking as if he were an old car trying to turn over on a winter's morning. The gleaming fork Illya Podipenko had clasped in his hand slipped precipitously out of his fingers, clattering loudly and embarrassingly against the edge of his nice china plate.

"What-what did you say?" at last he managed to sputter breathlessly, hacking conspicuously into his napkin, furiously lapping water from the glass in front of him.

Katya smiled, intentionally letting the words of her question hang between them. "Don't be silly, Illya, you heard me. I simply asked when was it that you first realized that you had fallen hopelessly in love with Lena Sharapova?"

"Lena...who?" the man mumbled uselessly, his mind thick as a bog. He looked across at the young woman with his brain stuck in neutral.

"Sharapova! Please, Illya! Don't treat me like a child. I was an 'A' student in your class. I attended all of your lectures. Lena Sharapova, whose life you saved two years ago in Moscow, remember? A direct descendent of Rasputin. When you uncovered the plot to murder all Rasputin's heirs, in order to steal all those priceless Fabergé eggs and you became a state hero. Seem vaguely familiar?"

"Ah, yes, yes, of course, *that* Lena Sharapova. I must have misunderstood you." He prattled as blood pounded his temples. "I don't see how—"

"Whatever, dude," scolded the young lady, "men are like plastic sandwich bags. You hold everything in, but we can see right through you." She tipped forward, bringing her elbows onto the white tablecloth. She smiled coyly, her words were spoken in a conspiratorial whisper. "Was it love at first sight, Illya? That's so romantic! I am outrageously jealous of her, you know. I just wish you felt about me like you felt about her."

"What?" Illya noticed fingers on one of his hands independently twitching like boughs in the wind. "I was *not* in love with Lena Sharapova—"

Suddenly, a laugh emanated from Katya Tevoradze's spreading lips with such velocity that it quaked the crockery on the table between them. She quickly attempted to stifle the sound with the back of her hand. "Oh, for God's sakes, Illya, a woman can tell. Every time, and I mean *every* time you said her name during your university lectures, your eyes became all round as eggs and started to glaze over and spin like saucers. Then you began stuttering like a goose. I'd say you have it pretty bad."

"Have...bad...what?" He wished the blood would stop pounding like a derrick in his ears.

"Love, Illya, *love*! Isn't it grand! But at times doesn't it hurt!" The young woman reached a hand across the table to lightly stroke the back of Illya Podipenko's hand. At first, he reacted as if he had been pinpricked, but Katya captured his fleeing hand in midair and refused to let it go. "Come on, Illya," she spoke softly, "admit it. I already know, anyway."

For a long-suffering moment, all the man could do was stare across the table in an idiot's gaze. His heart was thumping inside his shirt. Katya's smiling, youthful face seemed surrounded in magnificent soft light, disconcertingly radiating an angel's innocent halo. He saw clearly that he was trapped like a wolf in the taiga. And like a trapped wolf, he was destined to eventually surrender to his inevitable fate, perhaps chew off his own leg.

At last, he said slowly, sitting back in the chair, "I didn't realize it showed so much. That's quite embarrassing. You say everyone in my class knew?"

Katya gently began backtracking, "Not *everyone,* goodness, no. Certainly not the ones sleeping during your lectures..."

Illya blinked, stupidly. "Well, that's good... I suppose..."

He attempted to gather himself. His young companion had him by the tail, and he knew it. "I don't know if you could call it in love exactly," he began an explanation. "I would say more like an idiotic schoolboy's crush, perhaps. Incredibly stupid on my part, of course. The wistful follies of an old man, I suppose. After all, she was one of the most beautiful women in all of the Soviet Union. And smart too. An English interpreter. She moved here, to New York, about the same time I did. She worked for the United Nations."

"Is she still in New York?"

"She is."

"Do you see her?"

"No. Well, I used to. My first year here, she gave me English lessons. But I haven't seen her in over a year. I understand that she married a diplomat and moved into a big house on Long Island. I am very happy for her. She deserves it. She went through a lot back in Moscow over the whole Rasputin-Fabergé Egg fiasco. I helped her out is all."

"Uh-huh," replied Katya Tevoradze, "a bit more than that I suspect, Illya. You saved her life and recovered that priceless Fabergé egg that rightfully belonged to her. She has to be eternally grateful to you."

"Well, I suppose..." Illya was balling his linen napkin in his lap. After a few moments, he sighed deeply and said, "In the Alice book, the March Hare said something very wise. He said, 'I have an excellent idea. Let's change the subject.'"

"So there it is, Illya."

"There what is?"

"An older man falls head over heels for a much younger woman. So I ask you, why then can't a younger woman, say me, fall hopelessly in love with an older man, say you?" Her eyelids fluttered innocently like butterfly wings. Under the table, her foot gave Illya's leg a romantic, conspiratorial rub.

For a long moment, Illya Podipenko's faculty of speech had deserted him, and he could do no more than gaze off into the ether, slack-jawed. Not knowing what else to do, he at last took to goggling at his watch.

"My, my, look at the time," he whistled. Then over his shoulder he hurriedly bellowed, "Check please!"

CHAPTER 4

Illya Podipenko and his new friend, Katya, entered through a rear gate that creaked when she swung it open. The two-story flat was on Brightwater Court near the playground. The townhouse had a brick base and white aluminum covering the second story. A room air conditioner poked out of one of the upper windows. In all, it was a clean, unassuming looking place to live and in a lesser location would fetch perhaps forty thousand on the market, but its Brighton Beach location near the boardwalk, beach, and ocean alone pegged the sellers' price at around six hundred fifty-thousand dollars.

Katya led the Moscow investigator through a small courtyard with uneven bricks, an overhanging tree, some potted plants, a small table, and two outdoor chairs. In the dark, Illya inadvertently plowed into a pair of metal garbage cans, and they clattered loudly. Close by, a wary dog barked.

"Sorry," he embarrassingly whispered to the young girl, who chuckled knowingly, having done as much herself a dozen times in the past.

She climbed three concrete steps and drew open a rear door to the townhouse that she had shared nearly her entire life with her grandfather and uncle. Her left hand sought out a light switch, which she flipped on, not that the single bulb at the top of the long wooden stairs offered suitable illumination. They stepped inside.

"This is where we found Grandpa Sandro's body." Katya nodded at the dark space at their feet.

"I see," replied Illya softly. He peered up through the dark at old wood stairs that seemed to climb unabated to the heavens. "It's like climbing Mt. Elbrus in the Caucasus," whistled the man from Moscow. "And you don't believe your grandfather accidentally fell down these steps?"

"I know he didn't. Grandpa Sandro was very much afraid of these steep steps. He never, and I mean *never*, used them. The same with Uncle Grisha. Look how dark it is, how steep the steps are. They are old men."

"Hmm," Illya allowed. "And what did the police say?"

"The police? They said it was an accident, that Sandro likely fell down the stairs. No signs of forced entry or foul play."

"Yes, of course." Illya paused clearing his throat. "Don't be too hard on the police, Katya. I myself would likely have reached the same conclusion. Look, there is no sign of forced entry. Is this back door always locked?"

The young girl paused then answered in a quiet voice, "Well...in theory, yes."

"In theory?" asked Illya Podipenko.

"Sometimes, I forget to lock it, I admit it. Hurrying out for my school classes, taking out the trash. Look, it's so hidden back here. You'd think that no one would be interested. It's not like our humble home appears that we would have a lot of valuables lying about, does it?"

"I suppose not," answered the Russian investigator. "Then you are convinced that it was foul play?"

"Not a doubt in my mind. I think it was a kidnapping gone wrong. The Matrabazi brothers. I believe they were going to force Grandpa Sandro to tell them about the supposed Stalin secret treasures that Sandro and Uncle Grisha would talk about when drunk in the brothers' nightclub."

"And yet, if they killed Sandro, they wouldn't get the information they wanted, would they? Why push him down the stairs? They needed Sandro alive. I believe you are right. They were trying to kidnap him, but at some point, your grandpa Sandro managed to break away and accidentally tumbled to his death down these stairs. The Matrabazi brothers had to realize that if Sandro were to die, so too would the valuable secrets he knew."

"Makes sense," replied Katya then hesitantly added, "It appears Uncle Grisha is now the last person alive who knows the secrets."

"We need to talk to him. He could be in real danger," said Illya Podipenko. "The Matrabazis aren't likely to quit until they know where the supposed Stalin treasure is hidden." He went quiet a moment, his face clouding.

"What?" Katya noticed.

"I fear you may also be in grave danger, Katya."

"But I don't know anything. Sandro and Grisha never talked to me about their secret."

"Yes, but the Matrabazis don't know that."

*****

"Uncle Grisha, you must leave here. You may be in danger."

The old man grunted stubbornly. "I won't do that, my darling niece," answered the old man, his words announced in a gravely voice, a consequence of a lifetime of no-filter Russian cigarettes. He sat hunched in a tattered overstuffed chair in his small but well-kept living room. A bottle of vodka teetered in his lap. His speech was slurred, his sad old eyes rheumy. For the first time, Illya noticed that the old man's forehead bore the puffed scars of a man accustomed to leading with his head in tavern brawls and other disagreements.

"You go, Katya, with your new friend, Illya. He will protect you. I am an old man. I can't run anymore. I will stay."

"That's crazy, Uncle Grisha! They will *kill* you. You know what the Matrabazi gang is like and what they did to Grandpa Sandro!"

"And that is why I am staying, my dear. If the cursed Matrabazis try anything funny…well, I will kill them before they will kill me." The old man from the cushion of the chair pulled out an old Russian pistol, a Nagant M1895, an officer's model, a double-action, seven-shot, gas-sealed revolver. He waved it in the air. Intently, Uncle Grisha's shifted his eyes to the man sitting across from him on a brown sofa. "You must take care of my darling niece, do you understand, Illya Podipenko? She is the last of our Tevoradze line here in America. Guard her with your life."

"Of course, Grisha, you can rely on me. I won't allow anything to happen to her."

"It's settled then," Grisha muttered in a fading voice. He shunted the gun back down into the seat cushion of his chair. His head bobbed. His eyes were bleary, and he looked unsteady in the chair. Illya thought that perhaps the old man had receded into a vodka swoon, but at once, his head came up and he stared into the distance. Grisha smiled obliquely. He turned his face to his niece.

"Katya, my dear, will you do this old man a favor and nudge the fire a bit, eh? As you well know, these old bones get cold at night, even in the summer." He watched as the young woman, as she had done nearly her entire life, took a pointed brass poker next to the small fireplace and gave the single log a jab. Orange sparks snapped up the chimney. "I do so love the warmth of a small fire." Grisha said to no one in particular. He watched his niece return to the sofa and fold herself close to Illya Podipenko. He thought he saw her place her hand on top of the man's.

"So, Uncle Grisha," she gently reminded the old man, "at the Dubenka Club this afternoon, you said you were going to tell us the story of how Illya's father, the famous Marshal Podipenko, was responsible for you and Grandpa Sandro settling here in America."

"Yes…of course," remembered the old man. He took a breath and shifted his weight, pitching forward on the edge of his chair. He gazed pensively into the flames then spoke conspiratorially, "I have many, many things to tell you tonight, some bad things that your grandfather and I have kept secret all these years. Forgive us, my dear, we did this to protect you for your own safety."

"I understand, Uncle Grisha," Katya softly responded. She and Illya exchanged searching glances. Flames crackled a log in the fireplace.

"What I am going to tell you, no one else knows. I am the last living soul on this earth who knows the truth." He lifted the bottle of vodka to his mouth and took a swallow. He sponged his lips on the sleeve of his shirt.

"The first thing that you should know," he began deliberately, looking across at his niece, "is that Stalin did not die the way they say in history books. The fact is, your grandfather Sandro and I *murdered* Joseph Stalin, the leader of Mother Russia." He then shifted his gaze to Illya Podipenko and hunched forward in his chair. "And your father, the hero marshal, planned the whole damn thing."

*****

"We loved your father, Konstantin Podipenko, my brother Sandro and I," Grisha said thoughtfully to Illya. He shifted in his chair and cleared his throat. "He was a young, great man, respected, courageous, trustworthy. As I said, your father was personally responsible for Sandro and I living our dream of coming to the United States. Did your father ever mention this to you?"

The Moscow militiaman shook his head no.

The old man sat back in the chair. He poured vodka into a glass and threw it down his throat. He hacked into the back of his hand, slapped his right knee, and continued his tale, "Your father was a young man, a genuine war hero. This was in 1943, so your father probably was about nineteen years old at the time when he was personally appointed by Stalin to his general staff. The boss brought Konstantin Podipenko to Moscow directly from his heroics at Stalingrad. Stalin found your father to possess all the qualities of an ideal Soviet soldier: intelligent, dedicated, and ruthless. And the fact that your father was the deadliest assassin in all of the Red Army was not lost on the boss. With his paranoia growing daily, Stalin wanted a man with your father's lethal skill set close to him, so he appointed your father as a deputy commandant of operations for the near *dacha* at Kuntsevo, which meant that all the *dacha* staff ultimately took orders from him. Guards, maids, kitchen staff, groundskeepers, everyone."

Grisha paused a moment then leaned forward. "You see, in Stalin's ego-driven, conspiratorial universe, he came to believe that your father was perhaps the one man in the whole of the great motherland that he could speak confidentially to. From the very beginning, your father never shied away from an audience with the great leader. He always spoke straightforward and unblinking to the boss, staring straight into Stalin's eyes as they talked, which he knew Stalin greatly respected. Stalin had grown to hate many of those in his inner circle of sycophants who shifted and shrugged and fearfully stammered when he spoke to them, their eyes wandering to the carpeting at their feet. Stalin knew that when he would ask a question of his magnates, they would respond only with what they thought the great leader wanted to hear. But your father was different. Your father told the boss what he thought. I once overheard him tell Stalin, 'Others will tell you what you want to hear, Comrade Stalin. I will tell you what is true.'"

"At first," continued the old man, "many of Stalin's political allies and military officers were jealous of the leader's close relationship with the young sharpshooter, Konstantin Podipenko. They feared the young man had too much influence over the tyrant. But over the years, those same people actually became quite fond of the young man. They learned that Konstantin was well and truly a good man, and a fair one, and his close relationship with Stalin rather than a threat actually could be quite beneficial to them. When they wanted or needed something, they would let Konstantin know, and if he believed in the request, he would recommend it to Stalin at night, when they were together drinking and discussing worldly matters in the leader's study. If Stalin, for some reason, balked at the young man's request, Konstantin would nod understandingly and quietly, gently remind the already paranoid dictator that he hated when the two of them disagreed on a matter and that, if necessary, Konstantin would be forced to have Stalin eliminated so that a more socially acceptable solution to his request could be reached."

Grisha offered a warm grin. "So your father became, in essence, Stalin's confidante and personal aide-de-camp at the *dacha*. Always with him. They took walks together in the gardens surrounding the *dacha*, among the lemon bowers and tomatoes plants and his favorite rose bushes and mimosa flowers. Konstantin would help Stalin prune his precious roses at night, a time the leader oddly preferred. They fed birds on the open veranda. They played backgammon or chess or shot billiards when time allowed. Your father would patiently listen as Stalin would sing one of his favorite Georgian laments like "Fly Away Black Swallow." They would discuss art and history. Sometimes, your father would accompany Stalin to the opera to hear Chaliapin sing in his deep, bass voice. Stalin even allowed your father to shave him with a straight razor and to put talcum powder on his face to hide the pockmarks for photographs and public appearances. Still, there were some of the magnates who remained quite jealous of your father."

"Goodness," Illya Podipenko remarked, "I had no idea."

"I suspected as much," knowingly smiled Uncle Grisha. "But do not judge your father harshly, Illya Konstantinovich. I imagine he purposefully kept this information from you. The less you knew, the better. Not that he was ashamed at what he did during those days of Stalin. I think your father feared that perhaps his son might grow up thinking less of him as a true hero."

"I wouldn't do that," Illya responded. He rubbed his face with his fingers.

"But you haven't heard the entire story yet, Illya. Are you certain you want me to continue?"

Across from him, Illya Podipenko nodded affirmatively. The college girl, Katya Tevoradze, moved even closer to Illya on the couch. She threaded her arm through his then said, "Oh, you *must*, Uncle Grisha! Tell us about the murder of Stalin! Tell us *everything*!"

For a long moment, Uncle Grisha with soft eyes peered across at his beautiful niece and her new friend. He smiled at them warmly. He shakily set the bottle of vodka on a table next to him. "Very well," he said. "I shall proceed."

"It had become a nightly routine," Grisha continued his tale, leaning back in his chair. "After a round of feasting and drinking and cruel shenanigans, the inner circle of magnates would at last depart Stalin's Kuntsevo *dacha* about four or five o'clock in the morning. Stalin, ever the insomniac who dreaded being alone, would then summon his young aide, Konstantin Podipenko, to his study. The young aide would enter and exit the room through a hidden panel among the bookshelves that linked the room with the kitchen area. Konstantin would usually deliver a bottle of Georgian *Khvanchkara* wine night after night, never seen nor heard by the guards standing outside of Stalin's door. Sometimes, the great leader would simply say to his aide, 'Stalin's Tea,' a private code word for a precise beverage Stalin enjoyed. Konstantin would arrange the boss's tea served in a glass in a silver holder. Stalin would squeeze a lemon wedge into the tea, then Konstantin would produce a bottle of fine Armenian brandy. He would pour half a teaspoon worth into the tea then gently stir it for the boss. Stalin always smiled and nodded and uttered, 'Ah, Stalin's Tea, have a sip won't you?' He made his aide, your father, sip first to demonstrate that the tea had not been poisoned. In later years, Konstantin would bring Stalin a boiling cup of water in which he would put drops of iodine. Stalin had come to believe, for whatever reason, that this mixture would stave off his dangerous and ongoing battle with escalating hypertension. He was wrong.

"Sometimes at night, the young aide would play the American gramophone that Stalin kept on a side table. They would sit and listen to the Duke's aria from *Rigoletto*, Stalin's favorite. Or Mozart's "Piano Concerto No. 23," which seemed to have a brief calming effect on the leader. At such times, the aide resisted playing another of Stalin's prized records, that of dogs comically barking to music. Sometimes, Konstantin would read from Bulgakov's *Day of the Turbins*, Stalin's beloved play. The *Vozhd* knew the play so well that he would speak the words right along with Konstantin Podipenko. Sometimes, Konstantin would read chapters from *The Last of the Mohicans*, another one of Stalin's favorites, or Rustaveli's Georgian epic poem *The Knight in Tiger Skin*. In later years, the boss would hand his young aide-de-camp some tattered pages he had kept hidden away in a drawer. They were published poems that Stalin had written in his youth when he wrote under the name of "Soselo." As Konstantin read "Morning" or "To the Moon," Stalin would lean his head back against his chair, close his eyes, and whisper word for word what Konstantin was reading aloud. Many nights following the poetry readings, Konstantin Podipenko would sneak Stalin into the *dacha*'s kitchen, where the boss would strip down to his undergarments and lay on a wood board above a large bread oven. Stalin felt that the heat would soothe his bouts of nerve inflammation.

"But mostly, Stalin and his young aide would just sit close and chat, the boss on his divan and Konstantin Podipenko in a chair across from him. They would discuss history, the war, poetry, art, and literature until Stalin would fall asleep on the divan, books scattered around him. As they chatted, Stalin would enjoy recalling the days of his youth in Gori and Tiflis, greatly embellishing his role in the revolutionary underground movement and the subsequent

Bolshevik takeover of Russia. He would speak long-ingly, wistfully, and fondly of the friends, comrades, and family members from those early days. In Stalin's senile dementia, Konstantin realized the old man had apparently, perhaps conveniently, forgotten that most of those people he now recalled so fondly he had tortured, liquidated, or sent to Siberia to 'count the birch trees.' As he chatted to his aide, the boss would at times sit stroking his mustache with a finger, always a sign of calmness in the man, and he would frequently sketch wolves' heads on a pad of paper or, in the last days of his life, simply review the latest interrogations of Jewish doctors scheduled for work camps or extermination.

"On the night of February 28, 1953, Stalin, as accustomed, entertained his ever-dwindling inner circle, Malenkov, Beria, Bulganin, and Khrushchev, at the near *dacha*. Molotov and Mikoyan were no longer invited to these nightly festivities, not a propitious sign for their futures. Earlier in the evening, the boss and his cortege had, as was the excruciating nightly ritual, watched movies, often Charlie Chaplin or American westerns or *Boys' Town*, at the Kremlin before jumping into waiting cars and being whisked the thirty minutes to the Kuntsevo *dacha*. There, for hours, they ate and overdrank, listening with feigned interest as Stalin babbled inflatedly about the old days and how he had grown to have unflagging faith in his own infallible greatness. The boss, once a saintly choirboy, would then launch into a song, usually a melancholy Georgian lament. In the end, this night was a good night, the magnates felt, as the great leader seemed to be in a passably good mood, no one had left the *dacha* on a stretcher. Having bid them all farewell, Stalin retired to his suite of small rooms.

"Around five o'clock in the morning, Sandro Tevoradze and I quietly entered one of Stalin's rooms through the hidden doorway that Konstantin Podipenko had previously shown us. As part of the plan, Konstantin had taken the night off. We breathed a quick sigh of relief as we saw that, according to plan, the great leader had fallen asleep on a pink-lined divan. We peered around the dark room. Sandro elbowed me, nodding toward the walls enclosing the small room. On the walls were dozens of strangely disconcerting pictures of young Soviet children Stalin had torn from magazines and pinned in random order. We shivered, and I noticed that my knees had begun clacking together so loudly that I thought the noise would awaken Stalin before we had the chance to dispatch him. The *Vozhd* lay on his back, snoring jaggedly.

"Like misty shadows, we slid furtively across the room, our hearts pounding. Sandro pulled a small kitchen towel from his pocket and mutely stood gazing down at the man who had ruled the Soviet Union for nearly three decades and murdered countless millions of his own people. He was disturbed by how shriveled the man was in old age. His belly had grown round, his face shrunken, his hair thinning and white, his withered arm appearing more stunted than ever. Sandro felt a tug on his sleeve that made him jump.

"'You realize what we are about to do is an act of cold-blooded, treasonous murder, right?' I whispered fretfully. 'We will change history. It's not too late, Sandro. We can turn back.'

"'Never,' returned the elder brother. 'Have courage, Grisha. We are doing the right thing. You know that he is an evil madman and must be stopped. Remember the Holodomor, Grisha, the Ukrainian genocide when this tyrant was responsible for our own parents' death by starvation in the labor camps in his monstrous ethnic cleansing of the Ukrainian people. Think positive thoughts, my brother. This time tomorrow we will be safely in the United States, where you and I have dreamed about living since we were young boys in the orphanage. Konstantin Podipenko has made all of the arrangements. We must trust him. We will be free, Grisha. We will live in New York. We will open the restaurant we always talked about.'

"I closed my eyes and exhaled. Perspiration sheeted my forehead. I blotted it with a shirt sleeve. 'Let's get on with it then,' at last I stuttered tensely to my older brother. Sandro nodded, then, with his full body weight, dropped heavily on the sleeping boss's chest, causing Stalin's lungs to suddenly expel a rush of air. Stalin's mouth flew open, and Sandro stuffed the kitchen hand towel into it, blocking the windpipe. He leaned forward and, with his free hand pinched together Stalin's nostrils. Suddenly, the leader's body pitched and thrashed and rolled in an effort to fill his suffocating lungs with air. His legs flailed about, and I laid across them, encircling them tightly in my arms. Stalin's eyelids flew open, his irises glowing yellow in surprise and menace and fear and hatred at the boys on top of him. Peculiar animal sounds emanated from his throat. But we held fast and soon, what seemed to me to be an hour or a week, the great leader's body at last surrendered, going flaccid in our grasp, his malicious eyes spooling back in his head.

"The deed was done. We, the two Georgian brothers, momentarily sat on the man's body, our clothes clinging with perspiration, our lungs screeching for air, our hearts thundering in our chests. Sandro removed the kitchen towel from the boss's throat, then we lifted ourselves from Stalin's body and began cautiously making our way across the small room when suddenly a terrifying sound, a demon's cry, froze us in our steps. Behind us, Stalin's body stiffly pitched upward. He swung out an arm, clattering over a glass of water from a small table. In the distance, a guard dog barked disturbingly. The boss somehow managed to hoist himself upward as close by we gawked on in debilitating fear. Stalin took a few staggering steps toward his attackers, pausing in palpable agony, yet stumbling onward like a clumsy toddler. Then at once, his eyes widened in something akin to depthless fear, and his throat began wheezing out horrible, disjunctive sounds. His round body thudded to the floor in a heap.

"'Fuck your mother!' Sandro Tevoradze whispered. Cautiously, he approached the body on the floor. Stalin had curled into a fetal position, his head resting on an arm. Sandro noticed that Stalin had soiled his pajama bottoms and was laying unmoving in a puddle of his own urine. His eyes were closed, his lips unmoving. His right arm and leg were stiff and unworkable as if he had suffered a massive stroke.

"'Come, come, Sandro,' I tugged at him. 'We must go. Now!' I heard the guard dogs continuing to bark in the distance. 'Look at him, Sandro. I think he has had a massive stroke. The old man is finished. He won't recover from this. We must go, Sandro!'

"The older brother agreed with a nod, and we promptly slipped like unseen apparitions across the carpeting and disappeared through the hidden door."

Presently, Grisha Tevoradze shifted his legs beneath him. "Well, you know the rest of it," he shrugged his shoulders. "Comrade Stalin that night had, indeed, suffered a deadly stroke from which he would never recover. He died a few days later. And my brother, Sandro, and I safely made our escape to America thanks to your, father Konstantin Podipenko, and his detailed arrangements. Helsinki to Berlin to New York. And here we were in America just twenty-four hours after causing Stalin's lethal stroke at his *dacha*. Our dream of living in this wonderful country suddenly realized! Your father remained behind, of course, working with Stalin's successors and being promoted through the Red Army ranks."

For a long moment, the room in the Little Odessa flat went silent as Illya Podipenko and Katya Tevoradze were processing the details of the incredible story that Grisha had shared with them.

At last, Illya said, "I don't understand, Grisha. Why did Stalin trust my father all those years before he died?"

Grisha hesitated, screwing up his face in thought. Finally, he answered, "I wouldn't necessarily call it *trust* per se. I would say more like Stalin *feared* your father."

"Feared him?"

Grisha nodded. "It was very strange," he continued on. "As I have stated, after the Great Patriotic War, Stalin had become quite ill and senile, also alone and isolated, fearful of everyone. And yet, at the same time, he hated being alone. That is where you father came in. You see, Stalin was a paranoid, at heart a coward, always fearful of conspiracies all around him. And rightfully so. The boss knew it was only a matter of time before one, or all, of those old men in the inner circle would conspire to remove him from power. This is one reason why Stalin murdered so many people close to him. He would preemptively get them before they could get him. Your father understood this, so he took a very brave, some would say foolhardy or even suicidal, gamble to ensure that Stalin would not one day make him, too, disappear."

Grisha took a moment, gazing into the flames in the small fireplace across from him, remembering. "It was in 1945, as I recall, after the war. Konstantin had been Stalin's confidant for some time. One night, after the usual inner circle of magnates had gone home, Stalin and your father were chatting, as they often would, sitting across from one another in

89

Stalin's study at his Kuntsevo *dacha*. Stalin seemed in a particularly good mood that night. At one point, your father stood up and, much to the boss's surprise, approached the divan and lowered himself next to the leader. Stalin's body stiffened, but Konstantin reached out a strong hand, tightly clasping the boss's knee. "'Comrade Stalin,' your father began, speaking in the informal manner of the Russian language, which the great leader likely did not appreciate, coming from an underling, trusted or not. Konstantin leaned close to the supreme one, whispering in his ear while Stalin shifted uncomfortably, 'I have come to notice that those who you take into your confidence, as you have me, often seem to eventually disappear, just vanish into thin air as though they never existed at all. Perhaps they were spirited off by Beria's men in the middle of the night for a bit of French wrestling at Beria's torture chambers. That's the term you like to use, is it not? French wrestling? In other words, tortured then beaten to death in a cold, grey cell.'

"'See here you fucking upstart,' Stalin spit out of the side of his mouth, 'I could seal you in an envelope.' He shifted about as if to stand, but Konstantin Podipenko latched him by the shoulder and pressed him back into the divan. 'I'd be very, very careful if I were you,' the boss sneered, struggling. 'You want to be fitted for a cell at Lefortovo? I will show it to you personally.'

"'That won't be necessary, Comrade,' smiled the younger man. He put his face so close to Stalin's that the pockmarks on the boss's face appeared like craters on the moon. 'I feel it is only fair to warn you that I have devised a plan of action, and it is this: should I one day inexplicably disappear, perhaps drop dead from a heart attack or get hit by a truck while strolling along *Tverskaya* or if I get so much as a strong head cold, my plan will be instantly set in motion. You have your five-year plan, I have mine, you see. And my plan is one that you, with all the might of great Russia at your disposal, will be powerless to stop. My plan will be executed quickly and quite lethally.'

"'The devil's mother!' Stalin hissed. 'You may quickly find yourself on the Trans-Siberian express with a one-way ticket to a labor camp near the arctic circle. I can arrange a room in one of our five-star Siberian resorts.' His eyes burnished.

"Konstantin Podipenko loosened his grip on the man and leaned back. He said, 'I am blessed with very loyal men, Comrade. As we speak, I have two hundred men who are just waiting for the opportunity to put my plan in motion. Tough men, brutal men. Men who fought with me at Stalingrad. My men are everywhere. Hidden and also in plain sight. They will be unstoppable.' Konstantin paused to light a cigarette from Stalin's pack of *Herzogovina Flor*. Then he casually asked, 'Do you know what a hemicorporectomy is, Comrade Stalin? No? I will explain. A hemicorporectomy is a technique used to cut a human body in half. A very sharp surgical knife is inserted between the second and third lumbar vertebra, severing the intestine at the duodenum. This is the only way a body can be divided in two without having to cut through bone. And this is what my men will do to you should I suffer any funny business at your hand. They will cut you in half, then they will pop out your eyeballs and cut off your head. All will be displayed on Red Square for the world to see. Right where your personal Russian idol, Ivan the Terrible, used to perform his beheadings. Our good Soviet citizens will pass by your body parts, stopping just long enough to spit on them or to kick in your face or shit in your mouth and piss in your empty eye sockets. You remember the worldwide humiliation of Hitler's good friend, Mussolini, in Italy? This will be much worse, even more degrading. And, of course, next to you for all to see will be the body parts of your beloved daughter, Svetlana. I fear that it will all be quite messy.'

"Konstantin paused. He blew out a smoke ring that casually drifted above the two men. 'Most of your underlings bring you problems, Comrade Stalin, I bring you solutions.' Beside him, he could feel the man's body pitching itself in shaking spasms. His face, blanched as old meat, began twitching. He seemed to be gasping for air. Then a strange thing happened. The *Vozhd* began to chuckle, his lips widening. Then came an irrepressible belly laugh, throwing his head back. All of a sudden, his withered left arm began involuntarily flailing about in the air. Stalin had no control over it. It was like his arm had a mechanism all its own. Stalin paused to look at it jerking about then shot a glance to the young man next to him. He once again was suddenly and uncontrollably roaring with fitful laughter, tears forming at the corner of his eyes. He vigorously clouted the knee of the young Army officer next to him, and Konstantin began to laugh as well. The two sat for minutes, roaring wildly, unable to catch their breath until, at last, Stalin managed to choke out some words between the rush of expelled air. 'I can respect a man who has reckless courage, young Podipenko, a man who tells me the truth. I must keep you close to me, like a shadow!'

"He grabbed the young man's arm, pulling it toward him. He unexpectantly gave his companion a kiss on his cheek. And the two were off again, smacking their thighs and stomping their feet on the carpeting howling like tundra wolves in laughter that pounded the walls of the small room."

"It was crazy," Grisha now chuckled to his audience of two in the small Little Odessa flat. "But I guess everything with Stalin was crazy. From that moment on, he trusted your father completely. Stalin loved men with courage. It was an insane time." The old man lifted his head and peered across at Illya Podipenko. He noticed that his guest was sitting silently, unmoving, his eyes blank, face shadowed. "You are troubled, Illya Konstantinovich, I can see that. Tell me your thoughts."

The Moscow militiaman began slowly, "I don't understand, Grisha. My father hated Stalin, that I do know. He didn't like to talk about those days with me, but I do know that he thought Stalin was demented and dangerous and if not stopped would eventually be the ruin of the Soviet Union. Stalin was killing millions of his own people. Why did my father wait so long to initiate his plan of having you and your brother, Sandro, suffocate him?"

Grisha Tevoradze for a long moment bowed his head and studied his feet shuffling atop the carpeting. He seemed to be attempting to choose his words with precision. At last, he looked up at Illya Podipenko, gazing at him through eyes that were noticeably tired and rimmed in red.

He shifted in his chair, chewed on his lip, then said, "I don't know exactly how to say this to you, my new friend Illya Podipenko. So I am just going to say it, the truth." He took a deep breath. Then he said in a low voice, "The truth is, Illya, the man who one day would become the great Soviet Army marshal, your esteemed father, the young man who was closest to Stalin, was, in fact, an American spy."

*****

"*What?*" Illya Podipenko's jaw unhinged. Next to him, he heard the young girl Katya gasp.

Uncle Grisha nodded. "Your father was in a very valuable position. He had become the closest person in the world to Stalin. The old man had grown senile, bitter, forgetful, alone in the world, abandoned by his family and the sycophantic magnates around him. Your father knew all of the boss's secrets, the only one who did. What better placement for the Americans than to have an informant stolidly next to the sole power in the Soviet Union? That made your father incalculably important to the Americans. Your father realized that the God Stalin, after the Great Patriotic War, had become dangerously paranoid. He was authentically crazy, suffering from medical dementia. He had hypertension and cerebral arteriosclerosis, reducing blood flow to the brain. He became more volatile and irrational than ever before. He had become astonishingly unstable, a threat to the Soviet Union and the world. Your father learned that Stalin was planning a mass deportation of all Jews in the Soviet Union to Siberia and Central Asia. And Stalin, horror of horrors, was also planning to go to war with the imperialist Americans! Remember, Stalin now believed himself to be an infallible leader and genius military tactician. The Great War had given him the giddy whiff of military power and invincibility. So in January 1951, Stalin called together all of his military brass and the defense ministers from the Soviet bloc countries under his dictatorial command. At that meeting, he ordered each of them to expand their military capabilities and prepare for an all-out war with the United States."

"That can't be so," uttered Illya, hollowly.

"Oh, it was so," assured Uncle Grisha. "Stalin's scientists, under Beria, had developed the biggest nuclear bomb in the world, bigger than the ones the Americans dropped on the Japanese. Stalin sent your father as his personal emissary to witness the first test detonation. It was at a settlement in the Kazakh steppes in the summer of 1949. The test was imminently successful. Konstantin reported back to the boss, who went feverish as a schoolgirl. Four years after the Americans dropped its big bombs on the Japanese, Stalin now had his own death bomb. And he was eager and determined to use it. He now had the power of great annihilation at his fingertips and a deep-rooted and expanding inferiority complex about the showy Americans. This was a turning point for your father. He knew that Stalin was determined to crush imperial capitalism forever. He realized that the cloudy-thinking Stalin clearly had to be stopped before he could launch a weapon that would devastate mankind."

"But when did my father become a spy for the Americans?" asked Illya, visibly troubled.

"Konstantin Podipenko, as you know, was always fond of the Americans ever since he was a child, and people would tell him stories of how the Americans shipped tons of food, clothing, and supplies for Russians suffering from famine following the Bolshevik Revolution and the civil war. After the Great Patriotic War, as you know, the defeated Germany was being divided up into sectors by the victors, Russia, the US, England, and France. This was 1947, and Stalin sent your father to Berlin to report back to him daily on the latest negotiations going on. While your father was in Berlin, he was approached by the American CIA. They offered him an arrangement, and he took it. They offered a large sum of money and their protection and, should the need arrive, a sanctuary country of his choice. But your father didn't spy for the Americans for these reasons. Your father was, above all, a true patriot and by 1953 had fully realized that the increasingly erratic Stalin had to be stopped from destroying the Soviet Empire. It was that simple. It had long been your father's wish to form a closer relationship with the Americans, a superpower relationship that would be mutually beneficial to both countries. But the delusional Stalin was intent on declaring war on the Americans. Your father was not going to let that happen. He told the Americans what must be done, and, of course, considering the circumstances, they agreed. So it was that on that fateful night in 1953, as your father had planned, my older brother, Sandro, and I snuck into Stalin's room and suffocated him while he slept, stopping his plans of bombing the United States."

Across from the old man, Illya Podipenko and his young companion, Katya, sat in oblique silence. Confused words and images darted about in Illya's mind like electrical impulses. For what seemed like minutes, his lips lacked the faculty to form even simple words. Seeing this, Grisha Tevoradze smiled to himself and reached across his hand holding the bottle of vodka. Absently, Illya accepted it with a massive swig, followed by a coughing spasm. Katya gently patted him across the back. When he did finally manage to speak, his words were rasped out with some difficulty.

"So my father was a spy for Americans?" he said solemnly.

"That is correct, my friend. It was the right thing to do. Stalin was dangerously unstable."

"I see. And did my father remain a spy through his entire Army career?"

"Pardon?" Grisha seemed momentarily confused. Then it dawned on him. "Oh, no, no, not at all. After Stalin's death, your father told the Americans he was through. No more spying. And the Americans agreed. Thanked him for his service. It ended amicably. Although, now that I think about it, one more time in your father's career he did pass along some valuable information to the Americans. It was in the early 1960s when your father was a lieutenant-colonel on Khrushchev's staff. He let the Americans know that the Soviet Union was putting armed nuclear missiles in Cuba. Again, your father did this in an attempt to help avert a possible nuclear war. Thank goodness he did. Khrushchev was becoming a bit of a saber-rattler himself. That deeply disappointed your father. He thought Khrushchev, following Stalin's death, had an unprecedented opportunity to forge closer ties with the Americans. But Khrushchev wouldn't listen. This was a slap in the face to your father, who, after all, was a man greatly responsible for Khrushchev becoming head of the Soviet Union."

"My father helped Khrushchev become head of the Soviet Union?"

"Of course. You don't know the story?" Grisha Tevoradze stretched his legs and sighed deeply. "Well, then, I shall tell you…"

"On the fifth day of the weary Stalin death watch at the Kuntsevo *dacha*, Nikita Khrushchev, then First Secretary of the Moscow Communist Party, was making his way to the front door to leave the near *dacha*. It was seven o'clock in the morning. He was going to make a quick trip to his flat in Moscow to freshen up before returning to the circus that was parading around the comatose boss, who lay in a fetal position, paralyzed on his right side, and snoring away on a divan. Khrushchev was accompanied by some security men and the *dacha*'s young deputy commandant, Konstantin Podipenko, who was seeing them out. Suddenly, at the front door, Khrushchev waved the others on, then gripped your father by the arm, pulling him into a cloakroom off the main foyer. He pushed his face so close to Stalin's aide-de-camp that a bit of spittle shot out when Khrushchev spoke, landing on Konstantin Podipenko's cheek.

"'You are loyal to the boss?' Khrushchev growled. 'I've been watching you, Comrade, and something about your presence and nosing up to Stalin these past few years just doesn't smell right to me. I have never figured you out, a brave war hero, a teenaged sharpshooter, a deadly sniper, a fellow Ukrainian yet! I have known you since I was a commissar during the great battle for Stalingrad when the earth shook. You played an invaluable part in Operation Ring, our plan to liquidate Field Marshal von Paulus's Sixth Army. One by one, you picked off Nazi soldiers and their high command officers who were hopped up on methamphetamines most of the time. We outlasted them. We starved the fucking Germans, and in the end, they were eating dogs, cats, rats, horses, and each other for survival. You were but a youngster then. They nicknamed you 'The Boy Assassin' with your Mosin-Nagant rifle staunchly killing Nazi leaders from your hidden lairs in the bombed-out rubble on the west bank of the Volga. You were credited with over four hundred kills in Stalingrad. They promoted you to major and gave you the Hero of the Red Banner medal and Hero of the Soviet Union medal with its gold star. Of course, we watched as you as you jostled your way into the boss's inner circle, becoming a close advisor to Stalin, in charge of *dacha* operations. And don't think that I didn't notice that you wisely planned to conveniently be away the night of the boss's current medical crisis?'

"'Even close advisors deserve a day off, Comrade Khrushchev,' Konstantin Podipenko responded evenly, 'certainly you would agree.'

"'Do not test me, young man,' hissed the short Ukrainian.

"To this, Konstantin Podipenko smirked darkly; he couldn't help himself. It had occurred to him that he was talking to a very round man inhabiting a very rectangular suit. He bent slightly to stare at the shorter Khrushchev right in his eyes. 'Nikita Sergeyevich, you asked me if I am loyal to the boss. If you must know, I don't trust the unstable and murderous old barbarian,' he whispered, 'just like you. Stop the crocodile tears, Comrade Khrushchev. You have grown to hate the Great Stalin for the years of humiliation he has wrought upon you. He made fun of you as a Ukrainian country bumpkin. He chided you about your short and round stature. He saw you as his personal court jester, his clown. He called you a little fool, berated you in front of the others. He once said you were as ignorant as the Negus of Ethiopia. At his dinners, he would command you to drink vodka until you drunkenly soiled your pants then forced you to dance the Ukrainian *lezginka* in front of the others. He would thump his pipe on top of your bald head and tell the others that 'It's hollow.' During the war, he once clunked his burning pipe against your head, leaving dark ashes, an act of egregious disrespect going back to Roman times, and everyone laughed. Of course, you never forgave Stalin for when your son, Leonid, was on trial for murder for having accidentally shot and killed a Soviet sailor in 1942 while drunk at a party. You asked Stalin to intervene on his behalf, and he refused. And you blamed Stalin because while you were doing your duty fighting in the civil war, in 1921, your first wife died of starvation during Stalin's forced famine in the Ukraine. I don't believe you ever forgave him for that slight.'

"This utterance with its effrontery and cold animus with which it was delivered caught Khrushchev off guard to the point that he actually stumbled a step backward and the young man had to grab the older man's lapel so he wouldn't take a tumble right there in the cloakroom. He leveraged Khrushchev close to him.

"'I must commend you, Comrade,' Podipenko said, 'you were right to have your doubts about me. You see, the reason that, as we speak, the boss is a barely living corpse, in his last hours laying there, curled like one of Haeckel's embryos in a urine-soaked coma and making incoherent noises is that I conspired with two of my loyal associates to murder him. And it appears in a short time from now we will have succeeded. You and I both know he is not going to recover from this massive stroke. He is lying in there paralyzed in his death throes unable to speak with leeches on his ears and neck. Doctors are administering mustard plasters and two enemas a day of glucose and cream with an egg yolk. They are injecting him with camphor. His lips have turned blue, and his facial features are becoming unrecognizable. He has already transitioned into Cheyne-Stokes breathing. Stalin is done. There is no miracle recovery. You don't need to put on a grieving act with me. I know that you and all of the others are overjoyed about the current circumstances. You have been living in fear of your own lives. You certainly must know that you and the rest were next on Stalin's list of those who should be made to just vanish into the abyss. He had plans to wipe out everyone around him, his inner circle, in his mind merely an act of civic hygiene. Don't waste your time denying it.'

"'Impudence!' Khrushchev snarled. 'As we say in the Ukraine, "Take my words and put them in your ears." I will so enjoy personally supervising your torture. I will have you beaten until your eyes pop out of their sockets before giving you nine-grams,' he added, meaning a bullet in the back of the head.

"'That is not going to happen, Comrade,' evenly replied the younger man, allowing a half smile. 'In fact, quite the opposite. You will see to it that I am quickly and routinely promoted. Perhaps one day to marshal, maybe I will become one of the youngest marshals in the history of our great motherland to be so chosen.'

"'Is that a fact,' Khrushchev growled. 'And why would I ever do that?'

"'By God's grace, you have somehow managed all these years to survive Stalin's rule. You must realize that you were likely the next victim on his list to be made to disappear. You know that human life held no sanctity to him. Do you really think you now can also survive the rule of your hated enemy Lavrenti Pavlovich Beria?' asked Konstantin Podipenko. 'You call the degenerate Beria *nechist* an unclean devil. You know whenever that snake-eyed sadist enters a room, he brings death and darkness with him. To Beria, you are immensely expendable, a threat to his much-coveted ascension to the throne. As we speak, while Stalin lay dying, the sadistic Mingrelian is already positioning himself to be the anointed next leader of the Soviet Union, and you and I know we cannot allow that to happen.'

"Konstantin Podipenko paused. He lit a cigarette, then continued, 'Let me ask you a question, Comrade Khrushchev. You do have ambition to be the motherland's next leader, do you not?' He needn't have awaited an answer and didn't. 'We both understand that Stalin's inner circle consists of tired old men. Going forward, there are only two real candidates to next rule our beloved country. You and your hated enemy, Beria. If Beria takes over, he will unite the state security organs behind him and unleash a murderous fury against his enemies, perceived and otherwise. I fear you will be one of the first on his list for liquidation. But how to eliminate Beria, eh?'

"Khrushchev was quieter now, at once engaged. He gawked across at Konstantin Podipenko while attempting to straighten his ill-fitting suit coat. 'Difficult,' he reluctantly acknowledged in a low tone, 'perhaps impossible. If Beria unites the security organs behind him, he will have gained unbridled control of the country. His secret police can smash anything in their way.'

"'True, indeed they can,' nodded the younger man, 'and yet perhaps there is still a way forward for you. There is a force in our motherland that hates Beria as much as you do. The Red Army. Soldiers have long memories. They remember when Beria's henchmen on Stalin's orders viciously slaughtered thousands of our good Red Army officers in Stalin's massive cleansing of the military.'

"'And Stalin ordered this right before the Great Patriotic War,' Khrushchev chuffed, shaking his round head. 'What idiocy! But how can you be certain that I have the backing of the armed forces? Are they willing to take on Beria's massive network of sadistic and unconscionable murderers?'

"'I can assure you that the military will be willing, Comrade. Simply a matter of self-preservation for them, for you, for me.' The younger man took Khrushchev's elbow and guided him further away from the cloakroom's open doorway. 'I have had conversations with one of our greatest military heroes, a trusted comrade of yours. He is completely on board, and a plan is already in motion, if you are smart enough to trust me.'

"Khrushchev was a silent a moment then nodded. 'We Ukrainians must stick together.'

"'And so, we must,' the younger man gently patted the shoulders of the future leader of the Soviet Empire. He did not mention that fact that Khrushchev at one time had been responsible for the starvation and murder of hundreds of thousands of his fellow Ukrainians. Podipenko leaned forward, uttering in low tones. 'Now, I cannot share all of the details with you, Comrade. The less you know at this time, perhaps the better. We want you to act normally so no one suspects a thing. We must let the dust settle for a while following Stalin's death, which will be any hour now. You need to have patience. Malenkov initially will take over during a short transitional phase, paving the way for your ascension. I will tell you only that the plan involves a hero in the defense of Leningrad and Moscow and my military leader in Stalingrad, Stalin's fireman.'

"'Marshal Georgi Zhukov!' Khrushchev blurted out, louder than he had intended. Podipenko winced and put a finger to his lips and nodded his head slowly.

"'Now listen, Comrade. You will attend a secret meeting in Bulganin's office. Bulganin will smuggle some senior military officers past Beria's state security troops guarding the area. Zhukov will be waiting there. At this meeting, all will be revealed, final plans discussed, dates disclosed, assignments will be made. Do you understand?'

"'Understood,' replied Khrushchev. He was fighting to stay calm, yet excitement brimmed in his eyes. He clearly now saw an entire world of possibilities opening up before him.

"'Good, well done,' replied younger man. 'On a future date selected, there will be a hastily called presidium meeting. At that meeting in a conference room in Malenkov's office, you will denounce Beria to everyone, using your most hated invective strewn with your strongest obscenities. You will claim that Beria has put his murderous security organs ahead of the interest of the Communist Party and of the motherland. You will call him a criminal barbarian and a Mingrelian butcher of millions of innocent Soviet citizens through his special brand of terror and repression, climbing to power over mountains of bodies and rivers of blood. And you may want to throw in that he is a degenerate sexually deviant pedophile, having raped scores of Soviet young schoolgirls while abusing his position of power. Then, at a selected moment, Malenkov will press a button under the table, and Marshal Zhukov and his military troops will storm the room. They will arrest Beria at gunpoint, and he will be carted away to the Lefortovo prison for a bit of French wrestling before transferring him to a secret military underground bunker near the Moscow River. Then, at a staged trial, your colleague, Lavrenti Beria, will be duly convicted on all charges, and the depraved Mingrelian will never to be heard from again as if this nonperson had been no more than an evil wisp in the winds of our history.'

"The Soviet Union's future Communist Party First Secretary stood for a while quietly nodding his head in understanding. His shoes awkwardly squeaked as he shifted from foot to foot. At last, he said, 'It seems you have thoroughly thought this through, young Konstantin Podipenko. Congratulation to you. But, tell me, you said that two of your staff actually were the ones who sneaked in and suffocated Stalin while he was asleep on his divan, causing his stroke. And where might these two brave young men be at present?'

"The younger man replied, 'They are safely out of the country. That is all you need to know.' Konstantin Podipenko knew that his accomplices, Sandro and Grisha Tevoradze, had by now most assuredly landed in their new home country of the United States.

"'And what of you, young Podipenko? Where are you going?'

"'Me?' He seemed surprised by the question. 'I am not going anywhere. I like it here, my motherland. I would miss it if I were gone too long. Besides, I am sure I can be of some use to you. Think of it, Nikita Sergeyevich. The rule of Stalin is over. Your place in Soviet history is yet to be written.'

"'I understand,' replied Khrushchev cautiously. 'Are you not worried that one day someone might find out the real truth about Stalin's death? That you had two of your staff suffocate the boss as he was laying sleeping on his couch in the little dining room?'

"'Not too worried, no,' the young man shrugged in a carefree manner. 'No one knows about the plot, do they? Just me, my two Georgian lads, and now… you, Comrade Khrushchev. And I am certain that you would not want any of us to divulge the real, hidden truth contributing to Stalin's unfortunate demise.'

"'And what is this hidden truth exactly?' Khrushchev probed.

"'My two Georgian associates observed you and the rest of your comrades-in-arms at Stalin's final dinner. They saw you.'

"'Saw me?'

"'Yes, watched as you slipped poison in the great leader's wine.'

"'What's that you say?' Khrushchev's face hardened in a hushed anger.

"'Oh, yes. A bottle of one of Stalin's favorites, *Madzhari*, a young Georgian wine. What irony,' Konstantin Podipenko allowed. 'On the very night I set in motion my plan to eliminate our mad dictator, you also attempted to murder him!' Podipenko threw up his hands as if in exacerbation. 'I mean, what are the odds? Two murder attempts on the same person during the same night?'

"Khrushchev's plump head became a beet. 'I should watch such impudence if I were you, my young friend,' he spat out this in a threateningly low tone. 'You better explain yourself quickly.'

"'I believe you conspired with your enemy, Beria, and likely the other vipers in the snake pit, to poison Stalin. Despite you and Beria being loathed adversaries, you each knew you had a shared interest in survival and you had better work together this one time for this one common cause of eliminating the boss. You knew that Stalin had become dangerously paranoid. You knew you were marked men. My guess is that the poison likely was supplied by Beria from the poison labs he operates. Perhaps it was hydrocyanic acid or potassium cyanide or luminal or, better yet, Warfarin you used in the poisoned chalice, you know, a blood-thinner also used in rat poison. Odorless and tasteless. It is a fine choice. You were rather insistent on having a final toast before you and the inner circle returned to your homes early that fateful morning. You rather determinedly poured the boss's last glass of Georgian wine. It was then that you slipped in the poison. My two colleagues saw you. It's all written down for safekeeping, in case we need to bring out the facts for some reason at some later date.'

"'Preposterous,' grumbled Khrushchev, with a guilty-as-charged lack of conviction.

"'Not so preposterous, Comrade. You see, something doesn't quite fit here. Our great leader this morning while lying curled up on the carpet from a stroke unexpectedly began vomiting blood and his stomach began hemorrhaging. These are not signs of a suffocation performed by my two attachments. These are signs of a poisoning. I have taken the liberty of sending some samples to a toxicology expert, a friend of mine. He will provide me with a full report. I think you and I both know what the test results will reveal.'

"The short Ukrainian went silent. It took a few moments, but at last, his red, puffy face slowly morphed to what passed for calmness. His thick lips tilted upward. His round head started nodding. 'I am beginning to see why the boss kept you close these past several years. You are an extremely resourceful and intelligent young man, Konstantin Podipenko,' he said slowly, 'not to mention ruthless and a brave soul to boot. Yes, I believe you are right. I could use a man with your unique qualities on my team. You could prove to be useful to me.' He went quiet again for a moment. Then he said sadly, wistfully, as if attempting to sum it all up, 'You know,' he began, 'to Stalin, we were all just temporary people, all possible next victims, all mere specks of dust, nonentities. We were only theoretically alive, among the living by chance. We all would be on his list at some point. When we left the near *dacha* early in the morning, we were never certain if we would return home alive. The truth is that after the Great War, Stalin was not quite right in the head, cracked as the Tsar's Bell. Only the devil knew what went on in that black mind of his. He thought he was going to live forever.'

"'I know,' responded Konstantin Podipenko gently, 'I know.'

"And the rest, as they say, is history," at present sighed Uncle Grisha, stretching his body in the chair. "When the military stormed the room to haul the befuddled Beria away at gunpoint, they removed his belt and cut the buttons from his pants. Poor Lavrenti. He was forced to shuffle about holding up his pants with both hands. Not only did this help hinder any escape attempt, it also added a degree of abject humiliation, which I am sure our Red Army boys enjoyed."

Illya Podipenko was quiet, pondering Uncle Grisha's tale. He absently looked on as Katya arose from the couch and approached the fireplace. She used a brass-covered steel poker with a looped handle and a long, sharp prong to prod the burning logs then returned to sit next to the Moscow investigator.

Illya said, "So my father quit spying for the Americans when he was on Khrushchev's staff?"

"Pardon?" Grisha Tevoradze seemed muddled by the question. He gathered himself. "Oh, yes, of course, Illya. The fact is your father would come to be quite disenchanted with both sides. Khrushchev became erratic and bellicose, sending the Red Army into the Soviet Union's satellite counties, East Germany, Bulgaria Hungary, Czechoslovakia, forcibly putting down angry protests in those countries regarding Soviet rule. This is not how your father envisioned a thawing of the Cold War. As for the Americans, well, your father couldn't believe it. He had alerted the Americans about Stalin's impending death and advised them that this event would create an unprecedented opportunity to ease tensions and forge closer ties between the two countries. But the American president, Eisenhower, and his Secretary of State John Foster Dulles did nothing. They sat on their hands. They seemed perplexed and overwhelmed by the situation, stupefied about what course of action to take, so they took none. They slipped into diplomatic paralysis about how to respond to the new situation. There was no sense of urgency. Neither Eisenhower nor any of his high-level cabinet members attended Stalin's state funeral even though many world leaders were there. It seemed that the US leaders were incapable of grasping the new political landscape. Churchill wisely read the global tea leaves and called for a summit with the Big Three to discuss future paths. But the US crapped on the suggestion. Your father became disheartened and disillusioned with the politics of both countries. Not long after Khrushchev promoted your father to marshal in 1961, he resigned from Khrushchev's staff and became an instructor at the Frunze Military Academy. He did this until his retirement some years later. As you know, he lived out his last days at his personal *dacha* near the Arkhangelskoye estate, cynical and detached from the politics of the Cold War."

Quietly, the old man sat shaking his head. He stared into the small flames of the fireplace until his eyelids began shuttering themselves. His chin lowered to his chest, and the two across from him heard the sound of snoring.

They sat wordlessly until at last Illya turned to whisper to the young girl. "Should we wake him?" he asked.

"No, let him sleep. He will be all right." Then she was suddenly on her feet, her hand tugging the Moscow investigator from the sofa.

She said eagerly, "Come, Illya, I will show you my bedroom."

*****

They trundled up the carpeted front stairway to the flat's second story. There was a narrow hallway that led to two bedrooms, Grandpa Sandro Tevoradze's on the left, Katya's on the right. The girl flipped on an overhead light.

"This is my room," she announced proudly. Illya regarded a neat, cared-for room more generous than he had expected. It had a couch, a study desk, a bookshelf, a brightly painted chest of drawers, a closet, an end table with a funky lamp, a feminine canopy bed covered with a thick, Russian-designed duvet, and a bathroom off to the side. The taupe walls announced a teenager's room, with taped posters of rock stars, culture icons, and entertainment celebrities. Over the study desk was a large black-and-white poster of

Albert Einstein with his wild white hair, gray mustache, and a long tongue playfully thrust out of his mouth. At the bottom of the poster was a quote *"Only two things are infinite: the universe and human stupidity. And I'm not too sure about the former."*

Next to this was a matted and framed illustration of lyrics to a song that Illya did not know. He squinted forward to read the words aloud.

"What song is this?" he asked Katya.

"*Rumble Doll* by Patti Scialfa, one of my favorites."

"It's nice, I like it."

The girl smiled and strode to the bed, sitting. "This is where I sleep."

"I guessed as much," answered the man from Moscow.

She patted the duvet. "Come, Illya, sit beside me."

He ambled unsurely and sat. She put her head close to his and whispered, "This is where I dreamed about you so many nights."

"Ah, nightmares, I apologize." His lame attempt at lightness betrayed the awkwardness he was feeling.

"Do you want to lay down with me?" she whispered sweetly.

Illya could feel the girl's warm breath on his neck. His body stiffened. "Oh, look," he pointed at a small bookshelf across the room. "*Alice's Adventures in Wonderland*." Gawkily, he hefted his body off the bed and dashed across the room. He dandled the book in his fingers. "Marvelous," he said. "I like the twin short, round boys. What are their names?"

Katya shook her head forlornly and smiled. "Tweedledum and Tweedledee," she said. She arose from the bed and approached the fidgeting Moscow militiaman. "But they are not in this book."

"What? Surely you are mistaken!"

The girl bent, retrieving another book. "The twin boys appear in the follow-up book, *Alice Through the Looking Glass*."

"Ah, my mistake, sorry," Illya forced an embarrassed grin.

The girl took him by the arm. "Come," she said. "If you are afraid to lay down with me, I will show you Grandpa Sandro's room." She guided him out of her bedroom. She said, "You should be a character in the Alice books. Mr. Scaredy Pants."

Illya paused in the hallway. "Forgive me, Miss," he dramatically sniffed and affected a professional tone, "but my pants are not now, nor have they even been, scared."

Grandpa Sandro's room was even larger than Katya's. There was a clean hardwood floor peeking from beneath traditional Kashan rugs. There was a desk, bookshelf, nightstand, rocking chair, polished armoire, and a large bay window with a view of the boardwalk, beach, and waters of the Atlantic. On one of the walls was an icon of Yevgeny Aleksandrovich Rodionov, a Russian soldier who had been taken prisoner by Chechen rebels during the First Chechen War. He was later executed in captivity for refusing to convert to Islam and defect to the enemy side. What really caught Illya Podipenko's attention was an expansive alcove next to the window. It appeared to be Grandpa Sandro's homage to America with an American Flag, history books, a map of New York City and surroundings, a reproduction portrait of George Washington, a signed photograph of Ronald Reagan, a winged statue of a bald eagle, a large replica of the Statue of Liberty, a bronze statue of a cowboy riding a bucking horse, and a framed, smiling photo of Sandro with his brother, Grisha, and granddaughter, Katya, with Ellis Island in the background.

Illya thought Grandpa Sandro looked like a Siberian Cossack with a shaven pate and a sweeping black mustache. He was waving a tiny American flag.

"Goodness," said Illya Podipenko, "it appears that your grandfather was indeed quite a patriot."

"He was passionate about America, I told you," said the young woman, briefly lifting her face close to his. "He and Uncle Grisha were devoted to their new adopted country." She was quiet a moment. "This is where I will put the urn with my grandpa's ashes." She reached her hand out toward Illya, and he took it softly. He was about to say something when Uncle Grisha's voice rang out from below.

"My darling Katya, where are you?"

"Up here, Uncle Grisha," she called back. "We're coming." Looking over at Illya, the young woman smiled and shrugged her shoulders. "Duty calls," she said.

They found the old man standing at the fireplace, randomly prodding at the small flames with the brass poker. "Here, Uncle Grisha, I'll do that," said Katya, taking the implement from his hand. "Go sit. There is your vodka on the table next to your chair."

The old man obeyed. He thumped his body into the armchair and swashed from the bottle of vodka. Illya and Katya took their seats across from him.

"My brother, Sandro, and I only saw your father once more," said Uncle Grisha as if answering a question someone had asked. "It was 1960. Your father was part of the delegation that accompanied Premier Khrushchev on his visit to the United Nations here in New York. That was the time Khrushchev famously took off his shoe and pounded it on the podium for all the world to see. At one point, your father sneaked out of some high-level meetings and visited us right here in Little Odessa, in this very flat. He sat right where you are sitting now, Illya. My, we had a grand time, hugging and delivering vodka toasts and recounting stories from our youth in faraway Russia. He had not yet been promoted to the rank of marshal but soon would be. We all got appropriately drunk that night, but to this day, I do remember him speaking quite fondly of a son he had. The boy's name was Illya Konstantinovich he told us, and he was, I believe, about nine years old at the time. Your father was so proud, Illya. He said his son was destined to become a famous Red Army officer. It was a magic night."

With that, Uncle Grisha warmly smiled to himself, and his damp eyes seemed to gaze absently past the two sitting across from him to some undefined specter on the wall behind them. He remained lost in his own thoughts for a long period until, at present, he shook his head and leaned forward, elbows on knees. "It is time," he said in a soft voice, "that you learn another important truth. I am the only one alive who knows this secret. The Matrabazi brothers want to know the secret, so that is why what I am going to tell you can be dangerous. They will stop at nothing to learn what I know."

"We understand, Uncle Grisha," said Katya, "but you are scaring me."

"I apologize, my beautiful niece. But the secret must be told. It cannot die with me. We are talking about millions, perhaps billions, of dollars in hidden treasures, all appropriated by Joseph Stalin."

"Stalin?" cut in Illya Podipenko. "I thought he detested money."

"That's true, he did, for the most part," replied Uncle Grisha. "Stalin was very Bolshevik about money. Money meant nothing to him. He didn't like it. He considered it as the very symbol of capitalism, which the Bolsheviks disdained. He contemptuously referred to money as 'monetary tokens.' Of course, when he was in power, he didn't need money. He could have anything he wanted. In fact, for years he threw all of his pay packets inside a desk drawer. Your father, Konstantin, stole all of Stalin's money out of the desk drawer, about seventy-five thousand rubles, and gave it to my brother Sandro and me to start our new life here in America. We opened a restaurant next door to this flat. We called it 'Iveria,' which is the ancient name for Georgia."

Katya said, "So this two-story flat and the Iveria restaurant you started here with Grandpa Sandro was at least partially paid for by Stalin's own money?"

Uncle Grisha chuckled at that. "See, Katya, there is some justice in this world after all." He leaned back. "I can't tell you why Stalin surrounded himself with untold treasures. My brother thought maybe it was psychological. Stalin was dirt poor nearly his entire life. Plus, these treasures mostly came from his adversaries. Perhaps the riches were to Stalin some sort of personal trophy over his vanquished enemies. Who could ever tell exactly what was going on in that sociopath's mind?"

"Where did all of these treasures come from?" asked Illya Podipenko.

"Many different sources. Lenin always needed an endless stream of money to fund his Bolshevik revolution, and Stalin provided much of it. In the early days, throughout the Caucasus, Stalin and his criminal compatriots held up banks and trains filled with gold and stagecoaches carrying miners' wages and even mail ships carrying treasury funds on the Black Sea. Most of the proceeds Stalin sent off to Lenin. Some Stalin stashed away. He would kidnap children of wealthy tycoons for ransoms paid in rubles and diamonds. He would extort money from oil barons like the Rothchilds in Baku by saying he would end strikes by workers or sometimes he would just threaten to blow up their oil wells. Of course, he made sure that he got his taste of all of the diamonds and other gemstones that the Romanov women were secretly wearing under their dresses when they were brutally gunned down that fateful night in that basement in Yekaterinburg. During Lenin's rise to power, the Bolsheviks treasonously received money from Russia's war enemy, Germany.

"The Kaiser's Germany wanted an internal war in Russia and for the Bolsheviks to overthrow the Tsar's government, so Germany channeled more than fifty million gold marks to the Bolsheviks to fund their cause. Stalin made certain that some of that money found its way to him. They plundered the royal palaces for jewelry and gems as the Romanov dynasty fell. In 1936, Stalin interceded in the Spanish Civil War on behalf of the Republicans and offered his services to hold onto Spain's massive six-hundred-ton gold reserve for safekeeping so it wouldn't disappear during their war. More for Stalin to personally expropriate. Later, during the Great Patriotic War, the United States sent $11 billion in financial aid to Russia to help in the war effort. Stalin kept some for himself. And, of course, the big one. Stalin appropriated for his personal treasury some of the spoils plundered by his Russian Red Army troops after the fall of Berlin at the close of the Great Patriotic War with Germany. But not only in Germany. He appropriated wartime treasures from Japanese-occupied parts of China and Korea. He procured mostly gold, diamonds, and emeralds for himself. Some priceless artwork, a few furs. And there was more, but the point is, throughout his career, Stalin amassed a vast fortune and hid it all away."

"And no one knew?" asked a stunned Katya Tevoradze.

"No one who remained alive," answered her uncle. "Remember, Stalin trusted no one. In his paranoia, he feared conspiracies everywhere. It wasn't until Stalin appointed your father, Konstantin Podipenko, to his personal staff after Stalingrad that the *Vozhd* thought he had found the sole man that he could trust."

"And where is all of this Stalin treasure today?" inquired Illya Podipenko.

"Well, now, that's the thing." Uncle Grisha scratched his bald head and took a deep breath. "Stalin had hidden his plunder in different places across Russia, you see." He turned his eyes toward Illya. "But six months prior to his death, he called your father, Konstantin, into his study and told him all about the hidden treasures and the locations. For whatever reason, Stalin now wanted those possessions gathered into one single location, close to him. Who knows why? In any case, he gave a precise map to the locations of all of the hidden locations and gave Konstantin access to special trains and automobiles to retrieve all of it. Konstantin took my brother, Sandro, and me with him. It took us about six weeks to go to the various locations, find the treasures, load them up, and bring them back to Moscow."

"How many different locations were there?" asked Katya.

"Four. The first was the most difficult. In his younger days, Stalin had hidden treasures in the mysterious caverns in the mountain near Gori, the Georgian village where he was born. There were so many caverns in those mountains they called it 'the City of Caves.' But to Stalin's credit, the map he had drawn for us was perfect. He had hidden his loot behind a large bolder in a small cavern that was difficult to access and few knew it even existed. The second hidden site was near the Georgian capital of Tiflis on Holy Mountain near a white marble church where Stalin's mother, Keke, was buried. The third hidden site was near Sochi on the coast of the Black Sea. It was one of Stalin's favorite vacation homes called Red Meadow, high on a hill. Near the main *dacha*, there was a smaller summerhouse where a towering Oak tree stood. Stalin sardonically called it his Mamre tree, referring to the biblical Oak of Abraham tree where Abraham pitched his tent and met the three angels. Stalin buried his loot at the base of this tree. The fourth and final hidden location was in Moscow at Novodevichy Cemetery at the ancient monastery. It was buried in an unmarked plot next to where Stalin's second wife, Nadya, was interred, her large monument with marble roses carved on it."

Contemplative silence enveloped the room. At last, Katya asked, "So where is this single location that all of this treasure ended up?"

Uncle Grisha was about to answer when suddenly two men came roaring into the room through the door that led to the rear staircase. They were shouting orders in Georgian. Illya saw that it was the giant Carza Matrabazi and his brother, Silva, the idiot from the Dubenka Club. The giant was lumbering toward Illya and Katya on the couch. The Moscow policeman hefted up and bounded toward the giant, addressing him with a shoe tip to the testicles that seemed to have scant impact on the invader except to further anger him. Carza lashed out an arm and backhanded Illya nearly halfway across the room. Prior to the back of his head smacking into the corner of a table as he whooshed in free flight past where Uncle Grisha was sitting, he could see the old man struggling against Silva Matrabazi, who had clasped him under the armpits. Somehow, Uncle Grisha freed a hand. He managed to crush down on the attacker's scaphoid bone, the cashew-sized super sensitive carpal bone on the radial side of the wrist at the base of the thumb. The man screamed aloud and immediately allowed the weapon to clatter from his grip. Uncle Grisha then frenziedly began rummaging the seat cushion for his pistol. He found it, and with his right hand, he hefted the gun upward. He managed to thrust the barrel of the pistol into his attacker's mouth, pulling the trigger.

A blast rang out in the room and the back of Silva's head sprayed the far wall with red serum and silvery fragments. He crumpled to the floor like a sack of dirty laundry. Dazed, Illya Podipenko tried to heft himself upward, but his legs gave way. Blood trickled from his forehead into his eye. His chest beat unmercifully as through clouded vision he saw the giant across the room hoisting the young girl in one arm. She was thrashing her fists futilely against the giant's head and chest. The giant turned and clumped toward where Uncle Grisha was slumped in his chair. He bent over using his free arm to swoop up Grisha Tevoradze. As Carza the Creature stomped toward the doorway with a thrashing body pinched up under each arm, on the floor, Illya's hand foraged wildly for Grisha's gun. He found it, raised the weapon to eye level, and pulled the trigger. A bullet snapped into the back of the giant's left knee. It momentarily hobbled him, but he kept moving forward. Illya placed a second shot in almost the same spot, then a third shot behind the Creature's right knee. The giant halted, yowling in anger, saliva leaking from his jowls. He swung around toward Illya, and as he did, he launched Uncle Grisha hard against a wall, his head banging so viciously that it sounded like a melon dropped onto hard pavement. The old man's body slumped to the floor, unmoving. With streams of spittle flowing from his open mouth, Carza stomped toward the Moscow investigator; the girl Katya raised both of her arms above her head and wiggled her body free from the giant. She tumbled to the floor, searching for anything to stop the attacker. Her eyes found the sharp-tipped fireplace poker.

As the giant was leaning over to gather up Illya Podipenko by his collar, the girl snatched the poker and bolted across the room. She leaped on the giant's back, and with arms held high in the air, she let out a scream, and gathering all of her strength, she leaned sideways and thrust the tip of the poker through one of the giant's earholes at such an angle and with such force that the tip of the poker exited through an eye socket. Blood spouted from the giant's head. He bolted upright and let out a wounded animal's howl. He tossed the girl from his back and began stumbling aimlessly across the room, arms outstretched, the fireplace poker jutting from his gushing eyehole. Pierced on the very tip of the poker, a solitary eyeball eerily jigged in the air three inches from the giant's face. At the giant's feet, Illya Podipenko steadied the gun in his hand. A shot rang out, and a bullet thwacked into Carza's forehead. A moment later, he crashed to the ground like a hewn oak, dead.

Illya let the gun clatter to the ground next to where he sat. His temples were pounding, his constricted throat heaving for air. Across from him, he saw the young girl sitting upright, her face red, her arms clasped around her knees. She was battling to catch her breath, and she surveyed the tumbled room in front of her.

"Well, that happened," she uttered. "A friggin' dumpster fire."

Illya stumbled across to the girl, thumping down on the floor next to her. Together, they sat attempting to suck oxygen into their lungs. At last, Katya nodded her head in the direction of the giant's body on the floor.

"Look at you, Illya Podipenko! You are my hero. You shot the bitch, saved my life. Old school. I love it!"

"Me the hero?" he wheezed out. "You are the one who rammed that fireplace poker through the giant's earhole. You know that's probably going to leave a mark."

"Hate when that happens," the girl replied, and they sat next to each other laughing until Illya felt the strength to clamber to his feet, pulling the girl up with a heave.

She said, "You know, Homer Simpson once said that there's nothing wrong with hitting someone when his back is turned. So at least I got that going for me."

Illya nodded. "Well, then, it appears our work is done here," he observed, viewing their surroundings.

"Yeah," the girl responded, "I think the bad guys are mostly dead."

Suddenly, the girl was stumbling across the room toward where her uncle Grisha lay lifelessly. "Call 911," she shouted over her shoulder to Illya, who already was digging his mobile phone from a pocket. Katya sat to cradle her uncle Grisha's head in her arms.

"Uncle Grisha, I am here," she whispered to him. "Just hold on, we are going to get you to the hospital." She saw her uncle's lips barely moving, and she leaned her head closer. "Uncle Grisha, what are you saying?" She put her ear to his lips, concentrating.

Before the old man slipped into unconsciousness, Katya said, "I don't know what that means."

CHAPTER 5

The emergency waiting room was abuzz with night-time activity, as usual, at the Coney Island Hospital on Ocean Parkway, just minutes from the Tevoradze flat, across the Belt Parkway. Staffers in white smocks and blue scrubs scurried from here to there while bawls of the newly injured distantly rang out from the admitting area.

Illya Podipenko and Katya Tevoradze sat close, anxiously waiting. They had been there for more than two hours. Katya sat with an unread magazine across her lap. Illya glanced at his watch for the umpteenth time. He hadn't thought to wipe the crusted blood from his forehead. He took Katya's hand in his.

He said thoughtfully, "Your uncle Grisha seems like a tough old Georgian. He'll pull through."

The girl nodded absently. Her face was somber, and she hadn't spoken much until finally she said, "He whispered something to me, you know. Before he fell into unconsciousness."

"What did he say?" The two exchanged meaningful glances.

"I'm not sure. It was hard to understand. It sounded like he said 'Statue of Liberty.'"

"Statue of Liberty?" answered Illya. "Are you certain?"

"Well, I think so. I mean that's what it sounded like. It doesn't make sense, does it?"

"Not exactly. But we will figure it out, you and I. Don't worry about it, Katya. For now, let's concentrate on Uncle Grisha regaining consciousness."

"Yes, you're right, of course." She was quiet for another spell, resting her head on Illya Podipenko's shoulder. She cast her eyes about the waiting room. "They did a good renovating job," she sighed at last. "The waiting room was destroyed by Hurricane Sandy in 2012."

"Spend a lot of time here, do you?" Illya tried to make light.

"Little as I can." She weakly smiled. She turned her beautiful face upward, her eyes searching his. "I have already lost Grandpa Sandro, I can't lose Uncle Grisha too. I'll be all alone."

"You won't be alone," Illya gently assured her.

She leaned in, tenderly kissing Illya on his cheek. "My hero," she whispered.

"I keep telling you, *you* are the hero, not me. It was you who extracted the giant's eyeball with a fireplace poker. Remind me the next time you have a fireplace poker in your hands to give you a wide berth."

Katya chuckled. She was about to say something when Illya patted her knee. "The doctor is here," he said.

The two stood as a dark-skinned man approached them wearing a white surgical cap and a surgical mask hanging loose around his neck. "My name is Dr. Arjun Bhavani. I am a traumatic brain surgeon here at the hospital." His voice was soft and somehow reassuring. He shook each of their hands. "Well, our job is finished for now. We have done the best that we can."

"Is my uncle alive?" nervously asked the young girl.

"Yes. We have moved him to ICU. He had a very serious fracture of the skull. He is in a coma, and comas are tricky things. We've seen some cerebrospinal fluid buildup in the cerebral ventricles, causing increased pressure and swelling in the brain. There was some bleeding too. We are doing our best to reduce this. We do have some measurable activity in the brain and the brainstem, so that is positive. But with these cases, you never really know. His advanced age may work against him. We are monitoring him for seizures, which can happen in cases like this."

Katya smiled bravely. Illya put an arm around her shoulder and drew her near. The doctor stood quietly, his hands clasped behind his back, his eyes dark and compassionate. He continued, "Skull injuries like this can tear the layers of protective tissues surrounding the brain. This can enable bacteria to enter the brain and cause infections. A dangerous infection of the meninges can spread to the rest of the nervous system, if not treated. After a few days to a few weeks or months, a person may emerge from a coma or enter a vegetative state." He sighed deeply. "It is a waiting game now. Rest assured we will provide your uncle with the best medical care possible. My advice to you would be to prepare for the worse and pray for the best."

*****

Katya Tevoradze had parked her aging blue Focus behind two police squad cars from the sixtieth precinct along the street in front of the house she had grown up in with Grandpa Sandro and Uncle Grisha. Along with Illya, she ducked under the yellow security tape and entered the front door of the flat. It appeared that the activity was just finishing up. The two men in hazardous gear had already removed the dead bodies of the Matrabazi brothers. Places were marked on the floor, photos were being taken. Katya noticed that two younger men were having a low-toned discussion in the far corner of the room. One of the men Katya recognized as the same police lieutenant who was in charge the night the body of her grandfather Sandro was found at the bottom of the stairwell. The other man Katya did not know. It was this man who was now approaching Katya and Illya as they were lingering in the doorway observing the activities. He was a tallish, handsome young man with chiseled features and dark hair, a thick beard stubble, and full shoulders. He was wearing a blue nylon jacket with FBI written on it.

"Who is *that*?' Katya breathlessly inquired of her companion. She inhaled deeply.

Illya drew back his chin and stared at the young girl. Her eyes were round as marbles, and her skin had become noticeably florid. Smilingly, Illya replied, "You are not going to faint, are you, my dear?"

"I wouldn't bet against it," the flushed girl whispered. She could hear her own chest thumping.

"His name is Noah Carter. He is a friend of mine, an FBI agent. I called him. I thought he could be of some service to us. The police are going to be asking you unending questions considering that this is the second time in four days they've had to come here to collect dead bodies. I asked Noah to intercede."

"*Intercede*," Katya absently swooned as if the word was flush with romantic meaning. "And he is a friend of yours?"

"Please, Katya, you are dribbling on the carpet," Illya pointed out then turned and opened his arms wide, giving the FBI man a warm hug. "Thank you so much for coming, Noah," he said, "I know you must be very busy."

"Never too busy for a good friend, Illya." He smiled back. "As you can see, we've secured the scene and will have our forensic guys do their thing. I've talked to the local police lieutenant in charge. I told him we would be taking over the case now. He was perfectly agreeable. I don't think he wanted to mess with the Matrabazi family anyway, which is fine because we do. We've been chasing the family around New York for months. They have been on the FBI's radar for quite some time. Most of their illegal activities are federal crimes, so it is in our jurisdiction."

Illya was about to say something when he felt a meaningful elbow plunk to his ribs. The young girl next to him was vigorously clearing her throat for attention.

"Oh, sorry, sorry," Illya called out, "how rude of me. Noah Carter, this is Katya Tevoradze. She is a college student at Columbia. She lives here in this flat. It was her grandfather Sandro who was murdered a few nights ago and her uncle Grisha who was attacked tonight and is currently in a coma at the hospital."

"A pleasure," said the FBI man extending his hand. "I am so sorry about your current circumstances, Ms. Tevoradze. We are here to help you in any way we can."

When she took the young man's offered hand, she found herself sensually clasping onto it longer than accepted in polite society, or *any* society, really. Illya noticed that the girl's knees seemed to momentarily warp, and he secured an arm around her for support.

"Please," the girl rattled from her throat, "you can call me K-Kath, er, Kris—"

"Katya," Illya jumped in to save her, his grip tightening around her.

The girl reddened. "Yes, yes, of course, Katya. That is my name."

"And you may call me Noah." The agent's smile was warmly engaging and full of perfect teeth. His chin, the girl decided, should be on a marble statue somewhere. He then asked her, "Do you have a place to stay tonight?"

With that, the young girl went into full collapse mode, and Illya Podipenko swaddled her like a newborn and guided her to the nearest chair, where she slumped down unceremoniously, her knees splayed apart, her mouth agape.

Illya whispered, "You must rest, Katya. Try doing so with your legs together and your mouth closed. It offers an enhanced first impression." To which she merely let out a moan.

He returned to the FBI agent. He smiled. "Don't judge her harshly, my friend. She's had a bad couple of days. Normally, she is a very intelligent, very persistent, and a very brave young lady."

They both stole a look at her. She sat as if a Thorazine patient, staring blankly into nowhere, her mouth having slacked open once more.

"Yes, I can see that, Illya," Noah smiled, offering a wink. "Very attractive too. So she will be staying with you tonight?"

"She will. At my flat near the university. I have an extra bedroom." Illya wasn't entirely sure why he had added the last part so defensively.

"Totally understand," nodded Noah Carter. He put a hand on the shoulder of the man from Moscow.

"So tell me, Illya, what on God's green earth is really going on here?"

"Well, it is complicated," Illya puffed his cheeks. "Perhaps better discussed over vodka."

"Oh, I like the sound of that," Noah answered, agreeably. "Lead the way, my friend."

*****

They had settled in at a small kitchen table. The room was attractive with wooden cabinets, throw rugs, and a large butcher's block table in the center of things. Illya and Noah Carter sat glasses in hand, a bottle of chilled vodka between them. As the FBI man listened, the investigator from Moscow summarized the strange activities of the past few days. He described how the girl Katya, a Columbia student who attended his lectures, had approached him while he was sitting on a bench in Central Park with a wild story of her grandfather Sandro's peculiar death at the bottom of steep back steps in the house where they were currently sitting and about their visit to the Dubenka Club, owned by the Matrabazi brothers, where Illya had first met the girl's Uncle Grisha; how, when drunk, Sandro and Grisha apparently had foolishly talked about some secret treasures only they knew about that Stalin had apparently stashed away in different locations around the Soviet Union and how the two men, under the supervision of Illya Podipenko's own father, Konstantin, had amassed all these treasures into a single location right before

Stalin's death. He did not mention how Sandro and Grisha had attacked Stalin as he was sleeping, causing the leader's massive stroke that ended up killing him.

"Now, that is quite a story, Illya," said Noah Carter. "So all of this is about some secret treasure Stalin had hidden away decades ago?"

Illya nodded in the affirmative. Amiably, he poured both of them a follow-up tot of vodka from the bottle on the table. "Now worth billions apparently. That is why the giant and his brother, Silva, broke in here tonight. They were going to kidnap Grisha and the girl and force them to tell them where all of this so-called Stalin's treasure is today. But the girl doesn't know anything. Her grandfather and uncle never told her about it."

Noah looked at Illya a moment without saying anything. Then, "And you believe their tale to be true, that Stalin had hidden all of this treasure?"

"Crazy as it sounds, I do."

"Of course." Noah Carter was quiet a moment. "Did your father, the marshal, ever say anything to you about this treasure? It sounds as if he supervised gathering all of the hidden treasures in one location, all on Stalin's orders."

"Never mentioned a word. I don't know why. Maybe he wanted to shelter me from it. Or perhaps he was going to tell me and never got the chance before he passed away. I really don't know."

"I see." The FBI man rubbed his face with his fingers. He sighed heavily. "And before Grisha Tevoradze lost consciousness during the attack tonight, was he able to say anything that would shed light on where the Stalin treasure might be?"

"He said Statue of Liberty," a voice said.

Both Illya and Noah Carter turned their heads toward the kitchen's doorway. The young girl, apparently now having successfully gathered herself, stood cross-legged, leaning up against the doorframe. Her hands were tucked into the pockets of her shorts. "At least, that is what I thought my uncle said. He whispered it to me before he slipped into unconsciousness."

"Statue of Liberty," repeated Illya Podipenko. "I don't understand. Does that mean anything to you?"

Katya shrugged. "Nothing beyond the obvious. I know it was one of the favorite places for he and Grandpa Sandro to visit. They took me there many times. Other than that, I don't have any idea how it ties into Stalin's so-called hidden treasure." She was quiet a moment then added, "But I am pretty certain about one thing."

"That being?" asked Illya.

"I'll bet that Lady Liberty is the first place you and I are going to visit tomorrow morning."

"That's my girl," proudly responded Illya Podipenko, slipping a wink to the FBI agent.

CHAPTER 6

"Illya, this is incredible! This is where you *live*?"

"Welcome to my humble home, at least for the next two years while I lecture for the FBI." Illya had done well for himself. He lived in Upper Manhattan in a roomy flat off Amsterdam Avenue near the Cathedral Christ of St. John the Divine, within walking distance of Columbia University.

"Not so humble!" the girl cried out and began to excitedly swirl across the thick beige carpeting as if auditioning for the Kirov. She pirouetted around a brown, right-angled leather settee and lightly skimmed her hands across the books that were perfectly sequenced by ascending height on a light wood bookshelf. On a table, she saw a sculpture of a double-headed eagle from the old days of the Imperial Tsars. A carpeted wood staircase climbed to a second story. She peered at the fascinating artwork on the walls, and when she noticed the white louvered shutters covering a large casement window, she ran to it and pulled the shutters open. Golden-lit windows in somber buildings near and far winked at her through the night. "You can see the university from here!" she uttered breathlessly.

"Yes, you can. I can't complain. Columbia treated me very well. And for the next two years, the FBI is paying, so not too bad for a short, fat balding Muscovite."

"What? I think you are *cute*!" She had lightly glided up behind him and whispered the words in his ear.

"Cute, yes, well, let's not start all that again." He paused a moment, smiling. "Besides, it appears I might have some competition now."

She sniffed. "Why, Illya, I am quite sure I don't know what you are talking about."

"Really? Because I do not recall actually seeing a girl drool before."

"Please, Illya! I had a mint in my mouth, that's all."

"Uh-huh." He noticed the girl's cheeks had flushed. She was making circles on the carpeting with a toe. The two people looked at each other.

The girl said, "Well, FBI Agent Noah Carter was quite handsome, you must admit it."

"I do admit it."

"And he seemed quite intelligent."

"Quite."

"And his body was amazing, all those muscles!"

"If you like that sort of thing. And he is not married."

"I was working my way around to asking that."

"I figured."

"Well, he seems to check all of the boxes."

"Every one, apparently."

"Illya, you are making fun of me!"

"I wouldn't."

He watched the girl glide across the carpet toward him. She warmly reached out her arms and hugged him then stepped back, loosening the bun on top of her head. She shook her curly tresses free, and they fell to her shoulders. She rested her head against Illya's chest. She said, "I think you are jealous."

"Very." He gently stroked the girl's hair.

Katya pulled back and looked into his face. "No, you're not. You are too happy to be jealous. You are grinning like Alice's Cheshire Cat. You are actually enjoying this."

"Remember in the restaurant. You told me that you thought you could tell that I was in love with Lena Sharapova? How my face and body language gave me away when I spoke of her in my lectures. Now I know what you meant. I saw your face, your eyes. Your entire body crackled with electricity tonight when you met Agent Noah Carter for the first time. Your skin flushed, your pupils dilated, you kept leaning your body into his as you talked. Classic signs. That was love at first sight if I have ever seen it."

"It was that obvious?" purred Katya Tevoradze.

"Well, not that the Hazmat crew in your flat would notice. After all, they were busy bagging up a giant with a fireplace poker sticking out of his ear."

"You know what, I don't care. It was storybook. One look and I was swept off my feet. That's not a crime, is it?"

"Not a felony, certainly. No need to go on the lam, as Americans say." He sighed and gave the girl a kiss on top of the head. He became serious. "Listen, we have a big day tomorrow. We'll visit the Statue of Liberty, see if we can make sense of the words your Uncle Grisha whispered to you tonight. Seem like a plan?"

Katya nodded into the man's chest.

"Good," he replied, "then I think it's bedtime."

The girl tilted her face upward. She cast a quick smile and put a hand on his chest. "I thought you'd never ask," she breathed softly, looking at him carefully. "You know, Thursdays are pajama-optional."

The man smiled benevolently. "I am afraid I've got you there, young lady. Today is only Wednesday."

"I know," the girl closed her eyes and purred sweetly. "On Wednesdays, pajamas aren't even an option."

*****

Katya Tevoradze seemed despondent.

Illya Podipenko had taken her hand and guided her down a hallway. He stopped at a doorway on the right and said, "This is where you will sleep tonight. I will be here, right across the hallway."

"But—"

"Now, Katya," he spoke softly. "We must do what is right. You get a good night's sleep. Dream sweet dreams about your FBI Agent Noah Carter."

That had been an hour ago, and presently, Illya Podipenko was hopelessly tossing and turning in his own bed. He intertwined his fingers behind his head, his mind rousing around recent events and Uncle Grisha's wild conspiracy tales about he and his brother, Sandro, and Illya's father, the marshal. His mind randomly flared images of Stalin's death and of his supposed hidden treasures and of the home invasion by two of the Matrabazi brothers that put the young girl's uncle in a coma. Answers were not forthcoming.

At some point, Illya, hovering on the edge of slumber, became aware of a perceptible shift in the bedroom's air currents, an unseen presence close by. The air carried an ambrosial scent. He lifted his head, looking over his shoulder. In the dark he was surprised by a human outline.

It was the girl.

"Katya, you gave me a start."

"Please, Illya, I am afraid and cold. I need to be with someone tonight. With you."

"But, Katya, this doesn't seem right."

"Please, Illya, let me sleep with you. No funny business, I swear. I just want you to hold me."

On his back, Illya studied vague shadows across the ceiling of the room. At last, he let out a sigh. "No funny business," he reminded her.

"I swear, as sure as ferrets are ferrets."

"Now? You are quoting Alice's White Rabbit at this hour in the morning?" Through the shadows, he studied the dark silhouette hovering above him. He could see the white teeth of her smile.

"Well, all right." Illya pulled back the sheet and blankets. "I suppose you'd better jump in then."

The words had barely escaped his lips when the young girl shouted out, "That's what I'm talkin' bout" and surged like a wave into the bed, at which time Illya Podipenko let out a screech that could have split glass. "The devil, Katya, your toes are ice blocks!"

"I told you I was cold," she snuggled in. Her head sought the man's shoulder, her body wedged against his. She cooed, "There, that's better. Your body is so warm, Illya!"

"Hot flashes," he advised her. "It comes with age."

"You're funny." She laughed, jostling her body even closer to his. "Hmm, this is nice. We should have done this sooner."

"We just met twenty-four hours ago," Illya reminded her.

She answered wistfully, "It seems like a long time ago. I can hardly remember a time before you." They spent several minutes indulged in silence. Then Katya Tevoradze reported, "Alice in her Wonderland adventures once said, 'When I used to read fairy tales, I fancied that kind of thing never happened, and now here I am in the middle of one!'"

"Some fairy tale," Illya hmphed out. "More like a nightmare. You are sharing a bed with a pudgy, balding, vaguely literate, aging Russian man who stumbles in the mornings just trying to get both feet in his underwear."

"I know, right? You're the worst."

"Perhaps you should move closer to the opposite edge of the bed," offered Illya.

"Yeah, that's not going to happen," whispered Katya, compressing her body firmly into the man next to her. "You didn't get the memo?"

"Apparently not," sputtered Illya Podipenko.

Neither could sleep. It was creeping close to four o'clock in the morning, and they lay watching lights from outside seep through the window blinds to jig across the walls and ceiling. Katya Tevoradze's head rested cozily on Illya's chest. He was gently stroking the top of her head.

Finally, she said, "So how do you know Agent Noah Carter?"

"Really? This the best time to discuss Agent Carter?"

"Yes, it is."

"I see." Illya chuckled. "I foolishly thought a better time might have been any time that is *not* four o'clock in the morning."

"No, four o'clock works nicely."

"I stand corrected. Well, then, let's see," Illya began, "Noah had apparently come to know about what happened two years ago in the murders of the Rasputin heirs and the recovery of the previously unknown Fabergé eggs. He read everything he could about the case. He even began sending me e-mails in Moscow asking about certain details of our investigation. I answered him, of course, and we just became e-mail acquaintances. Then when he learned that I was going to lecture for two years at Columbia University about the case, he signed up for my inaugural class. We became close friends, and it was Noah who recommended to the FBI that I lecture about the case to new FBI recruits following my two years at Columbia. So he gave me two more years in New York. I can't complain."

"And you are certain that he is not married?"

"I am."

"That's awesome."

"I suppose so…he is a bit older than you, remember."

"Good. I like older men, I prefer them. Grew up around them my whole life. They have experienced life. It's romantic. Age difference doesn't matter. Like you and your true love, Lena Sharapova."

"Goodness, don't start that again."

"Well, you are in love with her, are you not?"

Illya went silent then said, "I love her, yes, but I am not *in* love with her. I mean, what's the use? Look at me and look at her. Talk about an age difference!"

"So you are not in love with her?"

"Well, I certainly was dazzled by her. Still am. She is one of the most beautiful and intelligent people I've ever met. She is now married to an American diplomat. I am happy for her, I truly am."

"Uh-huh," Katya offered, sounding less than convinced. "What about other lovers?"

"What?"

"Come on, Illya, you heard me. You can tell me, I am an aspiring adult. I am almost twenty-one years old! Go ahead, tell me about all of your lovers. Make me extremely jealous."

Illya sighed deeply. Finally, he said, "Well, I shan't deny that, in my youth, I may have had an intrigue or two with the odd low women who fell my way."

"My, how romantic! I don't understand why you never married."

"I *was* married once."

"What? You never mentioned that! How'd that work out for you?"

"It was a long time ago, around the time I joined the Moscow militia. I wasn't always bald and round, you know. In my youth, I had long, wavy, dark hair. Unfortunately, most of it was on my back."

"For Pete's sakes, Illya!" The girl delivered a rib shot.

The man winced and laughed. "Her name was Tanya. She worked for a magazine. She was very pretty. We were young. Neither of us realized the long hours I would be working. A lot of late nights in police work. And, of course, danger. She couldn't get used to it. I don't blame her."

"How long were you married?"

"Less than two years." Illya allowed a smile. "I always tell people the story. Right before we broke up, she gave me a book entitled *Everything Men Know About Women.* It consisted of a hundred and twenty blank pages. That's all. I read the book cover to cover.

Several times. And one time, she had asked me to buy her an expensive pair of Christian Louboutin shoes. I saved and saved and finally I could afford to get her those shoes. I bought them from a fashion store on the *Arbat*. So the day I gave them to her, she put them on, looked at herself in the mirror, and walked out the door. And that was the last I saw of Tanya. Afterward, of course, I dated a lady who was a personal trainer and a hooker. Can you imagine? All that time I visited her, I never knew she was a personal trainer."

"You are impossible, Illya! That's can't be true!"

"But it's a good story."

*****

Katya Tevoradze slumped down on a bench, blue around her lips from the sugary shaved ice she had been sucking. Earlier, she had chucked down a powdered funnel cake. She was dressed in tight beige shorts and a turquoise tank top with matching-colored socks rolled down to the tops of her running shoes. Sunglasses roosted on top of her head. Next to her, Illya Podipenko slanted against a metal railing, blankly staring off into the water of New York Harbor. A new, red ball cap the girl made him wear was pulled down low on his forehead. She had surprised him with it, having purchased it at the gift shop. On the front of the cap, it said "Lady Liberty."

"For pity's sake," she moaned, "who knew detective work could be so friggin' exhausting!"

"It's not for everyone." Illya smiled with a slight nod of his head. He was absently watching freighters, tugs, and sailboats sluice through the waters of the East River. In the distance was Governor's Island and, further, the Brooklyn docks. They had been at it for nearly four hours and had nothing, save for the ball cap, to show for it. *What did Katya's Uncle Grisha mean when he uttered the words Statue of Liberty to his niece?* Illya wondered to himself. *Had the girl misheard him? Maybe he had said something else, not Statue of Liberty?*

Whatever it was he had said, it brought Illya and his new, young friend, Katya, to the place they were right now. They had taken the ferryboat from the Battery Park pier on the southern tip of Manhattan. Katya had been excited, chattering about trying to determine what her uncle Grisha meant in his whispered words to her before he was taken to the hospital. As they approached Liberty Island, both she and Illya had fallen into a reverent silence, taking in the magnificent view. The statue's foundation and pedestal faced southeast, greeting ships entering the harbor from the Atlantic Ocean. Against a blue sky, the golden torch in Lady Liberty's right hand seemed to illuminate the low white clouds floating above her.

First, they tackled the many levels of the tall granite pedestal by elevator, stopping and wandering about each of the six levels. At the second level they spent time on the balcony and in the museum and wandered the Fort Hood level before finally reaching the pedestal's top observatory deck. They looked out to the crowded shores of New York on one side and New Jersey on the other with Ellis Island floating off in the distance in the Hudson River.

Then the real work began. The three hundred and fifty-four steep, narrow and upward spiraling steps to the statue's crown had Illya Podipenko pausing often to fetch air into his lungs and wipe droplets of sweat from his forehead. From the top, they could look to where a line of cars was snaking along the double-decked Verrazano-Narrows suspension bridge connecting the boroughs of Staten Island and Brooklyn. The girl explained to the skeptical man from Moscow that seasonal contractions and expansions of the steel cables caused the double-decked roadway to be twelve feet lower in the summer than in the winter.

"That is a valuable piece of information," Illya huffed out, bent over bellowing for breath. "You don't suppose they provide oxygen masks up here, do you?"

"That's hilarious," Katya replied. She patted him on the back. "But perhaps our time would be better spent looking for clues."

"You look. My vision is fading."

"Illya, be serious. We have to find out what my uncle Grisha meant when he uttered the words Statue of Liberty."

"You are right, of course." He stood up straight as he could and peered out over the vista of water, shoreline, and skyscrapers. His chest was still thumping. "I once read that there at least forty buildings in New York City that *have their own* ZIP code," he managed to breathe out.

"Is that a clue?"

"Probably not. Just something I read."

"Not helpful," she replied dejectedly.

For thirty minutes, they ambled in a circle around the torch overview pondering the expanse of scenery. "You see anything?" he asked.

"No. You?"

"Not really. A lot of water. A lot of buildings. Some bridges, some islands. No clues." He paused a moment. "There is one thing, though."

"What?"

"There is a man about fifty feet behind us. He has been following us. Don't look."

"Gray pants, white golf shirt, sunglasses?"

"You noticed?"

"Of course. I am aware of my surroundings, Illya. My grandfather and uncle taught me well. It's a Georgian thing, know what is around you at all times. You recognize him?"

"No. You?"

"No."

Illya looked forlornly at the circular metal staircase. "Let's begin our long trek down, shall we?"

Following their adventure to the top of the statue then back down again, Illya and the young girl had strolled the entire fourteen acres of the Liberty Island park surrounding the statue, stopping periodically to rest their tired legs. Silently, they had been studying the island's landscaping and environs. They had sought shade on a bench beneath an old beech tree and watched pigeons peck their beaks into the green grass. Katya had stopped at a kiosk to purchase a brochure on the history of Lady Liberty and a second kiosk to buy her cup of blue shaved ice. The man in the sunglasses lingered, never far away.

Presently, the girl hefted off the bench and deposited the remains of her ice cone into a nearby rubbish bin. She leaned against the fence next to the Moscow investigator and began thumbing through the brochure.

Eventually, she asked Illya, "Does the name Bedloe mean anything to you?"

"Pardon?"

"Bedloe. Does it mean anything to you?"

"I don't think so. Should it?"

"It was the original name of this island. Bedloe's Island. I am just throwing out ideas here. See if anything can help lead us to solving the puzzle. Maybe, I should just be quiet."

Illya smiled broadly. He leaned sideways and surprisingly gave the girl a kiss on her forehead. "Not a bit of it, my dear child. One never knows what might pop up as a clue. You keep digging." He rubbed his face with his hands and turned around. "Why don't we concentrate on the statue itself. What do we know?"

Katya flipped to a new page in her brochure. "Well, the statue represents *Libertas*, a Roman goddess of Liberty. Her right hand is holding the torch above her head. In her left hand, she is carrying a tablet inscribed with the Roman numerals July IV MDCCLXXVI. That is the date of the US Declaration of Independence, July 4, 1776."

"Make a note of that," offered Illya Podipenko. "Perhaps those numbers are a clue, perhaps a combination to a lock or something. What else?"

"At her feet is a broken chain, half-hidden by her robes."

"Okay. What about her crown?"

"There are seven rays forming a halo."

"There are seven seas, seven continents. It may mean something."

"But what?" asked the girl.

"The sad truth is I don't know yet. But we cannot disregard anything at this point." He was about to add another thought when he felt something punch hard into his back.

"Stay still. Don't turn around." Illya knew without looking that it was the man in sunglasses who had been following them. "You and the girl will accompany me to the ferryboat. My brother, Dato Matrabazi, wants to see you. One wrong move and I will kill you right here."

Illya nodded to Katya, and they both turned slowly. The man in the sunglasses nudged Illya onward. "Yet another Matrabazi brother?" Illya asked quietly.

"Good guess. Palo, the second youngest. You killed our two other brothers, Silva, and the giant, Carza. Dato is very angry. He wants to torture you himself. He is very good with blades. And, of course, with this one," Palo brushed a finger across Katya's cheek, causing her to flinch and indignantly swat his hand aside, "we want answers. We want to know where Stalin's treasures are hidden, and we will force her to tell us in the most gruesome and sordid ways."

"She doesn't know anything," Illya countered, walking forward.

"We will see about that. Keep moving—"

Suddenly behind him, Illya heard a *pffft* sound then a yawp of pain. Against his legs, he felt Palo Matrabazi's body collapse to the ground. Behind him now was a man in a white shirt and dark suit. He had a bull neck and a blondish crew cut, built like a longshoreman from the Brooklyn dockyards.

"Help me get him to the bench, quickly," the man ordered Illya.

Stunned for a moment, Illya took the legs while the younger man placed his hands under Palo's armpits, and, together, they hoisted him to the bench. The young man folded Palo Matrabazi's body into a sitting position and tilted his head downward as if the dead man were simply enjoying a nap in the Liberty Park sunlight. He took a deep breath and turned to Illya and the girl with a grin. He swiftly flashed a gold badge. "Robert Johnson, FBI. Agent Noah Carter assigned me to watch over you two today. We need to move fast. The next ferry is about to leave. Let's go."

*****

They were hurtling recklessly eastward on Neptune Avenue, whizzing past Coney Island brownstones and small shops, weaving in and out of the pathways of slower-moving vehicles, at times disdaining red lights and stop signs as if they were merely motoring suggestions. The FBI agent was driving, his left elbow poking out of the window next to him. Illya and Katya sat speechlessly jostled together in the back seat of the dark blue Audi. Agent Johnson had parked his car near Battery Park. Once he secured his passengers, he had sped through the Carey toll tunnel under the mouth of the East River to the Prospect Expressway then followed the Ocean Parkway south, past the hospital where Katya's uncle was lying in a coma, then past the Belt Parkway.

"We want to thank you for coming to our rescue back there," Illya tried to shout above the din.

"Not a problem," the FBI agent yelled over his shoulder. "Any friend of Agent Noah Carter is a friend of mine."

"He is a good man. Have you known him long?" Illya noticed that the man was sweating heavily.

"We joined the bureau about the same time."

"I see. And that was a one of the Matrabazi gang accosting us at Liberty Park?"

"Yeah, Palo Matrabazi. He is one of the four brothers in America, with another one, the oldest, in the Soviet Union."

Illya tried to hunch forward. A tire hit a pothole so fast that his head nicked the ceiling of the Audi.

He winced in pain. "You can drop us off at the young lady's flat on Brightwater Court."

"Can't do that," the driver mumbled in response.

"Pardon?"

The driver slammed a right turn off of Neptune Avenue. "Agent Carter wants to see you now. He says it is urgent."

"I understand." Illya was quiet a moment. "So did you go the college with Agent Carter at Yale?"

"I sure did."

"That's nice," responded Illya. He shot a puzzling glance to the girl beside him then reached into his pocket. He stealthily removed his mobile phone, hiding it between his thighs. He hit a few buttons then dropped the phone on the floor between his feet.

"Where exactly are we meeting Agent Carter?" he asked aloud.

The driver suddenly swerved right into a small street then slid a sharp left into an alleyway. "We use an abandoned warehouse behind that automobile storage facility just ahead. We use it for secret meetings."

"Agent Carter has secret meetings in an old warehouse in West Brighton just off Neptune Avenue?" Illya asked the driver, enunciating as clear as he could.

"What?" the driver asked.

"Nothing. It's not important."

Just past the automobile storage facility a run-down three-story warehouse came into view. The building had broken windows and a tottering roof and appeared in long disuse. The Audi braked into a sliding stop over gravel, spitting a scud of dust and grit into the air.

The driver unfolded from the car and opened the rear door. "Come with me," he ordered.

"You say Agent Carter is going to meet us here?" asked Illya Podipenko.

"That is what I said."

"Can the girl stay in the car? She doesn't need to be in the meeting."

"She comes with us."

With hesitation, Illya emerged from the back seat with the young girl in tow. He tucked his mobile phone into one of his socks.

As they followed Agent Johnson toward a doorway of the warehouse, Illya leaned close to the girl, whispering in her ear, "Noah Carter did not go to Yale."

"No? A pity. It's a decent enough school."

"That's not the point. I asked our driver, Agent Johnson, if he had attended Yale with Agent Carter. He said yes. But Noah Carter didn't go to Yale. He graduated from Rutgers. You see the problem?"

"Rutgers sucks?"

"No, no, I am sure it is a very fine school. The point is Agent Johnson lied to us."

"Now that *does* suck."

Illya paused in mid-stride, his eyes searching the girl's face. "Katya, I am not kidding around.

Something is not right here. I think we could be walking into a trap. The Matrabazi brothers."

"That *really* sucks."

"You are not scared?" He was stunned by her composure.

"So-so. I try not to show it."

"Pardon?"

"I am with you. What could possibly go wrong? I saw what you did with your mobile phone. So far, these Matrabazi guys have shown themselves to be staggering idiots. What are they going to do, kill the goose that lays the golden egg? They think we know where Stalin's hidden treasure is."

"But we don't."

"Not yet. But they don't know that." The young girl threaded her arm through the Moscow investigator's. "Anyway, you'll think of something."

Illya stumbled forward. "By some off chance you didn't happen to bring that fireplace poker with you?"

"Sorry. The last time I saw it, the giant was wearing it as a hat."

"No talking!" Agent Johnson called over his shoulder as he yanked open a door to the warehouse. "Inside. Move it."

The inside was dark and dank. The door clanked behind them. Illya squinted his eyes to adjust to the half-light. He could make out a table in the center of the room, two chairs on one side, a single chair on the other. Nearby, he counted four men in leather jackets, gold chains, barked knuckles, and automatic rifles gripped across their chests.

"I don't see Agent Carter," Illya said.

"He couldn't make it," responded the supposed Agent Robert Johnson. "Shut the fuck up and sit in those two chairs." He seemed to have inexplicably morphed into a man who enjoyed being ruthless.

"Dial it down, dude," Katya scolded him. "Don't be that guy. No reason to be so crude. If you leave now, you can save yourself." She winked openly at the man from Moscow.

Illya took the girl's hand in his and sat down. He gazed around the warehouse. Pallets covered by canvas lined the walls, a giant electric winch loomed on a track above.

"Blanks," at last, Illya said, looking at Robert Johnson.

"Pardon?"

"You didn't really shoot Palo Matrabazi at Liberty Park. Those were blanks in your gun."

"You worked that out all by yourself?"

"You realize that I *am* a police investigator," he said with a tilting nod of his head. He stared at the man dubiously.

"No more talking. Dato and Palo will be here shortly."

He glared at the couple in angry irritation.

"As you wish." Illya looked over at Katya and confidentially nodded.

She smiled at him. "*The Princess Bride?* Seriously, we're doing this now? You do surprise, Illya Podipenko!"

"And when do Dato and Palo get here?" pushed the investigator.

"I said shut up," the man muttered, unamused.

"It appears you may have some developmental issues," threw in Katya. "Perhaps if you took more of a holistic approach to anger—"

"Did someone mention my name?"

The voice came from behind where Illya and Katya were sitting. They turned to see a lean man approaching in a slithering gait. He had dark slicked-back hair, tight slacks, a purple shirt, neck tattoos, and the swarthy look of a Silk Road trader.

Though it was early summer, he wore a leather jacket soiled from use, and he had gold-rimmed sunglasses perched on top of his head. Illya noticed his fingers were stained yellow from nicotine and his clothes reeked of cigarette smoke.

"I am Dato Matrabazi." He slid into the chair across the table from the couple. He folded his sunglasses, tucking them into the front of his shirt. His eyes were hard, and he regarded the pair with obvious contempt. He removed a Glock pistol from his belt and rested it on the table in front of him. For a long moment, his gaze drifted from Illya to the girl and back again. His wry smile was thin-lipped and unkind and showed narrow teeth. "I am very upset with you two," finally he said with a dull-eyed expression.

When his lips spread, a sparkle of a gold tooth blinked. He spoke English in a clipped accent. "You killed my younger brothers, Silva and the giant Carza. We Georgians have a tight family bond, and we believe in ruthless revenge. Unfortunately, you will have to pay for these senseless killings. I fear your deaths will be slow and very painful."

"Okay, now I gotta stop you right there," the girl suddenly called out. "In fairness, your two brothers raided our house. All we did was defend ourselves from them."

Dato Matrabazi placed his hands upon the table and folded them together. Each finger bore ink and a flashy ring, but he noticed the couple across from him staring at his watch. Dato gave a greasy smile. He twisted his wrist and held it up in front of him so Illya and his companion could get a better view.

"Ah, I see you have noticed my watch? This is a ten-thousand-dollar Swiss Bvlgari, a Serpenti Spiga model, a single spiral watch with an eighteen-carat rose gold bezel set with cut diamonds. Notice the black lacquered dial with golden radium numerals that glow in the dark. Twelve thousand dollars but free shipping. I also have a mansion and two yachts, a Ferrari Enzo, and a Bentley in Miami. I assure you, I wasn't able to afford these luxuries on a choirboy's wages. I have done some bad things, I admit it. But so far so good as the Americans like to say." He allowed a cruel smile.

"Your watch, classically understated," nodded Katya Tevoradze.

The girl's sarcastic comment seemed to hurt the Georgian mobster's pride. His leering smile quickly faded into lips pulled tight across his teeth. He shuffled his feet under the table and leaned forward. He kept his eyes on the couple while he lit a cigarette.

"I am going to ask you some questions," he uttered with a forced smile.

At that moment, the warehouse door flew open, and a shaft of sunlight surged in. Simultaneously, the men in the room whirled toward the doorway, cocking their guns. A man's silhouette stood motionlessly.

A voice said, "Sorry I am late, big brother."

"Ah, Palo, back from your adventures on Liberty Island! You are just in time. I am sure you recognize our guests. We were just chatting."

"Please proceed, brother."

Dato Matrabazi turned back to once again face the couple across from him. His gaze regarded his two guests with disdain. "As I was saying, I have some important questions to ask you."

"We don't know anything," spoke up Illya Podipenko, his eyes never leaving the man's.

Dato's dark eyebrows brushed upward on his forehead. "You don't even know what I am going to ask."

"Of course, we do," inserted the young girl. "You want to know about Stalin's hidden gold."

The Georgian allowed a surprised smile. "Well, now that you mention it, it is a fascinating topic, don't you agree?"

"We don't know anything," repeated Illya.

"I don't believe you." Anger flared in the man's eyes, but he took a deep breath to quell it.

"We talked about this," shot back Katya. "Look, I'm just going to say it. You and your gang of bungling morons give those of us with Georgian blood a bad name. You talk about family. You fucked up two kidnappings. Because of your incompetence, my grandfather is dead and my uncle is in a coma in the hospital. That's *my* family. You managed to silence the only two people on earth who knew the secret of Stalin's treasures. I would call that some kind of special stupid. Just sayin'."

"I should watch your tongue, young lady." Dato's face reddened. He clenched his fists on the table. "That sassy mouth of yours may get you into trouble one day."

"Not from you friggin' idiots. Proverbs 15:4 says, 'A gentle tongue is a tree of life, but perverseness in it breaks the spirit.' Besides, it's not my tongue that needs watching, it's yours. I know where my tongue's been. I can't say the same about yours."

"We don't judge," quickly chipped in Illya Podipenko, smiling pragmatically.

"I think maybe you do," snarled Dato Matrabazi. "Let's find out, shall we?" He shifted his eyes to where Agent Robert Johnson was standing and gave his head a slight nod.

The agent approached where the Moscow investigator was sitting and balled his fist. A wallop to the face sent Illya Podipenko's body somersaulting backward, his chair clattering to the floor.

The girl leaped up and began screaming at Dato Matrabazi. "I mean, what the fuck, dude! Do not touch him, you *Ublyudok*! He told you he doesn't know anything!" From behind her, one of Dato's men clasped her by the shoulders and thrust her back down into the chair.

Agent Johnson righted Illya's chair and hoisted the investigator's body, flopping him down. Blood seeped from Illya's nose and lips. At first, Illya regarded the man across from him in silence, then said, his speech labored, "To be honest, all things considered, right now I'd rather be hill climbing in the Pamirs or quail shooting in Zavidovo. But it is true, honest disagreement is often a good sign of progress."

"What?" Dato glared at him with a look of genuine puzzlement.

"Mahatma Gandhi said it. Don't blame me."

Katya chipped in, "I think we are just looking for a broader narrative here."

Across the table, Dato allowed a lupine smirk. "We can do this all day and night. It is up to you. We have plenty of time."

Illya said, "I heard a funny line. Life is full of misery, loneliness, and suffering, and it's all over much too soon. Woody Allen."

"We will friggin' kill you!" the girl added fervently, to which the Georgian once more nodded to Agent Johnson.

The man again molded a fist and drew it back menacingly but suddenly hesitated as a strange musical chime began jingling through the room.

Collectively, they glared at Illya Podipenko's feet. Dato stood, peering over the tabletop. "Apparently, your shoes are ringing," he said, evenly.

"It's my mobile phone in my sock," replied Illya. "Should I answer?"

"By all means," replied Dato Matrabazi, "but I would be very, very careful."

Illya bent, retrieving the phone. He wiped blood from his eye and squinted at the small screen. He smiled, chuckling to himself.

"Something amusing?" Dato inquired.

"Music. Listen." He put the phone on speaker and turned up the volume.

As soon as Katya heard the music, she leapt from the chair and, as if she had a microphone in her hand, began singing in a loud voice, her body parts thrashing about in a whirlwind of motion as if meaning to free themselves beneath her tight clothing.

"Oh my God!" the girl shrieked, raising both hands in the air. "Creedence. Bad Moon Rising. I *love* it! Whoo!"

"Sit, young lady." Data leveled his gaze then nodded his head toward Agent Johnson who pushed down on the girl's shoulder until she sat.

Illya hurried on, "Wait. There is also a text message. Should I read it?"

"You *must* share with the group."

Illya held a hand in the air and read slowly, *"A species of waterfowl in the family Anatidae."*

Dato shot a perplexed look toward Agent Johnson, who shrugged his shoulders, then back at the man from Moscow.

"And what does that mean exactly?" Dato inquired.

"Well, if I had to sum it up in a single word," the girl cut in, shooting a glance at Illya Podipenko next to her, "I would it say it means 'duck.'"

"What?" asked Dato.

"You know, *duck*!" With that, she gave an embarrassed little smile and shrugged her shoulders toward Dato, saying, "Dude, you are so busted."

Simultaneously, Illya and the young girl lunged forward, shouldering the table in front of them onto its side, knocking Dato Matrabazi to the floor. They dived behind the table, Illya covering the girl with his body as the room at once exploded into a deafening thunder of gunfire from heavy automatic weapons. Men were shouting, like invading Jihadists, the burst of bullets whizzing past in the air, spitting chips of concrete all around them, the groans of men's bodies smacking against the hard floor. The body of Agent Johnson flopped on its back two feet from where Illya and the girl huddled behind the table. Blood spouted from a hole in his throat which he tried to stanch with his hand. He was moaning and moved his head sideways to gaze at the Moscow investigator. His eyes were wide open in hatred and bewilderment. The man strained to raise his gun hand, but Illya Podipenko bent his knee and hammered the heel of his shoe deep into the man's temple. Agent

Johnson coughed a stream of dark fluid then heaved a final time as a last breath of air escaped his body.

It was suddenly quiet. Illya's head slowly appeared above the edge of the table. Everywhere, he saw men wearing blue nylon FBI jackets. Some men wore black full-combat uniforms. The assault team formed at two sides of the warehouse. Commandos carried automatic assault rifles with mags on their belts and spoke into headsets attached to their helmets. He noticed a half dozen repelling ropes climbing high up to smashed windows near the warehouse's ceiling. The silence was at first eerie. The air hung thick and had an acrid cordite stench to it.

Illya slowly rose, brushing off his clothing. "Like the friggin' Bolsheviks storming the Winter Palace in Peter," he said to Katya. He stopped to watch one of the FBI men approaching, a wide grin spread across his face.

Illya said, "A waterfowl in the Anatidae family?"

"I was betting you'd get it." Agent Noah Carter laughed.

"I didn't. She did." Illya pointed at the overturned table.

"I'm here," a voice said. Katya raised her arm above the edge of the table then stood slowly. She awkwardly attempted to straighten her clothing, and when her eyes met Noah Carter's, she blushed and grinned sheepishly. "That was friggin' awesome!" she shouted out.

"Nice work, Katya," Agent Carter complimented her.

"You got my phone call then?" Illya asked Noah Carter. "I dialed it from a car outside."

"Sure did. We heard what you were saying on our end, about the location of the warehouse. Plus, we locked on your phone with our GPS-tracking technology. It led us to the right spot." He gazed around the room. "It appears that we've got a bit of a mess to clean up."

"So who is this gentleman?" asked Illya, pointing to a bullet-ridden body on the floor. "Said his name was Robert Johnson. He posed as one of your FBI agents at Lady Liberty Park today."

"Him?" Noah Carter cocked his head sideways, gazing down at the body. "He is no FBI agent. He's a dirty New York City cop. He left the force a few years ago when he realized there was a great deal more money to be made working as muscle for the Matrabazi brothers." Agent Carter sighed and gave the warehouse a final sweep of his eyes.

After a few moments, he said, "Let's get you two out of here."

"Someone is missing," said Katya at once offered. "Dato Matrabazi, the head of the family."

The three began surveying the bodies scattered around the warehouse floor.

"She's right," nodded Illya Podipenko, "he's gone."

Noah Carter scratched the top of his head. "Well, crap, that's not good."

*****

Katya sat on her bed on the second floor of the Little Odessa house where she had grown up with her grandpa Sandro and uncle Grisha. She wistfully contemplated the small room. Next to her on the bed lay a suitcase packed with clothes and toiletries that she wanted to take with her to Illya's flat, where she would be staying until things blew over.

She sighed deeply. "So many memories here... so many."

"I know," Illya gently replied from the doorway. "Hopefully, you won't have to be gone too long. Once the FBI determines it is safe for you to return, we'll move you back in." Illya patiently toed the carpeting with his shoe. "You ready?" he asked.

The girl nodded. She rose and handed her suitcase to Illya. She climbed into a blue backpack and took a last glance as she turned off the light switch at the doorway. They started to move down the hallway when Katya paused in front of her grandfather's bedroom. She opened the door and flipped on the light. She spent a few moments scanning the room where her grandfather had lived for so many years before the Matrabazi brothers murdered him. She was about to turn off the light when, next to her, Illya Podipenko let the suitcase slip from his hand.

When it clattered to the floor, Katya jumped with a start. She shot a glance at him. His eyes were wide, and he stood pointing a finger into Grandpa Sandro's bedroom.

"The devil's tail!" he shouted aloud.

"Illya, what is it?" Katya asked, alarmed.

For a moment, the Russian investigator seemed to be struggling with words wadded deep in his throat, but at last, he brought them forth.

"It's the Statue of Liberty," he finally managed to rasp out.

"Oh my goodness, you are a genius, Illya!" the girl shrieked as she was dashing toward the Statue of Liberty that stood among the other Americana items that Grandpa Sandro had displayed in his memorabilia nook. She curled her fingers around the two-foot-tall statue and took it with her as she sat on the bed. Illya sat next to her.

"I can't believe I missed this," she said aloud, brushing her hands along the statue all the way up to the golden torch arched high above the crown of Lady Liberty. "But I still don't know what I am looking for."

"May I?" asked Illya Podipenko.

The girl handed the statue to the Moscow investigator and nestled close to him, her eyes brimming with adventure. As the girl had done, Illya lightly rubbed his hands over the statue, equally unsure of exactly what he was looking for. Then he turned the statue upside down. On the bottom of the statue's base, he saw a small black latch, which he moved with his fingers. The bottom of the base popped open.

"Illya, you've done it!" the girl cheered. "Look, there is something inside."

Carefully, Illya grasped at it with his fingers and removed it from inside the statue's base. It was thick and soft paper that had been folded on itself numerous times. He handed it to Katya, who carefully unfolded it and began to read aloud.

"My dearest Katya,

"What a joy it has been for your uncle Grisha and me to watch you grow and mature into a truly wonderful young lady. Out of the terrible circumstance of your parents' deaths, it seems the heavens opened and delivered to my brother and me a beautiful, wonderful, intelligent gift that would fill us with love and unmitigated joy for the rest of our lives.

"But now, my dear Katya, I must share some details of our lives that your uncle and I have kept hidden from you until now. We did so because we wanted to protect you from any dangerous situations that could befall you if you had the knowledge of what I am about to share with you. I promise you that what you are about to read is the absolute truth, and some of it may come as a shock to you. I only ask that you not judge your uncle and me too harshly.

"The first thing that you should know is that in 1953, your uncle Grisha and I were young men living in Moscow, and we took part in a conspiracy to murder the dictator, Joseph Stalin. At the time, we were part of an attachment to a Red Army officer, then Lieutenant-Major Konstantin Podipenko, whose wartime exploits were legendary. We were assigned by him to work in the kitchen at Stalin's dacha near Kuntsevo. We prepared meals for Stalin's nightly dinners with his inner circle, pigs at the trough, my brother, your uncle Grisha, used to say. Sometimes we would also serve at the boss's table. It was clear in those latter days that the boss in his senility was losing his grip on reality. He became forgetful, impulsive, and bellicose. He had heart problems and frequent fainting spells. But what was really alarming was his determination to forge a war between America and the Soviet Union, including use of nuclear bombs that had been developed under the Mingrelian Beria. Konstantin, your uncle, and I all realized that Stalin had to be stopped. And so, it was that in the early morning hours of March 1, your uncle and I sneaked into Stalin's chambers and suffocated him while he was sleeping. We partially failed in this attempt in that Stalin did not die right away, but he did suffer a severe stroke from which he would never recover. He would die five days later. With Lieutenant-Major Podipenko's help, your uncle and I then escaped to America.

"The second thing you should know is that, a few months prior to Stalin's death, again under Lieutenant-Major Konstantin Podipenko's direction, your uncle and I were sent on a top-secret, two-week mission along with Lieutenant-Major Podipenko to track down and secure various treasures that Stalin had appropriated during his lifetime. As you may recall from your history, Stalin was responsible for raising funds for

Lenin and the Bolshevik cause and subsequent civil war. Stalin turned over to Lenin most of his plunder, but not all. For whatever reason, he hid away some of the riches for himself. We were sent to four different sites where Stalin had hidden these treasures. We located the treasures, gathered them together, and returned them to Moscow. There were gold coins, numerous pallets of gold bars, paper currency, jewelry, invaluable gemstones, like diamonds, rubies, pearls, and emeralds, furs, paintings, and other assorted valuables. We hid away all the valuables in a single location at Stalin's dacha in Kuntsevo. Stalin had built a bomb shelter next to his dacha. The bomb shelter plunges ninety feet down into the earth and has walls of two-foot-thick concrete. There were ten rooms in the shelter for Stalin and his staff to work and live should the need arise. But Stalin had constructed a secret, hidden eleventh room that no one knew about. It is in this secret eleventh room that we stored all the gathered treasures. There is only one way to access this secret room. Once you enter the bomb shelter, take the elevator down then walk along the hallway between the rooms until you reach the far wall. On your left, you will find the tenth room. In that tenth room, there is a small drain in the middle of the floor. One must remove the drain cover and reach inside the drainpipe about an arm's length. There is a button that, when pushed, will cause the west wall of the room to slide open, revealing a secret room brimming full of riches like you have never seen before.

"Now for the third thing I must tell you, Katya. I am sure you remember the many discussions your uncle Grisha and I had with you about the fall of the imperial Romanov dynasty after three hundred years of family rule. In the summer of 1918, Tsar Nicholas II, his wife, Tsarina Alexandra, and their four daughters and sickly son, the heir, were cruelly and unmercifully exe-

173

cuted by a Bolshevik firing squad in the basement room of the Ipatiev house in Yekaterinburg, a city on the Eastern side of the Ural Mountains. What surprised the firing squad was how many of the bullets they shot did not seem to have an immediate deadly effect on the royal family. In fact, many of the bullets seemed to be simply ricocheting off the bodies and buzzing around the tiny room. That is when the firing squad got up close and fired point blank into the heads of the imperial family members then mutilated their bodies with bayonets. The reason for the bullets ricocheting is that the imperial family had sewn into their garments the family jewels, hundreds and hundreds and hundreds of them. When the firing squad realized this, they all began snatching up the diamonds and other gemstones from the dead bodies, which they had stripped naked. In Moscow, Stalin learned of this and sent an angry telegram to the commandant, Yakov Mikhailovich Yurovsky, warning him that the imperial jewels belonged to the state and not to the men of his firing squad. Stalin warned the commandant that he had better secure all the jewels from his men and deliver them to Stalin personally or he would be executed immediately. Yurovsky delivered the jewels, more than eighteen pounds of them were returned, most of which Stalin sent to Lenin to help the Bolshevik cause. Most but not all. Some of the imperial jewels Stalin kept for himself. These Romanov jewels became part of Stalin's personal treasure cache that we were supposed to hide in the secret room of his underground bomb shelter. But we did not add all the Romanov jewels to Stalin's hidden treasures.

"Konstantin Podipenko insisted that we take some of the imperial jewels with us to the United States and hide them away. This is what your uncle and I did. We hid the jewels in the Statue of Liberty where you found the letter that you are now reading. Just reach your hand further up inside the base of the statue and you will find a bag made of red velvet. Inside this bag are the Romanov jewels. Katya, these jewels from the imperial monarchy are priceless, and rest assured that neither your uncle nor I took a single jewel for ourselves. These jewels are now yours, sweet Katya. Do with them what you will, just please be careful to tell no one. These imperial jewels are of incalculable value. Learning of them, many evil people would like to get their hands on them and will likely go to great lengths to do so. I am sorry to have placed this burden upon you, but we did not have many other options. You are an honest, intelligent. and loving young lady, and your uncle and I have the greatest confidence in you doing the right thing. You have made us so proud, Katya. May you live ten thousand years!"

The letter was signed *"Your Forever Loving Grandpa Sandro."*

Sitting close together on Sandro's bed, an awkward silence drifted around the man and woman.

Illya thought that he noticed the letter Katya was holding flitter lightly in her hands. He heard a soft moan and saw a tear droplet spread across the paper.

He put an arm around the girl and pulled her close to him. "Sorry," he at last said. "I know this is difficult." He offered his handkerchief. She took it and used a corner to dab at her eyes. She nodded. They continued to sit wordlessly until the girl at last heaved a deep breath and tendered a taut smile to the man sitting next to her.

Finally, she said, "Let's go diamond hunting, shall we?"

Illya grinned. He took hold of the Lady Liberty statue and turned it on its crown. Cautiously, Katya reached her hand through the tight opening in the base of the statue. It was a cramped fit, but she slowly raised her arm higher within the statue, and moments later when she removed her arm, a red bag was balancing on her fingertips. She handed the bag to Illya.

Studying the bag in the palm of his hand, he looked at the girl and said, "Are you ready?"

"Oh, hell yeah," she responded gamely.

Illya slowly opened the mouth of the bag and tilted it downward. What came tumbling out of the bag onto the bed's comforter caused them to both gasp in wonder. A glinting torrent of various jewels lay sparkling on the bed, reflecting the overhead light in an unimaginable spectrum of colors—blues, reds, greens, yellows, and gold. The flash of diamonds alone was nearly blinding.

Katya put a hand to her lips. "My stars, Illya! Have ever seen such a thing?"

The man from Moscow tried to respond, but he sat transfixed, words rolling uselessly in his larynx. He merely shook his head side to side.

"Can I touch them?" she asked, breathlessly.

"Of course. They are yours, after all," Illya managed to reply.

The girl smiled and cupped her hands together in a gowpen. She swirled a mound of jewels in her hands then drew them to her nose as if to smell them.

"What beauty! They are magnificent," she uttered aloud.

"And they are priceless, a true part of Russia's Imperial history."

At once, the girl's eyes widened. As if the jewels had suddenly turned to fiery coals, she pitched them from her hands so impulsively it made Illya Podipenko flinch.

"I can't keep these!" she shouted aloud.

"Pardon?" Illya thought perhaps he had misheard her.

Katya stood and took a step backward. Color leached from her face. "There is blood on these jewels, Illya! The Romanov family was wearing these when those cowardly murderers slaughtered them in that basement room a hundred years ago. These jewels belong to the state, not me. We must return them!"

"But, Katya—"

The girl made tight fists and shoved her arms straight at her sides. "No, Illya. I do *not* want any part of these. They reek of deceit, conspiracy, and bloodthirsty murder. They are cursed. We must get rid of them!"

"I don't know, Katya—"

"Fine. Are we done here?" the girl had pivoted on her toes and started marching toward the bedroom door. "You keep them, Illya, if they dazzle you so much. I don't want anything to do with them. Ever."

With that, she departed the room without another word, snatching open the door, stepping through it, then swinging it closed behind her.

*****

"Perhaps you are right," Illya said later upon entering the downstairs room. He was carrying the red bag of jewels in one of his hands. The girl was slouched on the couch, absently thumbing through a magazine. "These are, indeed, Russian history. They belong to the state. I have reconsidered my earlier opinion."

With a smile, Katya Tevoradze closed the magazine and placed it on the table in front of her. Looking up at the man, she said, "Thank you, Illya. It is the right thing to do. We must make arrangements."

"Of course—" He was interrupted by a determined knock at the front door.

Katya said, "Who do you suppose that is?"

"That would be Noah Carter."

"What?" The girl's eyes widened.

"He texted me when I was upstairs. He said he was on the way here. He sounded as if he had something important to share with us."

Katya hurried to the door and opened it. In front of her stood the FBI agent. He seemed to be sweating and a reddish tint cast across his face.

"Agent Carter, come in," the girl said.

"Thank you," Noah rushed by. He approached where Illya was standing. He bent at the waist, catching his breath. At last, he said, "We need to get you two out of here right now."

"Pardon?" said Illya.

"Dato Matrabazi is on the warpath. His three brothers are all now dead, and he wants revenge. Both of you are in his sights. I think he wants to kill you even more than he wants the secret to the supposed Stalin's hidden treasures. We need to get you to a safe place as soon as possible. Dato has called in all of his street goons. We are going to go to all-out war with him. I fear it will very dangerous."

"We could go to my flat again," said Illya.

Agent Carter shook his head. "I don't think that is safe. He may know where you live. And even if he doesn't at the moment, he has the street pipeline to find out. I think somewhere out of the country would be best for you. At least for ten days to give us a chance to wage war on the gang. I have the highest authority and resources at my disposal to send you anywhere you want. Consider it a vacation, perhaps. I have already ordered a twenty-four watch of this apartment and an around-the-clock FBI presence at your uncle's hospital room. We will keep you informed if there are any changes. Any ideas on where you might want to go?"

Illya and the girl stood motionless. For a moment, they quietly stared at the red bag of jewels in Illya's hand. Then they turned to the FBI agent and simultaneously uttered a single word.

"Moscow."

CHAPTER 7

Moscow

"I met him once, you know?"

The girl's head was resting on Illya Podipenko's shoulder. The constant, low hum of the jet engines on the private plane arranged by FBI agent, Noah Carter, had made her drowsy.

"What did you say, Illya?"

"Stalin. I met him once." For thirty minutes, the Moscow investigator had been sitting quietly, gazing out the window at the stars in the dark night sky, the past flicking through his memory.

"That's random." The girl straightened up in her seat. "You've been thinking about Stalin?"

Illya nodded. "It was shortly before he died. It was January 1953. I was about two years old. My father took me to meet the great leader at his *dacha* in Kuntsevo. In his last years, Stalin basically ran the Soviet Empire from there, not from the Kremlin."

"So you met the devil's spawn in person?" asked the girl. "How'd that work out for you?"

Illya sighed, remembering. "Stalin sat me on his lap, feebly bouncing me on his knees. He looked old and had gotten pudgy. His face was pale and luster-less as a stone and frightfully pockmarked. By then, he wore ill-fitting dentures replacing his yellow, rot-ting teeth. But I could tell that the dentures were painful to him. His mustache had sharp bristles and smelled of acrid tobacco despite that by then he had mostly given up his chain-smoking. His eyes were a disconcerting amber color and were eerily vacant, like a man who had seen a lifetime of death and knew his was not far off. Strangely, he pointed to pictures of joyful Russian children he had torn from magazines and had stuck them to the walls of his dacha. I was terrified. I was reasonably certain that an evil creature had me in his clutches and that he was going to take a bite out of me right there. I don't mind telling you, I had soaking nightmares for years afterward."

"Good memories," Katya breathed out then added, "I heard many stories about Stalin from my grandfather Sandro and uncle Grisha. I believe I learned more about the real Stalin than some schol-ars. I had my own personal record of history." The girl went on to explain that her grandfather and uncle on a nightly basis would sit in their old chairs, sipping Georgian wine or vodka in front of their fire-place, regaling the young girl with all sorts of feral tales about Stalin, who they disliked unquestionably, as any loyal, independence-minded Georgian would.

"When I was younger, their stories unsettled me. But as I got older, I came to realize I was listening to history, *real* history from two men who experienced it firsthand. I found myself actually daydreaming of meeting the savage Stalin myself. I fantasized about walking right up to him and telling him what I thought of him, that he was Satan in a soiled tunic, baggy trousers, and Georgian boots who didn't rule a country but ruled one vast brutal prison. I would tell him that he was an unrepentant mass murderer of millions of his own people, including relatives, politicians, military officers, nearly an entire peasant class, Jews, and many others. He murdered millions more than Hitler did, and for that, he should smolder in hell for an eternity. That's what I would have told him."

Illya chuckled aloud, shaking his head. "Of that I have no doubt," he whispered, pausing. "You really are quite an amazing and fearless young lady."

"I know, right?" Katya smiled at the man next to her and leaned over, giving him a light peck on the cheek. "Anyway, I am glad you think so, Illya. It's my Georgian blood, I suppose." She once again rested her head on his shoulder. A moment later, she said, "There are so many rumors about Stalin. It's hard to tell what is truth and what is fiction."

"Such as?"

"Did you know that in his underground days, Stalin would sometimes dress as a Muslim woman in veils to escape the police?"

"Stalin in drag. Now that would have been worth seeing. What else?"

"Well, as you know, Stalin had a withered left arm that would not bend properly at the elbow. It caused him great pain in his later years. But what was the cause of this deformity? Stalin claimed that it was the result of an accident when he was a young boy and the injury was not treated properly and he developed blood poisoning. Some said it was the result of a brutal beating by his drunken father. I am not sure I believe these explanations. Sandro and Grisha believed he was born with the arm deformity, the result of a difficult birth, leaving him with a condition that was known as Erb's Palsy. What do you believe, Illya?"

"I don't know. I guess I always thought his withered left arm was the result of an accident in his youth."

"Oh, here is one I love," the girl continued on excitedly. "It concerns the relationship with his second wife, Nadya. There are so many rumors, and there is a degree of salaciousness to them, so you know it is fun."

"You can't go wrong with salaciousness," gamely acknowledged Illya Podipenko.

Katya began, "As you know, Nadya Alliluyeva was the daughter of Sergei Alliluyev and his wife, Olga. They were friends of the young Stalin and actually hid him in their home during his vagabond underground Marxist days. It was said that once, in Baku, the heroic Stalin had saved three-year-old Nadya's life when she was drowning in the Caspian Sea. When she was a young teenager, Nadya went to work for Stalin as a secretary. They were traveling on a special train to Tsaritsyn to arrange grain procurement during the civil war. One night, Stalin raped the young girl. The family learned of it and, in the Georgian fashion, insisted at gunpoint that the two marry. Which they did when Nadya was only sixteen years old and Stalin was twenty-three years older than her. It was a tempestuous relationship with jealousy and fighting. It was said that in 1932 after one nasty episode at a large party, Nadya stormed out of the party early and went home. She took a small gun that her brother had given her and shot herself dead. But the thing is, they found unexplained bruises on her body that were not consistent with just a gunshot wound. The rumor was that Stalin himself murdered her or had someone do it for him. Of course, the government told the public that Nadya died of appendicitis. They covered it up, lied to the people."

"Lying to the people and covering up the truth is what our government does best," Illya observed. "It is an art form, really. It might be mandatory as written in our constitution."

"But here is the good part, Illya," the girl excitedly forged ahead. "The rumor was that young Stalin had slept with Olga Alliluyev, the wife of his friend and underground compatriot, and, as a result of this lover's tryst, Olga later gave birth to a daughter, Nadya, who Stalin would later marry as his second wife, meaning he slept with his future mother-in-law and married his own daughter, who, later, he possibly murdered."

"And they say romance is dead," offered Illya Podipenko.

Katya laughed. "What about you, Illya? You must know a lot of insider stuff, considering that your father the marshal was Stalin's confidante all of those years. You must have some great stories."

"Strangely, no. My father almost never discussed Stalin with me. I don't know why. I suppose now that we know, courtesy of your uncle Grisha, that the marshal had actually planned the murder of Stalin and was an American spy might have something to do with it." He was quiet for a moment then said, "But there is one thing my father once told me that, in light of all of the new information about him, I find very odd. And ironic. My father told me about the time he actually saved Stalin's life."

"How ironic is it that your father, the very man who plotted Stalin's murder, also saved his life? That's dope!"

"I know. It was during the war, in 1943. My father was part of Stalin's entourage that had accompanied him to Tehran for the Big Three allied meeting with Roosevelt and Churchill. Somehow, I don't know how, my father received information from some Germans who hated Hitler that the Nazis were going to kill Stalin and the others at that conference. It was named Operation Long Jump, approved by Hitler and organized by a Nazi intelligence officer named Ernst Kaltenbrunner along with an Otto Skorzeny of the Waffen SS. When my father learned of this, he, of course, reported it to Soviet counterintelligence and the Americans in time to foil the assassination plot. So not only did he save the life of Stalin, but perhaps Roosevelt and Churchill as well."

"He was a pretty amazing fellow, your father," Katya said.

"That he was," agreed Illya. His voice then raised an octave in excitement. "Wait, I haven't told you the best rumor yet about Stalin. It's priceless."

"Tell me all, Illya," insisted Katya.

"All right. Remember how Hitler when he saw the war was lost committed suicide and his officers burned his body?"

"I do remember."

"Well, supposedly, when Soviet soldiers discovered Hitler's charred remains, they found the one, and possibly *only*, Hitler testicle. The soldiers put it on ice and shipped it back to Moscow, to Stalin. When Stalin received it, he promptly ate it!"

"Oh, yuck, Illya! That can't be true!"

"He said it tasted like chicken."

"That disgusting! You're making that up!"

His body shaking in laughter, Illya put his hands on his knees and sucked for air. It took him a minute to gain control of himself, and once he did, he said, growing serious, "I remember my father once telling me 'The Tsarist regime was repressive and uncaring about Russian citizens. Many people thought that replacing a regime that had ruled for three hundred years with a revolutionary guard would be essential. Only later did they find out that we had replaced the Romanov Tsar with even bloodier, more ruthless Bolshevik Tsars in Lenin and Stalin.'"

Illya was about to add something when the voice of the Air Force pilot came over the intercom. "We are making our descent into Sheremetyevo International Airport. On behalf of my copilot, may I say to our two VIP passengers, *Dobro pozhalovat' v moskvu*. Welcome to Moscow."

*****

As they disembarked the plane, Illya and Katya were met by two massively imposing gentlemen with square heads and creased raincoats.

"You will follow, please," one of them said.

"Your luggage will be taken care of," added the second man.

With that, the two turned on their heels and lurched ahead, Illya and the young girl sucked along in their wake. A moment later, they were whooshed through a side door and found themselves outside of the airport terminal, enveloped in the Moscow night. One of the men lifted his chin toward a sleek, black Chaika limousine with flapping flags and a forest of waving antennae sprouting from the back of the car.

"Subtle," the girl whispered to her companion.

As the couple stepped toward the car, a man emerged from the driver's seat. He also sported a trench coat and wore a gray fedora wedged low and tight against his forehead. There was something familiar about the man, Illya thought. He squinted through the darkness. His lips turned up in a genuine smile.

"Sasha, is that you?" he called out.

"The one, the only," the voice answered in a comradely cheer. He opened his arms wide. "Come, my good friend Illya, we hug!"

The Moscow investigator eagerly cantered toward the man, he, too, broadly spreading his arms. They embraced one another earnestly, and the man gave Illya a kiss on his cheek.

"I have missed you, Illya Konstantinovich!" the man whooped. "It has been two years! I didn't know if you would recognize me."

"Who could forget a face like this, eh!" Illya reached up and removed the man's hat. "Now let me take a look what the surgeons did to you." He cradled the man's cheeks in his hands and inspected the man's face, their noses nearly touching. Illya slightly turned the man's head to catch the light from the airport terminal.

"Uh-huh." He nodded his head in approval. "I see. Excellent, Sasha! The surgeons did a marvelous job. You can hardly tell," he said encouragingly. Both men knew Illya's evaluation veered sideways from the truth, for the man's nose was spread like a trounced fig flatly across his face, one cheekbone seemed higher than the other, and numerous reddish scars stretched in a triangle from the middle of his face to a point on his forehead close to his hairline.

"Handsome as ever!" announced Illya Podipenko.

"Thanks to you, Illya! You wouldn't believe the women I get now! They all want to feel sorry for me, mother me, take care of me. I don't mind telling you, my love life has skyrocketed like Soyez Seven." He winked joyously.

"Glad to be of service." Illya chuckled then felt a tugging at his coat sleeve. It was the girl.

"I don't mean to break up this love fest, but—"

"Goodness me, sorry, sorry," Illya bleated embarrassingly. "I am being very impolite. He reached out an arm and gently moved Katya next to him. "Sasha Petrov, meet Katya Tevoradze, an American college student of mine. Katya, this is an old friend, Sasha Petrov. Two years ago, we worked together on the Rasputin case."

Sasha extended his hand for Katya to receive. The girl looked up into the man's face, and for an instant, her breath involuntarily caught in her throat.

The Russian noticed and smiled. "Your friend, Illya, walloped me in the face with a woman's iron," he boomed as if proud. "Smacked me with a household appliance! Laid me out like a carp. Nearly killed me! Now when I sneeze, my nostrils whistle the Russian national anthem." At this, both he and Illya roundly bent double, bellowing uproariously at the memory, tears squirting sideways from their eyes. Breathlessly, Sasha Petrov continued, "Once I went to the medical clinic for a checkup. I told the humorless attendant that I had an appointment, and she said 'Which doctor?' and I said, 'No, a normal doctor would do.' She punched me so hard in the nose, I needed additional

surgery!" The two men cried so loudly distant people with luggage started to edge away. The two men
grasped each other's shoulders so as not to collapse in
a mewling heap on the airport bitumen.

Next to them, the girl stood arms staunchly
folded across her chest.

"Fond memories," Katya forlornly shook her
head. "And I would love to hear the entire story
sometime. But for now, could we please hop into the
limo? I'd like to see a bit of Moscow before winter
sets in."

*****

"My stars, Illya! It is so beautiful! So many
shapes and sizes and colors! It's like a fairytale land!"

"I'll admit it," Illya responded, standing next to
the girl on the outdoor balcony of their suite in the
luxurious Hotel National on Manezhnaya Square.
Illya's Russian friend, Sasha Petrov, had made the
arrangements for the couple to stay in one of the
hotel's finest suites. "It is one of the most magnificent
sights anywhere in the world."

They stood sipping wine from gold-rimmed
glasses gazing down at the expanse of Red Square
with the Lenin Mausoleum and the colorful, striped
onion-shaped domes of St. Basil's Cathedral in the
distance. Just west of Red Square stood the crenel-
ated battlement walls of the Kremlin, thick, red brick
walls dating to the fifteenth century with spired

towers topped by ruby stars that reached to the dark heavens above.

"Mao Tse-tung once visited Moscow," Illya recalled. "Do you know what he said?"

"Educate me," responded the girl.

"Mao said, 'The only thing to do in Moscow is eat, sleep, and shit.'"

"A true romantic," evaluated Katya Tevoradze. "And obviously a dear, dear communist brother-in-arms to the Russian peoples."

Illya smiled. "At any rate, we will get a closer look tomorrow. We'll take a stroll after breakfast, and I can show you things. We won't be meeting my FSB friend, Sasha Petrov, until eleven in the morning in front of the State Historical Museum."

"What's that all about, anyway?" Katya asked.

"Pardon?"

"You and Sasha Petrov at the airport. Apparently, you once squished his face and now that dude is one of your best friends? And he is an FSB agent to boot?"

Illya looked at the girl and chuckled. "It is complicated," he said at last.

"So uncomplicate it," Katya spoke softly, gently folding a hand around the man's elbow. "Tell me everything."

Illya heaved his chest and expelled a long breath. "Well, it surrounds the Rasputin case and the Imperial Romanov eggs—"

"What with you *doesn't* involve that case?"

Illya laughed and gazed off into the distance. "Anyway, I was working the Rasputin case, and, much like you and I did at the Statue of Liberty, I noticed a man following me everywhere. Always in the shadows. Always lurking. I mistakenly thought he was there to interfere with my investigation or, worse, do me harm, just waiting for the opportunity. Across the hallway from where one of the Rasputin descendants was murdered lived a woman named Gadina Federovna. She had been ironing clothes at the time, and I told her I needed to borrow her iron. I tucked it up under my jacket and went outside. I walked a few blocks and noticed that the man was, like a specter, still following me. So I quickly ducked behind a corner building. When he approached, I jumped out and clocked him in the face with the iron. He went down in a heap. Unconscious. Blood spurting everywhere. Only later did I find out that Sasha Petrov was a federal security agent on President Putin's staff. He had been following me not to do me harm but to protect me in case some sort of danger threatened my investigation."

"You disfigured his face and now you are best friends?" Katya asked.

"When I learned who he really was, I felt shameful, of course. Guilt haunted me. I visited Sasha every day in the hospital, brought him small gifts. He eventually forgave me. In fact, he insisted on putting the guilt entirely on himself. He said he had been derelict in the execution of his assigned duties and that he deserved what he had gotten."

Katya said, "Goodness, that's quite a story."

"It's all true." Illya looked at the girl and smiled. "Thank the stars it all worked out for him. Afterward, Putin actually promoted Sasha and gave him such a jump in pay that Sasha could afford to move from his languid flat out near the old Khodynka airfield to where he now lives in a plush flat above a designer dress shop on the *Arbat*, a flat you and I together could not afford."

The girl was quiet a moment, then said, "And you trust Sasha Petrov?"

"With my life, Katya. And now yours." He kissed her on the forehead. She smiled and returned the kiss on his cheek. "It's been a long day. Let's go to bed."

The Moscow investigator regarded her thoughtfully. He asked, "What are the chances that tonight you will be sleeping alone in the second bedroom of this magnificent suite?"

Katya's blue-green eyes peered up at the Moscow investigator. "Slim and none, and Slim just left town."

"I don't understand. Did Alice say that?"

"Alice? Don't be silly, Illya. It was Muhammad Ali. When he was asked about the chances of Joe Frazier beating him in an upcoming boxing match."

"I still don't understand."

"Short version, I am *not* sleeping all alone in that second bedroom tonight. The bed in your room is plenty big enough for the two of us."

"Oh."

*****

195

"Did you know Lenin stayed here in the Hotel National in 1917 during the October Revolution?" Illya cheerily offered as they were finishing up a breakfast of buttery scones and cube-sugared tea in the hotel's beautifully ornate restaurant.

They were seated up against a huge window looking out onto Red Square and the Kremlin. The morning sky sheened a pale blue. The girl noticed that the man's eyes were maddeningly clear, and he looked refreshed and relaxed and ready to attack the day. "Room 107. Lenin stayed here for a week with his companion, Nadezda Krupskaya."

"I'll bet Lenin didn't make *her* sleep all of the way on the other side of the bed."

"Don't be so sure," responded Illya. "Did you ever see photos of Krupskaya?"

"Ha, ha," sulked Katya. She slumped with both elbows on the table, her hands shading her squinting eyes from the sunlight.

"Stalin totally disrespected Krupskaya," Illya continued on. "He once threatened her that if she didn't quit misbehaving, another wife would be assigned to Lenin."

"Soo interesting," moaned the girl. "Have you noticed that mornings come way too early in the day?" she croaked cheerlessly. "They should push them back a few hours. Each morning, I bargain with the devil for just fifteen more minutes under the warm duvet, followed by an all-you-can-eat buffet somewhere."

Illya chuckled. "Come, my gloomy little friend, let's take a stroll."

"You may have to carry me," she mumbled, "like any true hero would."

They entered Red Square through the Resurrection Gate, past GUM Department Store on their left and on their right Lenin's gray-blocked mausoleum and the spired towers of the Kremlin wall. The day was warm with a thinning sunlight and cooling wind that signaled autumn wasn't too far in the distance.

"This is the famous Red Square," Illya proudly pointed out to the girl. "It was from here, on November 7, 1941, at a huge military parade, that the Red Army soldiers marched directly to the front lines, and most likely to their deaths, during the Great War."

"Please, Illya," the girl whined, resting her head on the man's shoulder, "it is too early for history lessons." They wandered south, their shadows slashing along the cobbles, past the magnificent cluster of spired domes of St. Basil's Cathedral. The girl reached for Illya's hand. "It really is impressive, isn't it?" More awake now, she said to the Moscow policeman. "So many colors all swirled about. It reminds me of flames swirling toward the sky."

"Its real name is Cathedral of the Intercession of the Most Holy Theotokos on the Moat. It was commissioned by Ivan the Terrible in the mid-fifteen hundreds. It is quite remarkable that it is still standing today, considering the Bolsheviks and communists, once they took over the country, did away with religion. It is mostly a museum today, but in modern-day Russia, Orthodox Christian services have been restored. There is a famous photograph of Reagan and Gorbachev standing together in front of St. Basil's almost thirty years ago."

"I've seen that photograph. My grandfather cut it out of *Life* magazine. He was very proud of that moment."

"Strangely, it was actually Stalin, of all people, who saved St. Basil's from destruction. His Bolshevik urban planners wanted to destroy it and replace it with something else, but Stalin said no. They also wanted to destroy the Russian Bolshoi Theater and the Russian Ballet too. Lenin and Trotsky considered ballet and opera as unnecessary extravagances to Bolshevism. They wanted them demolished, but Stalin refused to destroy them."

"What a guy!" recited the girl brightly.

"Legend has it that when Ivan the Terrible first laid eyes on the finished St. Basil's Cathedral, he was so taken aback by its beauty that he had the architect blinded so that he might never create something so beautiful again."

"I guess that's why they never called him Ivan the Subtle."

They continued walking hand in hand through Red Square toward the Moscow river, where they paused to lean against a railing, watching the eight lanes of cars, trucks, and blue electric buses commuting across the concrete Bolshoy Moskvoretsky

Bridge. After a while, Illya Podipenko raised an arm, pointing a finger across the river.

"I used to live there," he said to the girl.

"Where?"

"There. Across the river."

Katya shaded her squinting eyes with a hand. "Next to that enormous concrete building?"

Illya laughed. "No, *in* that enormous building. That is where I grew up, where I spent my childhood."

"Quaint. A monolithic slab that takes up an entire city block."

"You should have seen it in the nineteen thirties when it opened. Basically, it was just a big concrete structure on a hill. But inside, the apartments were very nice. Spacious rooms, high ceilings, central heating, lots of light. There were five hundred apartments, all reserved for Moscow's elite, party commissars, old Bolsheviks, Marxist scholars and government bureaucrats, Red Army officers, opera singers, ballerinas, film producers, writers, doctors, you name it. Stalin's daughter, Svetlana, once lived there, the Khrushchevs too. It's called the House on the Embankment. There was a sports hall, tennis courts, kindergarten, library, a theater, launderette, and a kitchen from which meals could be ordered. It was a city within a city, a self-contained world off limits to outsiders. Stalin arranged one of the flats for my father."

"So avowed Marxists suspiciously living like Tsars? Who knew?"

"Hypocrisy at its finest. Welcome to the history of Mother Russia."

"You lived there with your father and mother?" asked the girl.

"Stalin awarded the flat to my father in 1946 after the war. Fifth floor, block 12. I was born in '51. My mother died when I was two years old. Her name was Sonya. She was a tall, blond beauty. She met my father in Stalingrad. Like my father, she was a famous Soviet sniper, a talented assassin, maybe the Red Army's best-ever female sniper. She had nearly as many Hero of the Soviet Union awards as my father. Sadly, I was so young when she died of cancer that I have very few memories of her. I remember her mostly from photographs. I was essentially raised by a nanny."

The girl recoiled. "What? You never told me that."

Illya nodded. "My father was rarely home. He had all of his duties as an aide-de-camp to Stalin and then Khrushchev. Sometimes, he would visit me on weekends."

"That seems sad," said Katya.

"I suppose so," Illya nodded. "But when he did visit, it was wonderful. We would play games. I remember, my father would take me to matches at the football stadium. We always had the best seats, in the government's box." Illya chuckled and continued, "When I was older, we would go hunting and fishing together. But the highlight of all of the marshal's visits home was something he called *zagadka*."

"Enigma?" the girl frowned.

"That is correct. Enigma is what my father called *our* game. My father would give me clues to unravel, trivia to answer, and riddles to solve. Word games. Math games. Scavenger hunts in which I would have to find items he had hidden throughout our home. He always challenged me mentally, and he was genuinely proud when I won, which I did often. He called me *volshebnyv chelovek*, the magic man." Illya paused in a deep sigh. "It was a great time."

The young girl put her arm through Illya's. "I think those games were why you became such a good investigator. You use your mind, you see things other don't, you solve crimes like you solved your father's puzzles."

"Could be." Illya smiled. "I still remember the first trivia question he ever asked me. 'Who was the only man to shake hands with Lenin, Stalin, Hitler, Himmler, Goering, Roosevelt, and Churchill?'"

"No idea," responded Katya.

"It was Molotov. His real name, of course, was Vyacheslav Scriabin. Stalin called him 'Molotstein' because he had married a Jewess. He also called him Stone Arse."

"Stalin gave him pet names. That's so cute!" Then she frowned and said, "You said you had a nanny. What was her name?"

"Inessa, I called her Inna. She was very young and very pretty. She was wonderful to me, like a real mother. And she was utterly in love with my father.

They tried to hide it, but I knew that they slept together when my father visited."

Katya was quiet for a bit. She stood at the railing tossing twigs into the river. A breeze blew a strand of hair across her forehead, and she brushed it back. Finally, she asked, "Is she still alive?"

"Inna? Indeed, she is. Quite elderly now, of course. After I left for my service in the Red Army, my father built a *dacha* for Inna and him near the historic Arkhangelskoye Estate. He and Inna lived there together out in the countryside until the marshal's death a couple of years ago. Actually, Inna still lives there alone. We shall visit her tomorrow."

Illya paused to thrust his hands into his pockets. He once again set his gaze on the massive building across the river. At last, he said, "You know, that building at one time was a house of horrors, in the 1930s, before I was born. It was sinisterly nicknamed the House of Preliminary Detention."

"That's a thing?" asked the girl.

"During Stalin's Great Purge in the 1930s, when he was murdering just about everybody from his past, he would have his secret police goons raid the building at night to cart off people he deemed no longer essential to life. The murder squad would pull up to the building in cars known as Black Ravens because of their silhouette of a bird of prey. Residents waited in agonizing, sleepless terror for the sound of an elevator opening, boot steps in the hallway, a rap on their door. Many of those unlucky enough to be singled out for that night's raid would be loaded into the Black Ravens and driven directly to a special execution yard on *Varsonofyevsky Lane*. There was a room with a sloping floor, which made it convenient for hosing down the remnants of those who had been breathing Russian citizens just minutes before. Their remains were dumped in Common Grave Number One at the Donskoi Cemetery. Later, a monument was erected that said, 'Here lie buried the remains of the innocent, tortured, and executed victims of political repressions.'"

"Sweet story," offered Katya with a disheartened thumbs-up sign. She hunched her shoulders, and Illya thought he noticed a shiver course through the girl's body.

Illya shrugged. "It is part of our Stalinist history. It was a time of unrelenting terror. Some people living in that building when they heard the elevator opening and boot steps pounding along the hallway were so scared they would have heart attacks and die right in their flat. Others would commit suicide by leaping out of their windows. In the morning, residents first thing would check neighbors' apartment doorways for sealing wax. If the doorway was sealed it meant that those who had been living in the flat just the day before would no longer be coming home. I once heard that during Stalin's purges, a single flat in that building could change occupants five or six times. There was even a rumor that there was a passageway under the river directly from the Kremlin to the backstairs of the House on the Embankment so that suddenly a murderous henchman could magically materialize in a resident's kitchen or bedroom."

"I think I just threw up in my mouth," Katya uttered, drawing her jacket around her as if a cold wind had just swept in. "You are trying to give me nightmares. I am *not* sleeping on the other side of the bed tonight. Like it or not, we are cuddling!"

The Moscow investigator smiled at her. "Now you know why Count Sergius Witt once said, 'All Russia is one vast madhouse.'" He saw that the girl fluttered once again. He put a consoling arm across her shoulder. "I can see that I have upset you, Katya, which, I admit, I didn't think was even possible. Come, we will cheer you up. There is someone I want you to meet."

The girl quickly swung away from the building across the river. Into the collar of her light jacket, she said, "Lead the way, Mr. Magic Man."

CHAPTER 8

They casually retraced their steps through the cobbled span of Red Square until they arrived at the entrance of the imperial State Historical Museum, a magnificent twin-towered structure of dark red-baked bricks covered in ornate turrets, medieval-style pinnacles, and decorative saw-tooth cornices looming on the west side of the square. Illya and his young friend, Katya, stepped inside, finding themselves in an entrance room of rich frescos, moldings, and carvings summoning Old World Russia. Vibrant morning light poured in through large windows in the air wells.

"Russian history lives here," Illya said to the girl, for some reason using a whispered, reverent tone, "from the very beginning. Forty-eight rooms, forty-four thousand exhibits. Hundreds of thousands of additional historic treasures in the museum's catacombs below where we now stand."

"That's awesome," Katya said, her excited eyes taking in the lavish architecture.

Illya nodded to their left, toward a kiosk that said "Information." They approached the kiosk where they found a woman plump as a guinea hen with a vanishing chin and wearing large red rhinestone glasses and dyed hair that seemed piled like a construction cone on top of her head. Sitting like imperious royalty, she was perched stiff and cold on a teetering stool, the cushion of which seemed to disappear up into some gaping area Illya did not wish to contemplate.

"Pardon," Illya leaned in close, "could you be so kind as to direct me to the curator, Viktor Ivanovich Marchenko?"

The woman churlishly ignored him. She was too busy foraging through an enormous purse teetering on her ample thighs.

Illya tried again. "Could you direct us to Viktor Marchenko?"

"*Nyet*," the woman barked. She seemed to have found what she was looking for.

"Sorry?"

"The curator is unavailable." She began pomading her round lips with a vigorously florid gouge of lipstick. She gazed at her reflection in a small mirror, smacking her lips together like a primping sturgeon, evaluating her craftsmanship. From her purse, she extracted a nail file and went to work on nails that looked like fishing lures painted neon.

"Could you at least check—"

"I said he is unavailable. Are you deaf, senile, or half-witted?"

"Sorry?"

The girl next to Illya Podipenko could take no more of the woman's contemptuous manner. She stepped past the Moscow investigator. "I got this," she said to her companion and leaned nearly cheek to cheek with the woman. "Look, Marge Simpson," she growled. "My grandfather and uncle helped murder Joseph Stalin. So I have that killer DNA in my blood. See what I'm saying? And this man, who you have ignored and offended, is not just some Vasya Pupkin out there walking the streets of Moscow. He happens to be a genuine hero of the state, Moscow militia investigator, Illya Konstantinovich Podipenko."

With the mention of the investigator's name, the nail file the woman was holding snapped in her hands like a sprig. Her head swiveled toward the man, her eyes through the thick lenses of her glasses suddenly appeared round as hen's eggs.

"*The* investigator Illya Podipenko?" she coughed out all breathy.

"You may have heard of him," Katya helpfully added. "He solved the famous Rasputin murder case and recovered the Imperial Fabergé eggs a few years ago. Ring a bell?"

The woman's ample breasts were visibly heaving beneath the pink blouse she was wearing. "Silly girl, *everyone* has heard of Investigator Podipenko!" She allowed a sigh as if she were a smitten teenager. "And here he is, so handsome too!" She ogled into the reddening face of the investigator, who awkwardly stood shifting his weight from foot to foot. He nodded his head hesitantly. After a few moments, the woman revisited present-day earth. "Oh, my stars, look at me, sitting here like a fool! You wanted our curator Viktor Marchenko? Let me get him for you, my dear, dear Investigator Podipenko."

As she was raising the telephone receiver to her ear, Illya shrugged and said, "Never you mind, dear lady. I know where his office is. We would like to surprise him."

"Surprise him, yes, of course. How fun!" She put pudgy fingers to her lips and made a turning motion as if locking a door with a key. "It will be our little secret, yours and mine," she panted, battering her eyelashes as if they were butterflies taking flight. Then she turned her gaze to the girl. At once, her lips dropped, her nose lifted smugly, and she took to examining her painted nails.

Illya and Katya swung around, clattering along the museum's hallway.

"You gotta love her," whispered the girl. "From the herding group?"

"Stay away when the moon is full and the wolf-bane blooms."

"I'm thinking that bitch eats her young."

"Marge Simpson? The yellow cartoon character with the stacked-up hair?" Illya uncertainly said to his companion. "And you have a killer's DNA in your blood?"

"Too much?" smiled Katya. "Sometimes, you gotta give them a little shot, a whack, let them know that you are there. She was a *suchka krashena*," added the girl, calling her a dyed-hair bitch. "My grandfather used to cite an old Russian proverb, 'You can't cut down trees without woodchips flying.' Know what I mean?"

Illya thought about this a moment then smiled. "A wise man, your grandfather," he acknowledged to his companion as they strolled through a massive room toward another wide hallway, "but you mustn't be too hard on her, Katya. She is, after all, a Russian." They passed dozens of exhibit rooms on both sides of the hallway, each a thematic showcase displaying the glorious culture and history of the Russian State from its ancient tribal beginnings. One exhibit housed ancient arms, rare samples of fabrics, clothing, and military uniforms. Another exhibit featured a collection of fine arts with paintings by celebrated Russian masters, and there was a massive room housing an exhibit of war battlements from the time of Ivan the Terrible. Just before the room exhibiting "Relics of the Russian State," there was a small set of stairs leading downward. Illya and Katya took the steps, entering a small dimly lit hallway. They came to a door on the left that said, "Viktor Marchenko, Curator."

The door was partially open. Peering inside, Illya saw his friend Viktor's lanky frame balanced on a wooden stool. His tall, angular body was draped in a white frock and bent over a table where he seemed to be diligently examining something. He wore a strap around his head attached to magnified glasses which made him appear to be a demented scientist swooshing beakers. He was shockingly thin, with a body of a dedicated vegan who had denied himself a lifetime of edible food.

"You go in first," Illya whispered to the girl. "I will hide behind the door, then I'll step into the room, surprising him."

Katya smiled and started to take a first step when Illya put a cautionary hand on her shoulder.

"Fair warning, my dear, Viktor can seem to be, well, at times…a bit high-strung, I suppose."

With that, the girl banged her knuckles loudly on the doorframe while simultaneously shouting out his name powerful as a ship's foghorn, "Viktor Marchenko."

This elicited a shriek so filled with terror and surprise that it could have come from an ass-pinched dowager. Whatever the man was working on shot airborne, and he reached upward with long, out-stretched fingers to pluck it out of the air, clutching it to his body. He swiveled around on the stool, his face red and seethed in anger.

"The devil's ass!" he screamed at the girl. "Do you know what you almost made me do? This antiquity is invaluable! It could have shattered into a thousand pieces!"

"*Mne zhal,*" answered Katya Tevoradze in Russian.

"Sorry? You are *sorry*, young lady?" The man hefted violently from the stool. He was tall and thin and lacked muscle definition in the chest and shoulders as if physical activity never really had been a lifestyle option. The top of his head seemed to stretch to the ceiling of the small office. He had a long hawk's nose and tufted black eyebrows that jounced on his bulging Lenin-like forehead when he talked. His eyes through the magnifying glasses looked as big as Russian turnips, and he was so undernourished that Katya feared if he turned sideways, he could well disappear into an alternate dimension. The man thrust out an arm that seemed remarkably to propel itself halfway across the room. His elongated fingers encircled what appeared to be a round black vase with a random design comprised of spidery golden cracks.

"Do you know what this is, child!" He affected the air of a boyar from the Tsarist days, and his bony hand shook the vase at the tip of Katya's nose. "No? Well, let me tell you. It's called *Kintsugi*, the ancient Japanese art of fixing broken pottery. This very piece dates back to the sixteenth century. We open a special *Kintsugi* exhibit in three weeks' time!"

Katya shrugged. "Come on, man. Looks like an old, broken vase to me," she uttered. "I believe when I was younger, I accidentally broke a similar vase in my grandfather's study. He just swept up the pieces and tossed them into the rubbish bin. No biggie."

Hearing this, the curator allowed an audible gasp, his face hued purple as a plum. His thin body tumbled backward, collapsing onto his stool. With his free hand, he slapped at his forehead. Slowly, he removed the magnifying glasses from his head and tossed them onto the desk. For a moment, he said nothing, merely gazing forlornly at the wooden floor at his feet. When he finally did speak, it was as if he were talking to himself.

"I blame our education system," he allowed with a resigned sigh. He seemed truly saddened by the current Russian youth. "No one cares today, no one wants to learn. Kids play video games, too busy ghosting strangers on the Internet. It is very sad." He was silent a moment longer then lifted his black eyes to the girl across the room. When he at last spoke, his tone was muted and patient, like that of a tutor addressing a slow child. "You see, young lady" he began, "the *Kintsugi* is a technique that Japanese artisans use to repair broken pottery rather than, as you so elegantly put it, toss it in the rubbish bin. The Japanese painstakingly rejoin the ceramic pieces with a camouflaged adhesive, using a special tree sap lacquer dusted with powdered gold, silver, or platinum. Once completed, beautiful seams of gold proudly glint in the conspicuous cracks of the ceramic piece, giving it a one-of-a-kind appearance. The more cracks, the more gold seams, the more valuable. This artistic practice celebrates each artifact's unique history by emphasizing its fractures and breaks instead of hiding or disguising them. In fact, *Kintsugi* often makes the repaired piece even more beautiful than the original, revitalizing it with a new look and giving it a second life. The practice is related to the Japanese philosophy of *wabi-sabi*, which calls for seeing beauty in the flawed or imperfect. The Japanese are very proud of the art." He lifted sad eyes toward the girl. "Do you understand what I am telling you, young lady?"

"A thousand percent," Kayta replied. "Sometimes, people are like that, aren't they? Flawed and imperfect yet beautiful. Broken then put back together again stronger and lovelier than ever before."

The curator knotted his brow then slowly shifted his gaze toward the girl, his eyes filled with sudden wonderment. "That is very profound, Miss—what did you say your name was?"

"I never said."

"What is it then?"

"Katya Tevoradze."

Viktor Marchenko drew his chin upward, his eyes contemplatingly roaming the ceiling of his office. "Tevoradze, Tevoradze," he quietly uttered under his breath, a long finger drumming at his lower lip. "Your roots are Georgian?" he quizzed.

"Yep, a *Cherkess*, like Stalin."

The mere mention of the *Vozhd's* name caused the curator to pucker his anus, inadvertently stiffening in his chair. His forehead became suddenly wet. His head swiveled about the room as if expecting dead apparitions to materialize from the surrounding walls. He looked back at the girl, and suddenly, a pitch of anger tipped his words. "Why are you *here*, Katya Tevoradze? What do you want from me?"

It seems I've brought you a piece of *Kintsugi*."

"Pardon?"

"In human form. A lifetime of cracks and dings and lines, but now better than ever. A new friend of mine. An old friend of yours."

"See here, young lady, I have neither the time nor patience for childish pranks—"

In that instant, the squat body of Illya Podipenko appeared from behind the doorway in a flourished ta-dah gesture. He strode into the room next to the girl, his arms widespread, a broad smile curved across his face.

"It is me, my friend Viktor Marchenko. I have returned to Moscow. I have come for a visit!"

The words had barely passed his lips when suddenly a squeak pierced the room as if someone had foot-stomped a dozing cat. In a single, unthinking motion, Viktor Marchenko absently flung the priceless Kintsugi into the air, which Katya fortuitously dived forward to catch in her hands. His legs like stilts seemed to traverse the room in two bounding steps.

"Illya Konstantinovich," bellowed the curator as he unfurled his arms around the visitor, crushing him to his chest! "Can it be real?" Towering over a stiff-standing Illya Podipenko, Viktor began sobbing dramatically while sowing kisses on Illya's bald pate. He went to one knee, resting his head against Illya's jacket.

"My old friend," he began wailing, "how long has it been? Two years, surely! I have missed you!"

"I have missed you, too, my friend," Illya replied uncomfortably. His forehead wrinkled, and his eyes widened as he peered across at Katya Tevoradze, shrugging his shoulders as if to say, *"Well, this is Victor. Please understand, he is an emotional sort of fellow."* He dabbed at the curator's bony shoulder with an empathetic hand.

"Come, my friend, let's chat, eh?"

In a start, Viktor surged to his feet, heading back toward his desk. Along the way, he unceremoniously snatched the *Kintsugi* vase Katya was holding as if he were poaching a soccer ball from a street urchin. He carefully placed the antiquity on his desk, astonishingly produced a white handkerchief from his coat pocket, and began vigorously dusting the vase as if the girl's fingers may have deposited communicable smudges on his prized relic. The task completed, he peered across to where the Moscow investigator was standing and, with two fingers tapped at his throat, silently inquiring in the Russian way, *a tot perhaps?*

"I have a bottle that I have kept in the bottom drawer for special occasions. It is an experimental vodka called *Atomik Vodka*, made out of water from the Chernobyl aquifer with wheat grown from a farm within the exclusion zone. They say it is safe, but they also admit they may have many more years of testing remaining before they can be absolutely certain. Anyway, if you feel adventurous…"

Illya smiled and shook his head no. "Appealing as it sounds, it is a bit early for me, my friend. In any case, I must be sober as a judge for the next few hours. We have a meeting with President Putin."

"Putin?" Marchenko's body tautened. "What Putin? *The* Putin? *Our* Putin?" He breathed out a rush of air, visibly distraught.

"Yes, Viktor, *our* Putin. Katya and I have a meeting with President Putin in," Illya glanced at his watch, "in thirty minutes."

The curator once again pulled out his handkerchief and dabbed at his forehead. "Nothing... *adverse*... I pray?"

"No, no, my friend. Just a cordial meeting. Which reminds me, Viktor, I wondered if I could ask you a few questions prior to our meeting with the president."

"You have questions?" Viktor inquired cautiously.

"Yes, about Stalin."

"*What*!" The curator's body became taut as wire, and he gracelessly tottered backward away from Illya as if his visitor had inadvertently uttered an incantation certain to summon the devil himself. He landed on the corner of his desk, his eyes wildly flickering toward the corner shadows of his small office. His chest visibly quaked, and his words whooshed from his throat in silent blasts of air. "I know nothing of the *Vozhd*, Illya Konstantinovich. Nothing, you understand? He is in the past, best forgotten!"

"Dude, sorry to interrupt," the girl unexpectantly offered up, "but this *is* a history museum, is it not? It is *all* about the past. You *celebrate* it."

"Silly girl," Viktor hissed dismissively, throwing a grave squint in her direction. "Not that kind of history."

Katya pursed her lips. "Oh, I was way off. I wrongly assumed that history was history. Even if it is somewhat unpleasant."

"Now see here, young lady—"

"Please, please," interjected Illya Podipenko, "we are all friends here. Let us be civil, shall we?" He faced the curator and spoke gently. "Now, Viktor, I just wanted to inquire about one thing. Our history tells us that young Stalin was the money raiser for Lenin and the Bolshevik cause. In this capacity, he personally controlled and dispersed to the cause millions of dollars in rubles, gold, diamonds, and other treasures. I was wondering if you have ever heard or run across information that perhaps Stalin may have kept some of the bounty for himself, perhaps stored away in some secret location. I am just curious."

The curator blew out a breath and seemed to relax. "Well, as you know, the *Vozhd* had little care for money for himself. That was the Bolshevik way. That said, there are always rumors, of course. Particularly with the overthrow of the Tsar and the looting of Germany after the war. There was a lot of gold, jewelry, and other riches up for grabs. But I have never run across any information to substantiate claims that Stalin personally benefited from all of this." He paused, folding his heavy eyebrows. With a squinted eye, he stared across at Illya and said, "Why do you ask me such a question, Illya Konstantinovich? What are you working on, eh?"

The Moscow investigator scratched the top of his head. "Well, my friend, at the moment, I am not exactly certain. I believe it is possible that Stalin hid away some reserves for a rainy day as they say. I am looking into it. If I find anything, I will let you know."

"Always the hero." Warmly smiled Viktor Marchenko, then suddenly, his body went rigid and he leaped from the chair as if he were late for a train. He slapped at the side of the white smock he was wearing. "You have never seen it, have you, Illya! Pardon me for being so rude! You must come with me!"

With that, the curator clutched the *Kintsugi* vase to his breast, grabbed Illya by the hand, and began bounding toward the doorway of his office. He was hurdling steps three at a time with a tripping Illya in tow and Katya jogging behind to keep up. He was so achingly thin, Katya thought, that when he moved his body seemed to shape-shift like a hologram image.

At the top of the stairs, they jagged a sharp left and entered a massive exhibit room known as "Relics of the Russian State." The vast room had a rich interior decor of frescos, moldings, carvings, and other decorations, creating the unique atmosphere of the past. The room contained dozens and dozens of exhibits from Russia's long history, including a fantastic array of portraits of the Romanov Tsars, various thrones of Russian monarchs, yellowed manuscripts, and many authentic uniforms from various Russian eras. The centerpiece of the room was a lengthy, half-moon-shaped glass case inset with soft halogen spotlights.

In long strides, Viktor Marchenko approached the glass case. Once there, he attentively placed the *Kintsugi* vase he was carrying on top of an exhibit case then wheeled about, facing the Moscow investigator. He posed one hand against his hip while with the other hand he dramatically unfurled his long fingers in a circular gesture as if he were a proud impresario introducing his latest ingenue.

"Tell me what you think, Illya Konstantinovich. Be brutally honest!"

Illya, along with the girl, approached the large exhibit and peered through the glass at an astonishing sight. The five Fabergé Imperial eggs that were originally designed as a Christmas surprise for the Romanov Tsar's children were displayed in a long velvet-lined, tiered presentation with elaborate, inset lights, which highlighted the intricate gold work and countless gemstones that decorated each egg.

"My word, Illya," shouted Katya, "these eggs are magnificent! I've never seen anything like them. And it was you, Mister Magic Man, who uncovered these!"

Illya gave a modest nod. "Each egg is different," he said, "each one is specifically designed and named for one of the Tsar and Tsarina's children. The four eggs on the lower row were to be gifts for their four daughters, the Romanov Grand Duchesses, Olga, Marie, Tatiana, and the rascal Anastasia. The eggs are called by the girls' nicknames, Olya, Mashka, Tanechka, and Nasten'ka. Each has a special surprise inside the egg. Look at the Nasten'ka egg for Anastasia. The egg looks like a large rosebush, with green leaves carved in jade and the rose petals made of different shades of pink diamonds. But to see the surprise inside of the egg, push this button here."

Illya pointed to a lit red button on the exhibit, and Katya pressed it. Before their eyes, Anastasia's Fabergé egg glided open, revealing a smaller rosebush surrounded by three of the royal family's favorite dogs carved in various hardstones. Momentarily, Jimmy, Anastasia's favorite spaniel, began chasing her younger brother's spaniel, Joy, and her mother's Scottish terrier, Eira, in a mad circle around the rosebush.

Katya's mouth fell open, and she clapped her hands to her cheeks. "That is so cool," she breathed out. "How creative!"

"Now look at this one," Illya pointed a finger above the row of four eggs. Standing alone, majestically above the others, was a Fabergé creation double the size of its mates. The opalescent white enamel finish was nearly blinding.

"That one is called the *Naslednik* egg, designed for the heir of all Russia, the boy, Tsarevich Alexei." Spread over the heir's Imperial egg's enamel was a fine guilloche ground interlaced with chase gold. Set in the enamel surface were nineteen round miniature portraits by the famous artist Zuiev, each portrait of a Romanov Tsar, from the founder of the dynasty Michael Romanov, through Peter the Great, Catherine the Great, Stalin's favorite Ivan the Terrible and all of the others up to the heir's father, Tsar Nicholas II. The entire egg was supported on wings of a royal double-headed eagle, the imperial emblem of Tsarist Russia. The eagle, including a sword and scepter clutched in its claws, was entirely sculpted in gold.

"Go ahead, Katya," nudged the Moscow investigator, "see what happens when you push that button."

The girl complied. The heir's egg slowly opened, revealing inside a replica of the grand imperial Alexander Palace in Tsarskoe Selo near St. Petersburg. The palace was constructed of gold, diamonds, and platinum. In the courtyard of the palace stood a garrison of hand-painted, stone-carved Don Cossacks in light blue uniforms and tall hats. They were soldiers who would one day be under the command of the supposed heir to the throne, had the Bolsheviks not murdered the entire royal family in a Yekaterinburg cellar in 1918."

"Say what you will about royal excess," breathed out Katya Tevoradze, "the Tsar knew how to give a surprise gift!"

"That is the Imperial egg that eventually was passed down to Lena Sharapova," Illya said. He halfway thought of not even mentioning that fact, knowing that the very utterance of Lena Sharapova's name could engender a dramatic response from the young girl, disrupting the museum's subdued milieu. Surprisingly, her response was more moderate than anticipated.

"Ah, *your* Lena Sharapova, I see."

"Look," Illya said pointing to the next glass case, "there is a photograph of her."

The girl bent for a closer look. The oversized photo was of Vladimir Putin demurely smiling as he was shaking the hand of the Rasputin descendent on the occasion of the grand opening of the Fabergé Egg exhibition.

"My goodness, Illya!" Katya suddenly called out loud enough for sheepherders to overhear out on the steppes. "She is absolutely gorgeous! She may be the most beautiful woman I've ever seen! No wonder you fell head-over-heels in love with her!"

"Well, I…" Illya could feel his jowls flushing from his collar upward. He shot a sheepish glance to Viktor Marchenko standing off to his side. Illya offered a shrug of his shoulders as the curator's bushy eyebrows climbed upward on his forehead.

"She exaggerates," Illya offered with a russet face and feeble smile, to which the curator formed a suspicious expression that said, *You are a terrible liar, Illya Konstantinovich.*

The girl continued along the exhibition then stopped suddenly. She threw her hands to her mouth and let out a shriek louder than the first. "Illya, look at this! It is *you*!"

"Where?" inquired the Moscow investigator. He stood stationary, and the girl retreated her steps, plucking Illya Podipenko by the arm, thrusting him forward. She pulled up, pointing a finger upward. "Next to that statue?"

"Silly, Illya. No, the statue itself. It's *you*, Illya, see!"

Illya's mouth dropped. He found himself gawking at a five-foot-tall bronze statue of himself. He was posed with his hands clasped behind his back, his raincoat flapping in the wind. He had a fedora tucked down on his brow. Quickly, Illya threw a quizzical look toward Viktor Marchenko, who was standing, rocking on his heels, his lips curved upward in an observant smile.

"We do hope you are pleased, Illya Konstantinovich," he said cautiously. "It was meant to be a surprise."

"Well, you succeeded in that, Viktor, I must say."

"So handsome!" the girl cried out. To the curator's concern, she quickly boosted up on her tiptoes and gave Illya's statue a small kiss on the cheek. "And there is a plaque too! Oh, look, Illya, they have your birth year 1951, but the year of your death has been left blank. Isn't that *fun!*"

"Very charitable and optimistic as well," answered the investigator.

"Read the plaque, Illya, oh you *must*," pronounced the girl to which Illya Podipenko shuffled his feet across the floor and edged his hands into the pockets of his trousers.

"I don't know—"

"Always so modest," Katya scolded the man. "Very well then, I shall read it. *Illya Konstantinovich Podipenko, Hero of the Russian Federation. One of Moscow's greatest militia investigators. Through diligent police work and persistent determination, he uncovered the existence, and the safe return, of five Imperial Fabergé Eggs commissioned by Tsar Alexander II to be surprise gifts for the five Romanov children. Illya Konstantinovich is the son of one of the Soviet Union's most decorated war heroes, Marshal Konstantin Podipenko.*

"Stars above, Illya. You really *are* a true hero!"

"I am not so certain about that," Illya shyly began. "I am just an imperfect, common jar of clay, like everyone else."

The museum curator quickly jumped in. "The statue was due to the benignity of our esteemed leader, President Vladimir Putin himself," Marchenko proudly reported. "The president personally suggested that we commission this statue of you."

"Putin suggested this?" asked Illya.

"He did."

"Has he seen it?"

"He has."

"I must thank him."

"You must." Then the curator quickly added, "And you must tell him how pleased you are with how it turned out."

"I will, for you, my friend."

"*Ya navsegda u tebya v dolgu*," Marchenko slightly bowed his head, "I am forever in your debt, Illya Konstantinovich."

Illya extended his hand. "Thank you, Viktor."

Illya and Katya turned to leave. As they did so, the girl swung a glance over her shoulder where the skeletal figure of Viktor Marchenko was standing, clenching the *Kintsugi* to his chest with one hand, waving a white handkerchief in farewell with the other. Tears reflected on his cheekbones.

"What the fuck is *wrong* with that guy!" she muttered to her companion, and before he could answer, Katya had turned and trotted back toward the museum's curator.

Illya looked on as she raised on her toes and began whispering something into Viktor Marchenko's ear, to which the curator's eyes soon seemed to bulge alarmingly from their sockets, and he stumbled backward as if he were going to flop to the ground.

"See what I'm saying, Big Guy?" she asked at the end then patted him on the chest and added, "Peace out."

A moment later, as Illya and Katya were leaving the building, the Moscow investigator leaned in and asked, "What did you say to Viktor to upset him so?"

Katya grinned. "I simply said, 'Dude, I greatly admire the *Kintsugi* vase that you are cuddling so tightly to your body it looks like you are going to rape it rather than just protect it. But why are you so afraid that it will fall to the floor and break into pieces? Didn't you tell us the very reason the vase was so valuable was that it was previously broken and put back together with strips of gold? So—and I could be wrong here—if you should, say, accidentally, drop that beautiful vase and it shattered into dozens of pieces, you could call in some Japanese dudes to reassemble it with even more cracks in it, using even more gold strips to repair it, thus it will become even more valuable than it is now. It is sheer economics, Viktor Marchenko! Go big or go home. See what I am saying?'"

Illya Podipenko could do no more than shake his head side to side, attempting to stifle his laughter until they had left the building. But as they were pushing open the door to leave, they suddenly stopped, stared quizzically at one another, and turned to peer over their shoulders. They could swear that they had heard in the far distance of the museum something that sounded very much like a piece of crockery splintering across a marble floor.

Katya smiled and leaned over to Illya and proudly uttered, "Boom! Nailed it!"

CHAPTER 9

Punctual as usual, FSB Agent Sasha Petrov met Illya and Katya in front of the Historical Museum and was now leading them inside the Kremlin through the former Senate building's side door into a carpeted elevator that rocketed them to the third floor. They walked silently down a fine, wide hallway of leather padded doors, pausing at the last one on the left, where they were met with a crisp salute from a soldier so young looking that Illya thought he should still be suckling at his mother's breast.

Sasha pushed some buttons on a keypad with blinking-colored lights, and the door soundless swung open. Illya noticed that his friend, illogically, still proudly wore a pin on his lapel of the sword and shield of the old KGB, now renamed FSB. Sasha ushered the visitors into a room that had reddish plush carpeting, tall windows with thick drapes, neatly stacked bookshelves, and a long, polished table that gleamed like a freshly waxed Mercedes. In one corner of the room stood the flag of the Russian Federation. Sasha waved them to two capeskin chairs on the nearside of the table.

Like a thrilled schoolgirl, Katya thumped down in the chair and leaned over to whisper to her companion, "Isn't this exciting, Illya! I feel as exhilarated as a cheerleader on homecoming night about to be ass-fucked by the offensive line."

The Moscow investigator closed his eyes and covered his ears with his hands. He shot a glance toward Sasha Petrov, who, having overheard what the girl said, seemed to suddenly have an involuntary gurgle emanating from his throat. His face beneath his hat had turned a crimson hue, and he slowly backed away from where the couple sat, alighting at last in a wooden chair near the doorway.

"Be on your best behavior, Katya," Illya urged the girl, "this is serious business."

"Totally, I'm all in, Illya. I'll use my indoor voice."

Illya was about to add something when his eye caught a shadow. He looked up and suddenly found himself staring into the face of Vladimir Vladimirovich Putin, President of Mother Russia. The man seemed to have appeared wraithlike out of thin air. He was standing behind the large table. He looked tan and fit and wore a shiny suit and a grin on his face that seemed genuine.

"My friend, Illya Konstantinovich," he said quietly, rounding the table and striding across the thick carpet, his smile brimming with good fellowship. His idiosyncratic walk was the familiar "gunslingers' gait" he was known for, with his right arm unmoving, held tight against his body, while his torso swayed along.

He thoughtfully extended his hand. "How good it is to see you again. What has it been, two years? You look good, healthy, happy. Tell me, you have found America to your liking?"

For an instant, the Moscow investigator considered his reply, sensing a trap question while President Putin lowered himself into his chair and poured mineral water from a bottle of *Borjomi* into four etched glasses on the table. Before Illya could give his answer, Putin looked past the Moscow investigator to where Sasha Petrov was sitting near the doorway. "Please, Sasha, no need to sit way back there. Bring your chair to the table and join us. You are part of this team, after all." Sasha smiled and dutifully carried his wooden chair to the table, sitting next to the young girl.

"And America?" Putin returned his gaze to Illya Podipenko. He locked his eyes on him and possessed the self-assured look of a man used to being in charge. A quiet fortitude wrapped around him like a cloak. He pushed a white bowl with apples, oranges, and bananas to the center of the table.

"Not so different from here," Illya responded in a reserved voice, smiling. "Sometimes crazy. Guns are part of everyday life, it seems. The state of Texas alone has so many armed deer hunters that it is one of the largest standing armies in the world. The most common phrase heard on the nightly news is *gunshots rang out*. And they seemed obsessed with breakfast cereals, dozens and dozens of different kinds filling the supermarket shelves as far as the eye can see, most of the cereals are made with heaps of sugar and other questionable additives, like glyphosate, an active ingredient in weed killer."

Momentarily, he went quiet then added, "I find it fascinating that in America, it is possible to get into your car and travel right across the country on an impressive interstate highway system from coast to coast without really seeing anything. You have to respect a country like that. But I must admit, I miss Moscow. What is it that they say? *'V gostyakh khorosho, a doma luchshe.'* Visiting is good, but home is better."

"Very good, Illya Konstantinovich, very good." President Putin seemed pleased. He tilted his head upward and smiled at Illya. "And you saw your statue at the Historical Museum? I hope you were pleased."

Illya took this not so much as a question but as a statement. The president had obviously already learned about Illya and Katya's visit to the museum and its curator, Viktor Marchenko. "Very pleased, thank you, Mr. President. But it was not necessary."

The president nodded but did not reply.

"He is very modest," chipped in the girl to which Putin offered a thin smile and replied, "All the great heroes are, it seems," he said quietly. He kept his eyes locked on the girl and said, "Please, introduce me to your young companion, Illya Konstantinovich."

Illya slapped his knee and said, "Forgive me, Mr. President, I was being rude. This is Katya Tevoradze. She lives in New York."

"Ah, New York," replied Putin pleasantly enough. He was silent a moment, but his eyes never left the young girl. "Tevoradze…your heritage is…Georgian?"

"And proud of it, Mr. President," responded Katya then added, "Sorry, perhaps I should not have spoken like that, I mean considering the current climate of relations between the Russian Federation and Georgia."

Putin waved a dismissive hand in the air. "Do not worry yourself, young lady. That's politics. Let the politicians do what they do. We won't let it interfere with our friendship."

The girl nodded then suddenly blurted out, "May I have an apple, sir?"

"Pardon?" the president raised an eyebrow, bent an ear.

"An apple," the girl responded, and as she did so, her hand had already ensnared a big, shiny one of which she took a bite so resolutely that the sound made all three men flinch in their seats. "I'm famished," she blurted out, hiding the white chunks at the sides of her mouth with her free hand.

Putin turned his gaze onto Illya Podipenko. Worriedly, he said, "Do you not feed this young lady, Illya Konstantinovich?"

Illya gulped and hurriedly replied, "We had breakfast at the National Hotel just a few hours ago, Mr. President. But she didn't feel up to eating much because she said mornings come too early and they should push mornings back a couple of hours, you know, for the betterment of all mankind."

Katya rushed to add, "You will find, Mr. President, that I am a deeply superficial person, as Andy Warhol once said."

"I see," responded Putin hesitantly, then after a brief while, he shrugged his shoulders and reached for the fruit bowl in front of him. He selected a banana and slowly began peeling it in his hands. He leaned back in the chair. "Tell me, Illya, your message said you had something of extreme importance you wanted to share with me. I am very interested in what you have to say. So if you will, please begin."

The Moscow investigator leaned forward in his chair. He could feel beads of sweat forming above his brow. He made sounds as if he were having difficulty clearing his throat. "It is very convoluted, Mr. President. It's hard to know where to begin." He appeared somewhat flummoxed and fell to an awkward silence as words coagulated in his throat. Seeing his discomfort, the girl jumped in.

"It is a complex cautionary tale, Mr. President," she began while chewing on the apple. "One that involves kidnapping, murder, secret hidden treasures, Stalin, Russian history, and," she paused to look directly at Illya, "a young girl's unrequited desire to make passionate love to an older man."

As these last words left her lips, the fleshy part of Putin's banana, like a rocket, audibly whistled straight up in the air, leaving the yellow peel uselessly abandoned and wilted in the president's hand. Ever vigilant, Sasha Petrov, his eyeballs distressingly bulging from their sockets, heroically snatched the missile out of midair before it could nosedive on the president's shiny tabletop. Awkwardly, Sasha handed the fruit to Putin, who accepted it expressionlessly then gamely deposited it back into the fruit bowl.

"Well played," Katya whispered to Sasha Petrov then offered gaily to the group, "Bananas, particularly ripe bananas, raise dopamine levels naturally, which is a pleasant thing for your brain. Also, they help you secrete mucus, which protects the intestinal walls from gastric acid, in case you were wondering. It is an old wives' tale that you shouldn't eat bananas and eggs together because of their different digestion rates. It is true that bananas have a higher glycemic index, which means they can be digested quicker than eggs, but, in practice, if you eat bananas and eggs together, they will both be totally digested together. So you needn't worry about the faux science. Oh, and there is a lot of water in a banana, percentage-wise, about the same amount of water as in a human baby. I mean, should someone ask."

The room went so silent that Illya could hear his armpits sweat.

"Is that so?" at last, replied President Putin. His face shaded slightly, his lips leaked a semblance of a smile, and he turned his eyes back to Illya Podipenko. "Back on topic," he stated, "it all sounds darkly intriguing, to say the least. Please, Illya Konstantinovich, take your time to gather your thoughts and continue your story."

Illya cleared his throat as next to him the girl interrupted. "Perhaps we should begin here," she hurriedly offered. From her jacket pocket, she retrieved a small red felt bag. She turned it in her hands then spilled perhaps two dozen jewels, including gleaming diamonds and emeralds, on Putin's table. They clattered together on the tabletop, catching light as they tumbled onward like shards of solid fire.

"Goodness," Putin exclaimed aloud. The fiery gems reflected brightly in the irises of his eyes. He turned his gaze to the young girl sitting next to Illya. "And what do we have here?" he inquired.

"Jewels," answered the girl, "but not just *any* jewels. These are Imperial jewels, the very ones once belonging to the Romanov family. The royal family had sewn these very jewels into the undergarments that they were wearing the night that Bolshevik firing squad massacred them in the basement in Yekaterinburg. At first, the shooters were confused. They kept pumping bullets into the bodies of the Tsar and his family, but the bullets seemed to be bouncing off of the bodies. That is because of these jewels. At any rate, when the Romanov family finally did succumb, the guards discovered the jewels hidden away in their clothing and, of course, procured them. Stalin learned of this and placed a call to the officer in charge. He told the officer that the jewels belong to the state, and the officer would do good in ensuring that the jewels were sent to Stalin for safekeeping."

Across the table, President Putin rolled a handful of gems in his fingers. His lips formed a modest smile. "Quite amazing," he breathed out. "And how exactly did you come to possess these priceless gems?" he asked the girl.

Katya glanced at Illya then back at Putin. "Well, Mr. President, that is a long and complicated story, perhaps best saved for another time. Anyway, these jewels are only part of the story. There is a lot more. Incredible treasures, priceless, all unknown in their existence, all belonging to the state."

The president formed a spire with his fingertip and rested his chin on them. "I would very much like to hear about these hitherto unknown priceless treasures of the state," he offered with interest.

For a moment, an awkward silence cramped the room, so Illya suddenly jumped in, saying, "We know from our history," began the Moscow investigator, "that Stalin procured financing for Lenin to fund the Revolution and the Civil War. He was very good at it. However, the funding came mostly from questionable pursuits. But it appears that Stalin may have kept some of the spoils for himself, for whatever reason. He hid away cash, gold, diamonds, and other treasures in a secret location. We believe we know where this secret location is."

"Would you care to share this information?" Putin inquired with an odd, thin, little smile that left little room for negotiation on the point. He rested his chin in his hands.

"We believe that this bounty is stored in a secret room in the bomb shelter that Stalin had constructed on his Kuntsevo *dacha* property during the war."

"Kuntsevo?" Putin sat back in his chair. "Are you certain, Illya Konstantinovich?"

"We are certain," jumped in Katya, "my grandfather left me a letter explaining it all."

"A letter," Putin nodded. "And who is your grandfather again?"

"His name is, or *was*, Sandro Tevoradze. Unfortunately, he recently died. He and his brother, Grisha, worked in Stalin's kitchen after the war then left Mother Russia to live in New York City. They carried Stalin's secret with them."

"And you are just now learning of this secret of Stalin's hidden treasures?"

"We are indeed," interjected Illya Podipenko. "We thought that you should be among the first to know. After all, the treasure belongs to the state."

Putin gathered himself, saying, "I appreciate the courtesy, of course. We had heard rumors about Stalin's hidden treasures, but we never put much credence in the claim."

Putin shifted his weight in the chair. He took a moment to study the visitors in front of him. After a while, he said, "It certainly is an intriguing notion, isn't it? That Stalin may have tucked away valuables that now belong to the state. I assume you plan on visiting the Kuntsevo *dacha* to check out the hidden room in the bomb shelter for yourselves?"

"Yes, sir," responded Illya, "if that is all right with you."

"Of course, with one condition," Putin hesitated.

"And what is the one condition, Mr. President?"

Putin smiled, "That I accompany you on this adventure. I should very much like to be with you, to see this hidden room for myself, and, of course, see Stalin's supposed hidden treasures."

"Of course, Mr. President," Illya answered with a smile. "It would be our honor if you should accompany us."

The grin on Putin's face was wide and genuine. "I could be of some help to you," he stated. "Kuntsevo is still guarded by our federal security services. I can smooth the way with them, so to speak."

"Splendid, Mr. President," offered Illya, raising his hands in front of him. "That would be very helpful."

"It is settled then." Putin pushed his chair back from the table and smiled at them. Then he gaily slapped the tabletop with his hand and quickly rose to his feet. He seemed pleased. "We shall take my car," he decreed bountifully. "Sasha will drive us."

*****

The spacious black Chaika, equipped with a reinforced steel frame and bulletproof windows, had been on the Minskoye highway for nearly thirty minutes when it turned left and entered a forest not far from Victory Park. Sasha Petrov sat alone in the front seat, piloting the smooth car while his three passengers chatted away in the rear seat. A sheet of thick plexiglass separated the driver from the passengers, blocking out the conversation from the back. But for the moment, the initial conversation had ceased. President Putin was silently reading something that Katya Tevoradze had handed him. Although Sasha Petrov did not know it, what Katya had handed the president was the letter that her grandfather had written to her, a letter that stunned Putin into silence. The letter revealed shattering events to Russian history: that Sandro and Grisha Tevoradze, under the direction of Stalin and his aide Marshal Konstantin Podipenko had gathered together all of the leader's treasures from four different secret sites and had stored them in a single, hidden room in the air-raid shelter at Stalin's near *dacha* in the Kuntsevo District; further, that Sandro and Grisha, weeks later, had attacked Stalin in his sleep, causing the dictator to suffer a fatal stroke; that Stalin quite likely also had been poisoned by Beria and Khrushchev; and that Sandro and Grisha had fled to the United States and that the hero Marshal Podipenko was, at least for a brief time, actually a spy for the Americans but only to keep his beloved Soviet Union out of a war with the United States.

At present, Sasha Petrov aimed Putin's car toward the hidden entrance of what was Joseph Stalin's personal residence near the former town of <u>Kuntsevo</u>, part of Moscow's Fili district. Much of the forest they had been traveling through was created by Stalin, having ordered thirty-year-old trees transplanted here from Moscow and Smolensk. Sasha was aware that their destination was where Stalin lived for the last two decades of his life. It was also here, at the so-called near *dacha*, where Stalin lived during the Great Patriotic War, and it was here that he played host to such august guests as Winston Churchill and Mao Zedong. And where Stalin died an agonizing death on March 5, 1953.

The thought illogically made Sasha's heart clang faster, and he gently pressed down on the accelerator. A quick glimpse in the rearview mirror showed him that his three passengers were locked once again in meaningful conversation in the back seat. Out of the gloom of overhanging trees, Sasha commanded the black car to a stop at a guard's station in front of a double-perimeter fence. Two uniformed guards snapped to attention, approaching the black car. Sasha smiled to himself. He had called ahead to alert the guards of Putin's impending arrival. He did not want the young men of the state security services to be caught unawares, perhaps lounging around listlessly drinking vodka and throwing cards into a hat. As the guards approached, Sasha lowered the car window and offered them a wink. The guard immediately snapped out a hand signal, and the motorized fence gate in front of them slithered open.

The Chaika swept through the gate and continued onward beneath tall birch trees that provided an impenetrable ceiling for the property. Moments later, Stalin's *dacha* edged into view, and Sasha wheeled into a parking area in front of the gothic building, which was simple in its two-story design. It was painted an unimaginative green color.

"So here we are, the near *dacha*," offered Illya, hefting himself out of the car.

Putin nodded. "Quite spartan as you can see. Stalin lived life as he preached, like a Bolshevik, simple tastes."

Illya took the young girl by the hand and helped her out of the car. She stood by the open door and inhaled the crisp air around her. Thick tree cover held out afternoon light, and a breeze luffed through the top of the trees.

"Roses," she said simply, "from Stalin's gardens. Wonderful."

"And look, there," Illya nodded toward the *dacha*, "on the left. That is the veranda where Stalin would work, summer or winter, strategizing about the Great War or making his death lists." The girl saw that Illya was standing stiff and unmoving while gazing at the building. She noticed a drip of sweat had formed at his temple, and she reached up a thumb to pat it away. "Ghosts?" she asked him quietly.

Illya nodded. "Once fear infests your shoes, you always walk differently," replied the Moscow investigator. "That time when I was two years old and my father brought me here…" His chest heaved. "I remember that enormous dining room with its rose carpeting, long table, and photographs of Lenin and Marx on the wall. I remember his small office, too, where he had cut out magazine photographs of Russian children and had taped these to the walls. It was frightening."

"Imagine, Illya," responded Katya Tevoradze, "your father and my grandfather and uncle worked for Stalin right here in that building."

"My grandfather too," added a voice. In unison, Illya and Katya turned to face the Russian president. "Yes, it is true," smiled Putin, "my grandfather was a chef, and he prepared many meals for Stalin at the dinners he hosted right here at the near *dacha*."

"Then surely your grandfather must have known our relatives," said the Moscow investigator. "My father, the marshal, for a time was in charge of the kitchen staff, and Katya's grandfather and uncle were part of that staff."

"I am aware of this, and I agree with you. They must have known each other." Putin turned, following Sasha Petrov who was guiding the group past apple and lemon groves and a small pond to a partially hidden gated concrete entrance built right into the side of a hill. The guards had already unlocked the steel gate.

They entered the door at ground level and walked down a flight of stairs to an elevator, which they boarded. The elevator would drop them eleven stories underground. During the short ride, no one spoke a word, but Illya noticed that he was nearly dancing on the balls of his feet, shifting his weight from foot to foot in excited anticipation of uncovering Stalin's hidden treasures. He also saw that he was not the only one in the elevator doing this. If you looked close enough, Illya observed, you could pick out the various telltale tics and body fidgets indicating that each person in the elevator was wired in nervous anticipation over what riches they may find in a hidden room in an air-raid bunker that Stalin had built for his personal use. Presently, the elevator door whooshed open and decanted the riders onto a long corridor with steel coating on the walls and rooms on either side. The ceiling, which hid a thick layer of reinforced concrete above it, had recessed lighting that shined brightly. Quietly, the group followed behind Illya Podipenko, who led them past hermetic doors of meeting rooms and offices and a large dining room cut into a concrete wall that was nine feet thick. At the end of the corridor, Illya paused in front of the last door on the left. He shot a quick look over his shoulder to where the Russian Federation president was following behind. The president nodded almost imperceptibly, and Illya pushed open the door. The room seemed smaller than the others. Against the far wall were a desk and two simple chairs. The rest of the room was empty.

Illya's eyes wandered over the room's ceiling and walls. At last, he noticed a rectangular Persian carpet on the floor. He bent over, sweeping the carpet aside to reveal a small drain in the concrete floor. He removed the drain's cover and reached in an arm. After a moment, he felt the button he was searching for and pushed it. A side wall began gradually sliding open, causing the floor to rumble beneath their feet. As the wall slid open, four heads eagerly peered around the corner to see what treasures had been uncovered. One by one, their facial expressions assumed a similar look—eyes wide and round, mouths gaping black holes, jaws dipped to their chests. They gawked at each other, stunned.

The room was empty as the Siberian steppe, blanched white as a bone.

Only one person was able to catch his breath sufficiently enough to speak. It was the president of the Russian Federation, and he surprised everyone when he uttered "What the fuck" into his shirt collar.

*****

The return trip to Moscow was noticeably less convivial than the trip on the way to the Kuntsevo *dacha*. For the first twenty minutes, no one muttered a word as if they all were suffering from some sort of collective shock about what they had seen, or more accurately, what they had *not* seen in the bomb shelter. They certainly had not expected to be greeted by an empty room.

After all, Sandro Tevoradze's letter to his granddaughter, Katya, had been unequivocal. There was a hidden room in the bomb shelter where Sandro and his brother, Grisha, had stored treasures stockpiled by Stalin. The two boys had gathered the treasures from four different locations around the country and placed the treasures in the underground room themselves! All under the supervision of Stalin's aide, Konstantin Podipenko. *And now the Stalin treasures had vanished?*

As the black Chaika passed through the Spassky Gate beneath the clock tower and slowed to a stop at an entrance to the former Senate building, President Vladimir Putin, as he exited the car, took Illya Podipenko by the arm. With an unblinking gaze, he pulled the investigator close and whispered into his ear. "I know that you will sort out this cock-up," he said to Illya, his lips slanting into a tight smile. He gazed at him through lidded eyes. From inside his jacket, he pulled a pack of cigarettes, *Sobranie Black Russians*, from the Ukraine. He lit a cigarette and paused a beat before saying, "You will find all that treasure you told me about. I have the utmost confidence that you will not disappoint me, Illya Konstantinovich." He let his words sink in.

Then he gave the investigator's arm a conspicuously hard squeeze as he headed off to his office, leaving behind him Illya Podipenko with his cheeks puffed out in exasperation.

CHAPTER 10

"What just happened?" asked Katya Tevoradze.

She was bracing herself in the passenger's seat as Illya's blue Moskvich clanked and hammered and bucked past the final Ring Road on Volokolamskoe Shosse toward the historic Arkhangelskoe Estate in the Krasnogorsky District, Moscow Oblast.

At the edge of the city, they bounced and flounced along in Illya's old car, which he preferred to call "vintage." The roadway was dotted with volcanic potholes scheduled for rehabilitation nine years ago. Outside the car, the day and city were fading, the sun skimming through distant trees. Eastward behind them, the city was dissolving in shadows, the city lights of Moscow receding, giving way to countryside. Gray clouds scuttled on the horizon as the Moscow investigator's automobile belched a purple line of smoke from beneath the hood. When Illya's car banged into an unexpected cavity in the rutted dirt road, the car's front bumper that had been attached with a twisted coat hanger smacked the ground so hard that it became unattached and went bounding off somewhere toward Volgograd.

"I am not entirely certain," Illya answered her question in a raised voice so he could be heard over the car's rattling like a crate of dishes. If his car had been one of Beria's neighbors, Illya thoughtfully pondered, it would have already been summarily liquidated. He was uneasily embarrassed about the transportation, which was little more than a combustion engine on wheels. Although he now was financially secure enough to purchase a new car, perhaps a Lada XRAY Coupe or a Nissan Sentra, he had trouble mustering any aspiration or ambition to do so. His jangling Moskvich had for years served him well and fit him like familiar old clothes. Still, he was thankful that his car didn't seem to perturb the girl too much.

"I pray my car does not offend your senses, Katya," Illya shouted to be heard. "I love this car. It's always an exercise in improvisation."

"I can see that," answered the girl. "It's homey. Where is the radio?" she asked, pointing to a black maw in the dashboard where a radio would normally reside but now a hole was leaking all sorts of exposed wires and cables.

"If I had to guess, I'd say hooligans ripped it out while the car was parked on my street in front of my flat when I was overseas, in America. Probably sold it at the Izmailovsky flea market one weekend. Appears they stole the side mirrors too. I will replace them in time."

"And windshield wipers?"

"Bastards ripped off those too. I will replace them as soon as I have glass put in the windscreen itself. As of now, with no glass in the windscreen, there is little use for the wipers."

"I hear you," Katya nodded. "What do you do if it rains?"

"Mostly squint," he replied.

"Makes sense. Just one more question."

"Of course."

"Is that an arm in the back seat?"

"An *arm*?" Illya took a darting peek over his shoulder. "You mean that thing wrapped up in plastic with all of the flies buzzing around it lying next to the empty bottle of Hammer and Sickle vodka?"

"That's the one."

"You know, I believe you may be right. I mean it certainly *looks* like an arm, doesn't it? I don't remember it being there before."

"Perhaps from an old case you were working on? You can order file cabinets today over the Internet."

"Could be an old case… I suppose. Or perhaps it is all that remains from some wayward hitchhiker."

"Apparently anything's possible in jolly old Moscow," Katya sat back and breathed in contentedly. "You know, after a while, the urine stench really isn't so bad."

Illya smiled, leaning over to give Katya's knee a comforting pat. "That's my trooper," he smiled. Then he straightened in his seat and said more seriously, "It is pretty obvious that someone removed Stalin's treasures from the secret room in Stalin's bomb shelter after your grandfather and uncle had stored them there."

"Yes," Katya shouted out, "but who? And why?"

"Only one person comes to mind," responded Illya.

"Your father, the marshal," Katya replied, and Illya nodded affirmatively.

"That's my thought. The marshal was in charge. He knew what was going on. He arranged for the treasures to be moved after your grandfather and uncle left for America. They never knew. That's why they thought all of the treasure was still in the hidden room in the bomb shelter. They didn't know any difference."

"And yet the question remains, why? What was the reason for moving all of the treasure?"

"Maybe it was Stalin's decision. This was a time right before he died when he was not in the best mental state. He was suffering from paranoia. His thinking was cloudy at best."

Illya threaded his car into a forest of pine trees and tall alders until finally he reached an entrance-way to the wooden *dacha* his father had built in a bend high above the Moscow River in the distance. The Moskvich coughed to a stop near a pond of wild rushes and dark, tea-colored water.

"Oh, my, Illya, it's *lovely*," the woman cried out. She was pointing excitedly at the rustic, two-story log house in front of them. The cabin was rimmed with a stand of slender, white birch trees that the marshal had planted around the house in the Russian way of protecting the inhabitants from evil powers. A dense forest of tall larch and spruce trees provided the dacha's backdrop, and the simple cabin with window boxes of purple bougainvillea sat on a small hill rise above the pond, whose waters played with the sunlight and appeared speckless and clean.

"This is where you lived with your father?"

"For a short while, yes, after the military. My father had this cabin built, his weekend *dacha* getaway. I loved it here. I have many memories of loud parties and card games, Cuban cigars, dancing to American music, my father the life of the party, hosting Red Army officers and American diplomats. There were cases and cases of expensive liquor, champagne, and Beluga Noble vodka and Golden Sterlet caviar and even more expensive, friendly, bawdy, painted women of suspicious morality. There would be early morning hunting and fishing parties and nude swimming in the pond. It was the best of times."

"Sounds like," said Katya.

The couple hefted themselves out of Illya's car and approached the pond in front of them. An arched bridge spanned the water, where tall cattails stood stiff and straight around the perimeter of the pond. On the opposite side of the pond was a well-weathered oak wooden dock that had seen better days. A skiff of doubtful seaworthiness was tethered to a wooden pylon. There was a ramshackle boathouse with a rusting wench hanging on an outdoor hook. Behind the boathouse, there were neat vegetable patches with potatoes and beans and thick larch trees that climbed side by side up a steep grade of long grass until they disappeared into a forest.

"What is that?" the girl inquired, squinting her eyes to a white crescent-shaped structure at the opposite end of the pond.

"That's a small mausoleum," answered Illya, "a memorial to my father and mother. Their ashes are interred in the building, resting next to each other for eternity."

"How romantic! But I thought your father's ashes were buried in the Kremlin Wall as befits a Red Army marshal and a Soviet hero."

"Well, let's just say that the actual ashes interred in the Kremlin Wall are those of my father's favorite dog, Dimitri, a Russian wolfhound. My father had arranged this with Inna and me just before his death. He did not want to be interred in the Kremlin Wall. He loved this place. So Inna and I made the switch. Dimitri had died a few years earlier and we kept his ashes on a mantle. No one knows this, just you."

"Your secret is safe with me." The girl smiled.

"Good," Illya seemed satisfied, "so we don't have to kill you."

Katya laugh sounded of youth and innocence. She put her hand in Illya's. "I'd like to see the mausoleum up close, if I can. Is that possible?"

"Of course," responded the Moscow investigator. "There is a path through the woods on this side of the pond. Come, follow me."

Illya led the girl by the hand as they surged along a gravel path that ran along the edge of the pond. Thick vegetation grew on all sides, giving the feeling that they could be isolated from the rest of the world.

The shadowed pathway was lined with larch, fir, and rowan trees that held the sunlight back. At the end of the path, an opening led to a long, crescent-shaped mausoleum with its white marble finish glinting in the late afternoon sun. A simple carved balustrade curved around the monument's semicircle. Katya suddenly broke away from Illya and rushed over to the memorial. She sat down on a wide marble ledge that ran the length of the sarcophagus.

"Illya, look, the view is awesome!" she joyously cried out, her eyes sweeping the vista.

The investigator ambled toward Katya and dropped down next to her. It was soundless except for the chirring of insects. Together, they enjoyed the warmth of the sun on their faces and gazed in silence at the panorama in front of them, the wind carrying the sweet scent of tall grasses and wildflowers from a seemingly unending meadow of waving green grass dotted with white-pedaled chamomiles with their yellow centers and bright azaleas. In the further distance, grassy fields waved with colorful fern leaf peonies, pink Rhododendron, and spectacular purple Crocus. In its still further reaches, the wild meadow eventually gave way to a thick forest of spruce and electric-colored maple trees, housing birds that randomly screeched aloud. On the far horizon, they could see village rooftops at a glinting yaw in the Moscow River.

They were sitting quietly side by side when a voice cut through the silence.

"Hello," the voice said, "Mind if I join you? I hope I am not interrupting anything."

Illya recognized the voice and, smiling, twisted his head around to see his friend, Sasha Petrov. He held out his arms in a welcoming gesture. "Come, come, Sasha, my friend, sit with us. We are just enjoying the sunlight and the serenity of nature."

The visitor sat next to Illya Podipenko. "To what do we owe the pleasure of your visit?" asked Illya.

"Nothing extraordinary." Sasha answered. "I just wanted to drop by to see how you were getting along and whether you needed me to do anything for you."

"We are doing fine, thank you, Sasha."

"Have you seen Inna yet? Or Boris?"

"Not yet, that is our next step." Illya checked his watch. "In fact, I think we should head that way now. Join us, Sasha."

The three stood, taking one last look at the beautiful tableau in front of them then turned to walk along the pathway toward the cabin that stood spare and clean in the sunlight. Rounding a bend in the pathway, they came in view of the pond to their left, and Katya pulled up, grabbing Illya's arm in a tight grip.

"What is *that*?" she gasped out, her voice in a whisper.

"Where?" replied Illya.

The girl had her arm raised, a finger pointing in the distance.

"There," she said.

Illya followed her finger. "You mean near to that beast splashing in the pond?"

"No. *The* beast in the pond!"

Illya raised a hand to his brow, shading his eyes. He squinted through the morning light.

"Goodness me. Looks like a bear, I'd say. And a big one at that."

"What is he doing?"

"Swimming or possibly bathing, it appears."

"What?" Her eyes were wide in disbelief.

"Or perhaps fishing for breakfast," threw in Sasha Petrov. He offered a wink across to Illya Podipenko, who hid a grin. They were having fun with the girl.

"Please, don't make any sudden moves or make any loud noises," warned Illya in a low voice.

"Why not?" cried the girl.

"Don't draw undue attention to us. The last thing we want is that beast charging us."

"Too late," commented Sasha as, suddenly, the bear seemed to notice the three people in the distance. His mouth opened wide, showing rows of sharp white teeth. He let out a tremendous bellow that startled birds in the trees. He lumbered out of the water, shook the water from his brown fur, and rose up on his hind legs. He roared once again and suddenly began charging on all fours toward the visitors.

"Illya," shouted the girl, "he's coming this way. What should we do?"

"I find prayer helps in times like these," Illya said softly as the bear rumbled nearer. "I guess I'll go try to cut him off. You better hide behind Sasha."

"What? He'll kill you, Illya!"

"Oh, ye of little faith!" Illya said to the girl then started trotting toward the on-charging bear. "Remember what the unicorn said to Alice."

"Wait, what?" The girl thrust herself into the arms of Sasha Petrov and buried her face in his chest. "You are quoting Alice *now*?"

Illya was plunging ahead, calling over his shoulder, "The unicorn said, 'If you believe in me, I'll believe in you.'"

As the bear ran forward, Katya could feel the ground rumble and hear what sounded like angry snarls coming from its mouth. With one eye peeled, she watched as the bear approached Illya. At once, the bear rose to a tremendous height on his back legs and wrapped the man around his shoulders with his front paws. Illya's legs gave way under the weight of the beast, and he collapsed to the ground, the bear on top of him. Katya screamed out as she could hear the shouting and bleating noises coming from Illya as he squirmed frightfully across the ground.

"Sasha, stop them!" she cried out. "The bear will eat him alive."

She immediately noticed that Sasha Petrov did not reply. Inexplicably, as she clung to him, she momentarily felt the man's body shaking in spasms.

What is going on? she wondered. *Is Sasha crying, or is he…laughing?* she asked herself. She pulled away and looked up into the man's face. He was smiling broadly and, chuckling.

He said to the girl, "The bear might lick him to death, but I don't think he'll eat him alive." He raised a finger, pointing. "Look, see what I mean."

Katya turned and faced the bear and Illya full on. She watched a moment longer then saw. Illya was struggling all right, but not defending himself from the bear's voracious teeth and jaws, but rather from a huge pink tongue that was lapping at the man's bald head as if it were a shiny lollipop. Illya rolled around on the ground unable to stop his convulsive laughter.

The girl broke away from Sasha Petrov. Her face was red in anger or embarrassment. She fixed her hands to her hips. She stomped a foot into the ground and called out like a custodial *babushka*.

"Illya, stop that at once. You get up from there right now. You are getting all dirty. Your clothes are a mess!"

"Tell that to the bear," breathlessly, Illya called back. Ruggedly, he grabbed the large animal behind his ears and gave the beast a kiss on the snout. He wiggled free from the bear's grasp and stood wobblily. He made an effort to smooth the wrinkles from his clothes. He accepted a handkerchief from Sasha Petrov to wipe his head.

"Katya," he breathed out, "meet Boris."

"This is the Boris you mentioned earlier?"

"The same. Boris the Bear. Raised him since he was a cub. He's just a big baby. Come here, give him a pet on the head. He won't bite."

The girl edged forward, unsure. She raised an arm to pet the bear's round head. Boris sniffed the girl's hand, his nostrils flaring. She gently patted the bear's head near the ears. Boris closed his eyes, and the girl swore to herself that she could see the bear's lips arch upward in a satisfied grin.

"Where did he come from?" the girl smiled.

"Years ago, my father was on a fishing trip at Lake Vygozero along Russia's border with Finland. Through the lake mist, he noticed something thrashing around in the weeds at the edge of the lake. He approached to see what it was. As it turned out, it was Boris who was just a young cub. He was all twisted up in a fisherman's netting. His mother and other bears were nowhere to be found. My father calmed Boris down and eventually cut him loose. The bear cub was exhausted and starving, so my father fed him fish from the ones he had caught earlier. From then on, Boris was attached to my father, and my father decided to bring him home with him."

"And you raised him?" asked Katya.

"We did. We named him Boris. He is a Kamchatka brown bear, not so different from your grizzly bear in America."

"Where does he live?"

"In the hills behind the cabin," Illya vaguely waved a hand in the distance. "He has a rock cave. It's actually quite nice. He visits every morning for breakfast. We keep a refrigerator on the cabin's front porch stocked with fish and elk meat we get from a butcher in the village. We also stock the pond twice a year. Boris helps us out, keeps the wolves away, keeps a protective eye on Inna, who lives alone. He would give up his life for her. He's a good old boy, very intelligent."

As Illya was talking, Boris wobbled over to where Sasha Petrov was standing. He grunted and rose, putting his paws on Sasha's shoulders. He flapped the hat off the man's head and, as had done with Illya, began licking Sasha's head with his tongue.

"All right, Boris, good seeing you too." Sasha laughed, patting the bear's massive chest. "Down now."

Boris complied to the command, and Sasha accepted his handkerchief back from Illya, which he used to wipe his head. He picked up his hat and placed it on his head. "He is very affectionate," Sasha thoughtfully explained to the girl.

"Boris loves Sasha," added Illya. "It's Sasha who feeds him a couple times a week."

Ten minutes later, three people and one bear were shuffling along the path skirting the pond, eventually climbing the stairs to the cabin's front porch and sprawling deck that encircled the front of the house. Illya made a fist and rapped on the front door with his knuckles. Momentarily, the door swung inwardly. Standing in the doorway was an older woman, who wore her thick, white hair pulled back into a tight bun. She was still attractive in her advanced age, and Illya could remember what a beauty she was as a young woman who was in love with Illya's father and who took care of Illya as a surrogate mother.

"My dear, dear Illochka!" the woman cried out. She threw her arms wide and drew the man to her chest. "How I have missed you! I was struck with joy when you texted me that you would be coming for a visit!" A tear streaked her smooth cheek.

"Good to see you also, Inna," Illya whispered to her. "I have missed you too."

They stood hugging in the doorway for a few moments. Then the man said, "Inna, I want you to meet someone very special." He reached his arm backward and pulled Katya closer to him. "This is Katya Tevoradze. She is a good friend of mine, a student in one of my lectures. Katya's heritage is Russian, Georgian actually, but she lives in New York, and it is her first time in Moscow."

The older lady reached out and warmly squeezed Katya's arm. "Welcome, my dear child," she said to her. "Oh, my, Illochka, she is as pretty as you said she was. And so young!" When she smiled, tiny, beautiful creases showed around her eyes.

"That she is, Inna. Truth be told, whenever I am near her, she makes me feel very old indeed." He smiled, leaning in and kissing Inna on her forehead. "The grounds appear well-looked after," Illya said, waving an arm across the pond and boat dock behind them and the forest in the distance.

"There is a man in the village," the woman replied, "the husband of a longtime friend of mine. He comes twice a week to take care of the place. He keeps the grass and bushes trimmed and the flower and plant beds weeded. He does his best to keep the pond clean by cutting back the cattails, and when something needs painting or repairing in the cabin itself, he takes care of that too. He brings me food from the village when I can't get out. And, of course, your wonderful friend, Sasha Petrov, here, what a nice man he is, also visits frequently and helps out where he can." She took Sasha by the hand and kissed it warmly. "So as you see, Illochka, I am being well looked after."

Boris the Bear suddenly forced his round head through the bodies. The woman laughed warmly and rubbed the bear behind the ears. "Oh, Boris, I haven't forgotten about you. You protect me, too, and I love you for it." She bent down and said in a half whisper, "I bet you are hungry, aren't you, Boris?"

"I'll get him a snack," said Sasha, heading for an old refrigerator not far from the doorway, next to a neatly stacked woodpile. Boris quickly lumbered behind him.

"Don't you get lonely out here all by yourself?" asked Katya of the older woman as they entered the *dacha*. "I would be frightened so far the city and being all alone."

"Well, I am not completely alone. I have my memories here to keep me company, good memories, wonderful memories of the marshal and his military cronies and their wives and girlfriends, all drinking and joking and telling old war stories. It was such fun in those days! And, of course, Boris comes by every morning to check up on me, to make sure everything is safe."

"So Boris still comes by?" inquired Illya.

"But, of course, Illochka! He's getting a bit older, too, but he hasn't slowed down much. I feed him breakfast every day. And you know Boris is not one to miss his breakfast."

"Goodness, this is beautiful!" Katya spoke lyrically. She was standing in the foyer of the two-story *dacha*, her eyes viewing the lower level's main room. It was large and wide open, with eight-foot windows lining the walls, filling the room with natural sunlight. The room was trimmed in blond wood. Bright, woven Turkish rugs rested on clean pine floors. At one end of the room, above a handsome mantle, perched atop a stone fireplace, hung a vibrant copy of the painting *Ivan Tsarevich Riding the Gray Wolf* by Viktor Vasnetsov. An ornate chandelier hung in the center of the room.

"Come, I will give you the cook's tour," said Illya, taking the young woman by the arm.

The dacha's white walls were decorated with the many awards given to Illya's father—Hero of the Soviet Union, numerous Orders of Victory, Orders of Lenin and Orders of the Red Banner, and the Order of St. George. His uniform was on display behind glass and bore both the Hero of the Soviet Union and Hero of Russia stars, plus so many other medals that they were stitched one after another in rows onto the breast of his coat. And, of course, in the center of it all was the Gold Star studded with diamonds given to Konstantin Podipenko when he was promoted to the rank of marshal.

The girl's eyes roamed photographs of Illya's father with Stalin, Khrushchev, Brezhnev, Andropov, and Chernenko. There was also a black-and-white photo of Illya as a baby surrounded by his proud parents, Konstantin and his young blond wife, Sonya, and another photo, obviously taken years later, in which Illya, who appeared to be in his early teens, smiling broadly with his father, who was in full military dress with his arm around a younger and very beautiful, Inessa. It appeared that they were about the climb aboard the old skiff Katya had seen earlier tied up on the dock in the pond. A picnic basket was on the ground next to the boat.

"I like old photos," Katya said to Illya. "It gives you a sense of time and place, of family, that's important."

"I agree," responded Illya as he ushered the young girl into another room; this one smaller, and it appeared that this was the room that the marshal used as his study. The room was bright in its sunlight, with small clerestory windows facing south ringing the top of the ceiling, allowing in additional natural light. A large wooden desk held a round lamp, a black telephone, a random stack of yellowing papers, and a decorated, lacquered box that contained cigarettes. Katya noticed that on the table lay a Russian translation of *For Whom the Bell Tolls* by Hemingway.

A full bookcase ran the entire expanse of the far wall. A nice-looking, textured pinewood wet bar was built into the wall with elevated shelving holding dozens of glistening bottles of hard liquors imported from America and pristine wines from Russia's Krasnodar region and Crimea vineyards. The bottles had colorful labels, and each stood shoulder to shoulder with one another like sleek Red Army soldiers at attention. Though she was not a drinker, Inessa the caretaker, dutifully took down and dusted each bottle on a weekly basis because the marshal would have blessed her for this kind act and attention to detail. In the corner on a round table was a large chess set carved in Onyx. Two wooden chairs faced each other across the chessboard and a lazy paddle fan circled on the ceiling above.

"I spent many hours at the board with my father," Illya said to the young girl. "I got to be reasonably good, but my father was a master. Sometimes, I think he just let me win so I wouldn't become discouraged about the game. Fun fact, Ivan the Terrible died of a stroke while playing a game of chess."

"That is fun," responded Katya. "Maybe he got the 'Terrible' nickname because he was beyond bad at chess."

"Do you play?" asked Illya.

"No, not really My grandfather and uncle tried to teach me, but I never had the patience to learn it well."

Illya was about to ask something else when the melodic tune of his cell phone filled the air. He saw who was calling and slipped a wink to Katya before answering.

"Noah, my friend," Illya called out, "how are things in New York?"

Hearing who was calling Illya, the girl clapped her hands over her mouth. Her lips swept upward in a reflexive grin.

Illya paced as he listened. His face seemed to tighten, bunching in concern.

"Yes, yes, I see, Noah." He scratched at the whiskers shadowing his chin. "Yes, of course, I will pass along the information. Ah, she is doing well, thank you for asking. Here, you can say hello for yourself."

Illya reached out toward Katya, nudging the cell phone into her hand. "It's Noah Carter," he whispered to the girl, "he wants to say hi to you."

Katya beamed as she took Illya's phone in her hand and began walking the perimeter of the room, at times spinning lightly on her toes as she murmured softly into the cell phone. Illya smiled to himself as he observed her; she appeared to be an enamored schoolgirl chatting up a favored suitor. At the end of the conversation, Illya saw that Katya's lips had formed the words "I love you" which she spoke into the phone before handing it back to the Moscow investigator and saying, "Well, I have good news and bad news. Which do you want to hear first?"

"I prefer good news," responded Illya.

"Noah said that my uncle Grisha is still alive in the hospital. The bad news is that he remains in a coma and has not yet awakened."

"I'm sorry," said Illya truthfully.

"There is more good news and bad news," Katya offered. "Good news first?"

"Let's."

"Noah also informed me that the FBI has rounded up most of the Matrabazi gang and have them behind bars. It will be safe for us to go home soon."

"And the bad news?"

"The head of the gang, our friend from the warehouse, Dato Matrabazi, was not among those captured. He has somehow escaped."

"That *is* bad news," Illya shook his head.

"It gets worse. Noah said the FBI received information that Dato Matrabazi boarded a plane destined for Moscow. So he is probably already here."

"You're right," acknowledged Illya, "that is worse news. Once here, he can join up with his brother Zaza's gang."

"And come after Stalin's hidden treasures," said Katya.

"Which means he'll come after us," Illya reminded the girl. "I need to warn Inna."

*****

Illya Podipenko was feeling troubled, and it showed.

"Are you all right?" inquired Katya. "You seem on edge."

"Do I?" responded Illya. He forced a weak smile. They were standing in front of the marshal's long bookshelf. "Sorry. Having Dato Matrabazi in Moscow gives me pause. He knows about Stalin's hidden treasures, and he undoubtedly knows about my father's relationship with Stalin. At some point, likely sooner than later, he and his brother's thugs are going to show up here wanting some answers about where Stalin's treasures are hidden."

"Do you really think so?" asked Katya. She was absently sliding her fingers along dozens of book jackets, first editions by Tolstoy, Gorky, Nabokov, Pushkin, Turgenev, Pasternak, Mendelstam, Bulgatov, Gogol, Chekhov, Solzhenitsyn, and Dostoyevsky.

Illya nodded affirmatively. "There really is nowhere else for them to begin their search."

"Which means they could be here at any time."

Illya nodded once more. "Which means we better start looking ourselves. See if we can find any clues to where the treasure might be."

The girl wandered across the room and gave Illya a warm hug. "I am so glad you've decided to send Inessa to spend a few days in the village with her friend. That was a smart move. No need to expose her to any possible dangers."

Illya nodded in agreement. He also remembered that he had to thank his friend, Sasha Petrov, for volunteering to take Inna to her friend's house in the village. Sasha's plan was to drop off the woman at her friend's then continue on to his home in Moscow for the night, returning to the *dacha* early the next morning.

The investigator shook his head and sighed. "Perhaps you should have gone to the village also. I fear for your safety."

"Don't worry about me, Illya. We are a team. We'll kick ass and take names."

"Your optimism shines," Illya acknowledged.

After a few minutes, Katya asked, "Do you think the treasure is somewhere here in the *dacha* or at least on the property?"

"I do," said Illya. "I don't know where else the marshal would have trusted to store it. If he had gone to as much trouble as he did to move it from Stalin's underground air-raid shelter at Kuntsevo, he would have moved it close by. A place that he knew, a place that was well-hidden, a place nearby so he could put his hands on the treasures quickly, if he needed to." Illya expelled a deep breath. "It is here. We just need to find out where."

"Maybe, this will help, Illochka" a voice said.

Both Illya and Katya turned toward the voice. It came from the doorway where Inna was now standing. She had an Astrakhan wool shawl over her shoulders and an old small suitcase at her feet. In one of her hands, she was holding what appeared to be a brown envelope, which she was held out in front of her. "I found this earlier this week," she said, entering the room. "It's for you, Illochka. From the marshal. I finally started going through his papers a couple of days ago to file them. I found this in the top drawer of the chest of drawers in his bedroom. It says that upon the marshal's death, this should go to you. I had never seen this before. I am so sorry, Illochka, that I am just now finding it. I wanted to give it to you before I left for the village."

"No, no, my dear Inna, it is fine. Not to worry." He warmly kissed the older lady on the cheek. He took the envelope from her and turned it in his hands before opening it. On the front of the envelope, Illya read the words in the marshal's handwriting, "For Illya upon my death. Your biggest challenge yet!"

"Uh-oh," Illya muttered aloud, "I am not sure I want to open his."

"Oh, Illya, you must!" cried out Katya. She walked to the investigator's side, leaning her body into his. Illya carefully tore open the envelope, removing a folded piece of paper. He read aloud, "My dear son, Illya. If you are reading this, then I have already died. Don't be sad. I lived a long, fun, and adventurous life. I have only two regrets: that your beautiful mother passed away at such an early age and that I did not spend enough time with you, my only son. I leave you now with the biggest and most important *zagadka* of your life. If you solve all of the clues correctly, you will find untold riches that I have hidden away for you. These riches are from Stalin's private collection that he accumulated for his personal means. No one else in Russia knows of their existence. Do with them what you wish. Knowing you as I do, I suspect that you will return them to the rightful owner, the state. But you must solve the *zagadka* first! Good luck, my son! P.S. Please see to it that Inna and Boris are properly taken care of."

Illya carefully folded the paper and placed it in his shirt pocket.

"So it *was* your father," said Katya Tevoradze, "who moved the treasures from the hidden room in Stalin's bomb shelter."

"Apparently so," Illya sighed. "Now all we have to do is find where he hid it."

"Well, you *are* the magic man, aren't you?" Katya offered demurely. "Work your magic, solve the enigma."

"We shall see."

"Come on, man. How hard can it be? Your father left you a few puzzles to solve. What's the big whoop? It's your father. He is not going to leave you puzzles that you can't solve."

"Well, he can be very tough. And remember, he wants the clues difficult enough that I hopefully can solve them but outsiders who perhaps would stumble onto the clues cannot. So the puzzles can't be too easy."

"I believe in you," Katya whispered and quickly kissed him on the side of his face. "Go ahead, what is the first puzzle? Read it to me."

Illya chewed his lip and looked across at the girl. "All right, let's have a go," he said softly. He was quiet a moment, reading the clue to himself, his lips moving. Then he smiled. "Okay, this one is fairly simple. He is starting us off easy."

"Read it to me. See if I can get it." The girl's words brimmed with adventure. Her eyes brightened, and her body began jiggling in anticipation.

Illya laughed. "Okay, settle down and concentrate. Here we go. It is a question, and the question is this, How many eyeballs are there in a full deck of American playing cards?"

"That's a good question!" Katya shouted happily. "How difficult can that be?"

"Don't get cocky," Illya sternly warned her. "My experience, if the solution appears too simple, it isn't. The marshal liked to design questions that have a trick within them, so forewarned is forearmed."

"All right then, we will take it slowly. How many eyeballs in a full deck of playing cards? Well, eyeballs appear on all of the face cards. There are jacks, queens, and kings, one in each suit, so in a deck of cards, there are twelve face cards. So that's twenty-four eyeballs, that is if all the faces had two eyes, which I know they don't. This is the trick part. Some face cards only have a single eye. The problem is, I can't remember which face cards, or how many, have only a single eye. Do you know, Illya?"

"I do. There are three face cards that have a single eye, the jack of hearts, the jack of spades, and the king of diamonds."

"I knew you would know." The girl grinned then became serious. "So there are twelve face cards, nine of them have faces with two eyes, that's eighteen eyes, and three cards have a face with a single eye, that totals three eyes. Therefore, eighteen eyes plus three eyes equal twenty-one eyes." The girl paused, throwing her hands in the air. "There you have it, Illya, the answer is twenty-one eyes, not so hard after all!"

Illya nodded. "I must say, your reasoning was very sound, my dear. Unfortunately, you didn't go far enough and your answer was, unfortunately, wrong."

"What? That's impossible. The math is there."

"Almost there, my beautiful little Archimedes," the man smiled, "but there is a further trick." From a drawer in front of him, Illya pulled out a deck of American playing cards. He spread the cards in his hand until he found a face card, the queen of hearts. He threw this down on the desk in front of him. "So how many eyeballs do you see on this card, my dear?"

"Two!" Katya exclaimed.

"Are you certain?"

"Yes, Illya, I am certain. The queen of hearts has two eyes. How many do you see?"

"Well, Katya," he said as he slowly rotated the card a hundred and eighty degrees. "I see four eyes, not two. You see the bottom of the card is the mirror image of the top of the card. Therefore, there are two queen's faces on a single card, not one face. Hence, there are four eyeballs on the card not two. So you must double your answer, not twenty-one eyeballs in a deck but forty-two eyeballs."

"That's not fair, Illya!" shouted the girl. She gave her companion a smart rap to his shoulder. "It was a trick!"

"Of course, it was a trick," answered the man, "that is what this is all about. They are tricks, puzzles, misdirection, brainteasers all meant to challenge me by my father." He paused and his chest heaved. "This one was an easy one. The puzzles will get harder. Are you still with me?"

"Until the end, my dearest," whispered Katya.

"Good," responded Illya as he was opening another folded piece of paper. He read it and smiled. "Ah, a question to answer. We have to answer it correctly before we can move on. So do you have your thinking cap on?"

"I do. Please proceed."

"Okay, here is the question, Why is it against the law for a man living in Moscow to be buried in either St. Petersburg or Vladivostok?"

The girl pursed her lips, her brow constricted in thought. "Uhm, I am not sure. You?"

Illya smiled. "Of course. It's not that difficult if you think about it."

"I *am* thinking about it. Nothing is coming to mind. So tell me, magic man. Why is it against the law for a man living in Moscow to be buried in either St. Petersburg or Vladivostok?"

"Because he is not dead. He is *living* in Moscow. Therefore, if he is still alive, it is illegal to bury him anywhere. You can't bury him if he is not dead."

Katya frowned and slapped a hand against the man's shoulder. "Not in Stalin's day!" Katya laughed. "Stalin probably preferred burying most of his enemies dead but perhaps not so opposed to burying a selected few of them alive."

"That's a macabre thought for such a beautiful young lady," offered Illya Podipenko. "All right, are you ready to move on to the next question?"

"Ready Teddy."

Illya read aloud from the piece of paper. "You must go on a hunt to find the two sisters living in twin towers. One sister is dark, the other fair. One is from the land, the other is from the sea. Great wealth is in one, and if you find it, you are to keep it."

"Oh, I like the sound of the last part," said the girl with enthusiasm. "The mention of great wealth always is a promising motivator."

"So you know who the sisters are?" inquired Illya.

"Not a clue. You?"

Illya smiled. "I think so, follow me." He took the young girl by the hand and led her out of the study, through the living room, up a hallway corridor, and into a kitchen that was open and light and had beamed ceilings. He sat Katya down in a chair at a breakfast table then settled in a chair across from her. They sat in silence, at last, Katya raised her hands in the air and said, "So?"

"You don't see it?" asked Illya.

"Please, Illya, I am about ready to pop a blood vessel in my temple."

"The answer to the clue. It's right in front of you."

"Where?" the girl responded, "next to the tall salt and pepper shakers on the table?"

"No," Illya chuckled, "it *is* the salt and pepper shakers. Remember the clue, twin towers, one sister dark and from land, that's pepper, and the other sister fair and from the sea, that's salt. There you have it, Katya. You did it!"

She beamed and said, "Salt and pepper shakers, of course! But I didn't really solve it, you did."

"Well, you get half credit just for being here."

"That's very generous of you, Illya," cooed the girl while her forehead was suddenly knotting in uncertainty. "Goodness, this is heavier than it looks," she said, handing the pepper shaker across the table to Illya Podipenko.

The investigator took it in his hand and smiled. "Remember the second part of the clue, *Great wealth is in one*. I am guessing gemstones." He removed a pair of glasses from his shirt pocket, unfolded them, and put them on halfway down his nose. He studied the pepper mill for a moment then turned it upside down, unscrewing the base of the object. He carefully tipped the pepper mill forward, and dozens of shiny diamonds and emeralds spilled in a luminous wave of glass across the kitchen table toward the young girl.

Katya screamed. "Good Lord, Illya, diamonds! Look how brightly they shine!"

The man smiled across the table as he studied the gemstones reflecting seductively in the blue irises of the girl's wide eyes. Almost in a whisper, he replied, "Yes, they do."

"And these we get to keep?" she asked.

"Yes, we do."

The girl let out a joyous shout, bolted upright, leaning across the table to plant her lips against his. "I love you, Mr. Moscow's Top Investigator!" she yelped out, causing Illya's cheeks to burnish pink and warm from his collar up.

"Wait. There is more, apparently," he managed to utter. He was unfolding a piece of paper that had been inserted into the pepper mill.

"Another puzzle to solve. It is a question, a brainteaser. We must answer correctly in order to move on."

Katya retook her chair. "Go for it!" she screeched vigorously.

"Okay, here it is. In the pond outside, there is a patch of lily pads. Each day, the patch doubles in size. It took forty-eight days for the patch to cover the entire lake. How many days did it take for the lily patch to cover half of the lake?"

"Oh, no," wailed Katya, "not a math question. I hate math. It makes my brain ache."

Illya reached across the table and patted the girl's hand. "Come, my dear, stay with me. Remember, we are on a quest to uncover untold riches. Do you want me to repeat the question?"

"Yes… I mean, no. I got it, forty-eight days for the lily pads to completely cover the pond. How many days for the pond to be half-covered, blah, blah, blah." She squinted up her eyes in thought, tilting her head upward. She balanced her chin on top of a fist she was making, elbow on the table. After a minute, she glanced across the table at the Moscow investigator, who was sitting quietly, an intriguing Mona Lisa smile turned on his lips. "You already know the answer, don't you, Illya? I can tell by the feverish look in your eyes. You are trying to hide it, but that look gives you away."

"I do know the answer, yes, Katya. It is not so difficult. Concentrate."

"I can't. I am too excited," she whined, hunching her shoulders. "You just tell me the answer, Illya."

His chest heaved in a sigh, and he smiled. "All right. Now follow me. On the forty-eighth day, the lily pads completely covered the pond, a hundred percent. Now, we know that every day the patch doubles in size, right? So we need to determine what day the pond was half-covered, knowing that it would double in size the next day to be fully covered. And the logical answer is that the pond was half-covered on the forty-seventh day, then doubled in size to be fully covered on the next day, the forty-eighth. So that is the answer, you see?"

"If you say so, magic man. My brain is about to burst, and I am starting to get dizzy. I am not as good at this as I thought I would be." She sounded discouraged.

"Nonsense," Illya comforted her, "you are plenty intelligent, one of the brightest young people I know. You're just getting warmed up. You want to find Stalin's hidden treasures, don't you?"

"I suppose. How much longer will it take?"

"I don't know. We have to keep following my father's clues."

"He put you through this kind of torture every week growing up?"

"He did. It was great fun."

"Hmm, no doubt," she purred, "no wonder you ran off and joined the militia!"

Illya took the young girl's shoulder and squeezed it softly. "Come now, Katya. This is why we are here. Unfold the next clue and read it aloud."

He handed her the piece of paper, which Katya unfolded in her fingers. She read, "More of the same is next. You must journey to a land of thirty men and two women, all are dressed in black or white." She repeated the clue to herself several times under her breath, just her lips moving to the words she was saying to herself. Suddenly, she clapped her hands together and shouted out, "I know this one, Illya! It's not so hard! It's the chessboard in the other room. A land of thirty men and two women, dressed in black or white. It has to be!"

"Well done, Katya," Illya offered enthusiastically. "I think you've done it! And, look, the clue says 'more of the same.' That might mean we'll find more diamonds that we can *keep for ourselves!*"

They entered the room in a trot, going straight to the small round table that supported the chessboard. They sat in the chairs across from each other. Instinctively, Katya reached for the black king with its large round base, sculped column with a carved cross on top. "Heavy," she smiled and handed it across the table, where Illya took it and spun it in his hands.

"You are right, very heavy," he responded and began twisting the base of the chess piece. His earlier prediction proved accurate. Sparkling diamonds spilled across the black and white squares of the chessboard. The girl squeaked in glee.

Illya said, "I feel quite certain you are not going to have any problems paying your next year's tuition to Columbia."

"Fuckin' A," the girl replied, shaking her head in wonderment. "This is awesome. I'm starting to like this enigma game better." She watched Illya take a small square of paper from the base of the chess piece. He handed it across for the girl to read.

She said aloud, "Charles the Great. The only one beardless." She frowned. "What the hell does that mean?"

Illya laughed. "It refers to Charlemagne, the French king, later an emperor of the Romans, during the Middle Ages."

"What does he have to do with anything?"

"Well," sighed Illya, "the good news we don't have to go far to find the answer. It is right here."

Katya's shoulders offered a shrug. "Here? Where? On the chessboard?"

"Not on it, *under* it."

"Under it? That doesn't make sense, Illya."

"It does if you know that there is a drawer in the table right in front of you."

She peered down, opened the drawer, and drew out a deck of playing cards. "Oh, no," she slumped, "not the cards again."

"Afraid so."

"And exactly what do the cards have to do with the clue, what was it, Charlemagne?"

"Yes. The only one beardless. Here, take a look." Illya began sliding through the deck of playing cards; as he did, throwing the kings face down onto the table. As he talked, he turned them over one at a time. "You see, Katya, the four kings in a deck of cards represent real rulers from history. The king of spades, for example, represents the biblical King David. The king of clubs represents Alexander the Great. The king of diamonds represents Julius Caesar, and the king of hearts represents Charlemagne, and Charlemagne is the only one of the four kings who does not have a beard. See." He turned over the final card on the chessboard between them, revealing the beardless king of hearts.

"How do you know all of this friggin' stuff, Illya?" bleated the girl. "Seriously, I worry about you."

The man laughed. "I don't know," he replied. "I read." He took the king of hearts' card in his hand and brought it close to his face. His eyes squinted at faded writing in the white margin of the card. "There is something here," he said to the girl. He once more placed his glasses on his nose. "Another clue."

"Read it out loud," Katya encouraged him.

"He murdered a quarter of the world's population," Illya read slowly. "Beginnings 48."

"What the hell does that mean?" barked the girl. "Who murdered a quarter of the world's population, Stalin? Mao? Hitler? Pol Pot?"

Illya shook his head. "No, all unquestionably profound mass murderers in their own right, but none could be credited with dispatching a quarter of the world's population."

"Who then?" asked the girl. "And what does Beginnings 48 mean?"

"Good question," Illya responded, rubbing his chin. He went quiet, thinking, tapping his fingers on the tabletop. When at last, he gave a quiet nod of his head and a smile.

The girl said excitedly, "I know that look, Investigator Illya Podipenko! You know the answer! So tell me!"

The man arose from the chair and approached the long bookshelf. He reached to the second shelf and pointed to a black book with a cross on it.

"Near the Bible?" asked Katya.

"No, *in* the Bible. Like so many things, the answer lies within," he said to Katya. "American version," continued Illya, returning to his chair. He sat, opening the book. "Unless I miss my guess, Beginnings 48 is Genesis 4:8," he said to the girl. "Here it is," he handed the book across to the girl. "You read, please."

Katya accepted the book and ran a finger down the selected page until she reached Genesis 4:8. She began reading, "'Cain spoke to Abel, his brother. And when they were in the field, Cain rose up against his brother, Abel, and killed him.'"

Katya looked up and scowled across the table. "I don't get it, Illya. Cain killed his brother, but that is only one man."

"Yes," Illya nodded, "but that one man represented a quarter of the world's population at the time. Remember, then there were only four people on earth, Adam and Eve and their sons, Cain and Abel. So when Cain killed Abel, he eliminated a quarter of the world's population. It was actually the first recorded murder in human history."

"You are ridiculous!" gushed Katya, sweeping back a lock of hair that had fallen across her face. A second later, her eyes grew wide. "Illya, there is another clue written in the margin!"

"What does it say?"

"It's in Russian. But I believe it says, "Follow Virgil!"

"Follow Virgil?"

"Yes, that's what it says."

"The Greek poet Virgil?"

"You're asking me?" Katya responded, shocked.

"Now, Katya, you are an A student," Illya patiently said. "Think and tell me what you know about Virgil."

"He is a Greek poet. He wrote *The Aeneid*. The story of Aeneas, the Trojan hero and demigod who leaves Troy, which has been destroyed by the Greeks, and sails to Italy where Aeneas' ancestors are destined to found Rome. He encounters many adventures along the way. That's what I remember."

"That's very good, Katya, I am proud of you," said Illya, which made the girl lower her head in a flush of pink cheeks and a small "thank you" tumbling from her lips, adding, "See, I am not totally useless to you."

"Never said you were," scowled Illya, shifting in the chair, "You must know that." He cleared his throat and spoke energetically. "Now, see that big, blue, bound-leather book up there," he said, pointing to the second shelf of the bookcase. "Bring it here, would you, my dear? It is *The Odyssey* and *The Iliad* by Homer and *The Aeneid* by Virgil all bound together into a single volume. Quite extraordinary."

The girl jumped up and pulled the book down from the shelf. It was heavier than she anticipated, and she awkwardly plopped it down on the tabletop with a thump. Illya sat up in the chair and began turning pages.

"What are we looking for?" asked Katya.

"I have no idea. Some clue to the next step. Looks like I have a bit of reading to do tonight. My memory of Virgil's story of *The Aeneid* is pretty thin." He was about to add something when he heard the chimes of his cell phone. Katya watched him answer it. He spoke softly, nodding his head, then hung up.

"That was Sasha Petrov," he informed the girl. "He's just checking in to see that we are all right. He dropped Inna off safely at her friend's flat, and now he is heading home. He reiterated that he plans to be out here early tomorrow morning to check on everything and help out where needed."

"You like Sasha, don't you?" inquired the girl.

"That I do. Trust him implicitly." With that, Illya looked at his watch and hefted to his feet. "It is late, my dear. Big day tomorrow. And it now appears that I have a bit of reading of Virgil to do tonight to prepare. So off to bed I go."

Katya approached and took his elbow. "Not alone, you don't. I am going with."

"Somehow I figured," Illya answered, fatigue suddenly pressing down on him.

CHAPTER 11

Morning winked early.

A thousand shards of pink pinned the clear blue sky above Moscow. The heavy air spoke of coming heat and a day of wet shirts across the back. The day's first sun swelled outside the window.

Sitting in an old undershirt and frayed suspenders across his bare shoulders, Illya was already at the small breakfast table, drinking coffee and munching on fresh bakery ginger cakes that Sasha Petrov had brought in earlier in the morning. In between sips and bites, Illya was turning the pages of *The Aeneid*. Although he managed to finish great chunks of the epic poem by Virgil in bed the previous night, he could not complete it all before his bedmate complained about the light being on and induced him to turn it off.

Said bedmate now entered the room in a sloping, shuffling, barefooted gait of someone suffering from chronic sleep deprivation. She had on what looked like one of Illya's sleeveless undershirts and little else. Her face was pale, her eyes ringed in black, her ruffled hair looking as if she could have been a descendent of the Gorgon sisters.

"Don't judge," she hazardously snapped at Illya as he poured her a cup of coffee and watched her flop down in the chair across from him. Blinding sunlight filled the room, slashing through window blinds on the east side of the cabin. She balled her fists and rubbed her eyes. Illya heard what he thought was an animal's snarl come from deep within his companion's chest. Then she said, her voice woolly with sleep, "It's too early for this shit. Haven't modern-day Russians ever heard of the crack of noon? I mean, what's the big friggin' rush? The country will still be here if we sleep in a bit." Lifting a single bleary eye, she inquired, "Are those fresh ginger cakes?"

"Sasha brought them. He got here early before sunrise. He stopped to get the ginger cakes on the way. He's a good man."

"Friggin' officer and a gentleman, if you ask me," said the girl, "except I might be too tired to eat."

"I seriously doubt that," Illya responded with a smile. He put a single ginger cake on a small plate and handed it across the table. "Here, eat up," he said.

She took hold of the baked good and feeling the warm texture of it at once seemed immensely more awake. She straightened in her chair and to all appearances inhaled it whole, like a blue whale gulping krill. A swill of coffee followed, then she wiped her lips and said to Illya, "So last night, in *The Aeneid*, did you find any of your father's clues to where Stalin's treasure might be hidden?"

"Not really, no," responded Illya, adjusting reading spectacles he had put on. "I mean, the Trojan hero Aeneas, following the sack of Troy by the Greeks, certainly had great adventures during his eventual travels to Italy, where it was destined that his ancestors Romulus and Remus would found Rome. At one point, a fierce storm knocks Aeneas and his crew off course and lands them in Carthage, where Queen Dido soon falls in love with Aeneas. When Aeneas determines he must leave her, Dido is devastated by his departure and kills herself upon a pyre by stabbing herself with a sword. He has more adventures on the way to Italy. Good story. But no clues, at least that I can unravel. Perhaps I am missing something." He pushed his glasses further up on his nose.

"I don't know," the girl shook her head. "You've been on the mark so far, dude. I believe in you, a thousand percent."

"Thank you, my dear girl. You are a comfort to an old man." He paused, his eyes contemplatively latched onto the far wall. He kept repeating his father's clue under his breath, "Follow Virgil." At last, he said aloud, shrugging his shoulders, "Who knows, maybe it's the wrong book?"

"Whoa, whoa, wait a minute!" The girl spun around. She leaped from her chair and determinedly marched straight ahead to the big bookshelf. "There *is* another book," she said excitedly, "and Virgil appears in it, plays a major role too. I saw it earlier when I was looking over the marshal's collection of books. Look, here it is!" She went on her toes to reach up.

She came away with a large book with a red leather cover. She turned it for Illya to read the front cover. "*The Divine Comedy*," she called out eagerly, not *The Aeneid*. "Virgil didn't write *The Divine Comedy*, but he certainly plays a major role in the story of Dante's *Inferno*. Virgil's soul guides Dante Alighieri through the nine circles of hell."

"Brilliant," shouted Illya Podipenko, "well done, Katya! I think you are on to something there. Let's have a look, shall we?" He held out his hand for the book, but Katya held it close to her chest as she primped toward where Illya was sitting.

"Uh-uh," she uttered coquettishly, "You take the book, you take me. That's the deal."

Illya looked up at her. "You drive a hard bargain, young lady. Come, sit on my lap. We shall look for clues together. But don't be too disappointed if we don't solve things right away. Remember what Dostoyevsky wrote in *Crime and Punishment*."

"Educate me."

"He wrote, 'You never reach any truth without making fourteen mistakes and very likely a hundred and fourteen.'"

"That's so negative!" wailed the girl. "Well, we will see about that." She folded lightly into the Moscow investigator's lap, the top of her head resting just below his chin.

"What do we know about this book, eh?" Illya pondered then began answering his own question. "We know that this is Dante Alighieri's epic poem *The Divine Comedy* from the fourteenth century, and this particular tale, Dante's *Inferno*, is the first one of three poems, the latter two being *Purgatorio* and *Paradiso*. The *Inferno* tells the journey of Dante through hell, guided by our friend, the Roman poet Virgil, who wrote *the Aeneid*."

"I remember that hell is depicted as nine concentric circles of torment located within the earth," Katya added to the conversation. "I can remember the depiction of hell creeping me out. I had to read the *Inferno* last year at Columbia for my world lit class."

"Very good, Katya, for remembering there were nine circles of hell. I am much impressed."

"I *am* an A student," she came back with faux huffiness.

"I remember." He was fanning through the book pages when he noticed something was written in one of the margins, and he quickly went back to it. "Look at this," he said, "it's a note in my father's handwriting. It says, 'Use what you know.'"

His response seemed to cause the girl to chuckle to herself.

When she continued on, Illya said, "Did I say something funny?"

The girl shook her head no, but she was still giggling.

"Katya," the Moscow investigator finally said, "you must tell me what is so amusing."

She managed to bring herself to a stop. She peered over her shoulder, up into Illya's puzzled face.

"I am laughing because I know something that neither you nor Mr. Negative Dostoyevsky knows."

"That covers a wide landscape," said the man.

"We are looking for Dante's hell, and I know where it is. *Use what you know*, your father wrote."

She pointed in the air toward the bookcase. "The entrance," she said, "the gates to hell."

"Near the bookcase?"

"No, the bookcase itself," she chuckled. "When I just now removed *The Divine Comedy* from the shelf, I saw something."

"What did you see?"

"On the wall of the bookshelf, behind where *The Divine Comedy* was an electronic keypad. So the know-it-all Dostoyevsky with all his negativity and fourteen mistakes and so forth can go suck ass. We will solve this mystery ourselves, you and I together."

"That's the spirit!" Illya boosted the girl off his lap. "Your optimism may exceed a person's legal limit." He rose from the chair. "Now let's have a look at this electronic keypad, shall we?" He approached the bookshelf and squinted into the dark gap where *The Divine Comedy* had been. Katya was right. Against the back wall, there was a keypad complete with blinking green and red lights. "Use what we know," Illya repeated under his breath. "I am thinking numbers, not words. Use what we know."

"What do we know?" Inquired Katya. "I feel like I don't know anything."

"No, no, you are wrong, Katya. Think. You know quite a bit from previous clues my father left for us. Think about numbers. What was the first clue he left us that dealt with numbers?"

The girl rubbed her chin and screwed up her face. "I am not sure. Was it the question about the number of eyeballs in a deck of playing cards?"

Illya smiled. "Yes, that was his first puzzle that dealt with numbers. What was the answer, do you recall?"

"I do. Forty-two eyeballs."

"Good girl. Nice memory. So forty-two is our first number. Now the second set of numbers—"

"I know! The pond scum!"

"The lily pads, yes," chuckled Illya Podipenko. "The question was how many days did it take for the pond to become half full of lily pads."

"I remember the answer," the girl said with enthusiasm, now obviously warming to the task. "Forty-seven days. I don't think I will forget that one."

"Once again, well done, Katya," grinned Illya Podipenko. "And now the third puzzle that involved numbers?"

"That's easy. The one about Cain and Abel. Genesis 4:8. So forty-eight is the number."

"I believe you are getting the hang of this, Katya. Excellent. So our numbers' code, what we know from the math clues in the order that they appeared is 424748. Go ahead, Katya, you earned it, tap that number in on the keypad. Let's see what happens."

Katya did so, and immediately, the bookcase creaked open, revealing a steel door behind it, which also chugged open. The activity made the wooden planks beneath their feet shudder and groan. The girl, with Illya at her side, approached the open door, which exposed wooden steps that disappeared down into what appeared to be some endlessly dark pit of misery from past days.

"Look," Illya pointed to a sign on the wall at the top of the stairwell. He read it aloud to the girl, "Abandon all hope, you who enter here. Look for four."

"Encouraging," chuffed the girl.

"A quote from Dante's *Inferno*."

"I know. Except the *Look for four* line. That he added."

"Then let's remember the number four. It will likely come into play later." Illya put his arm around the girl's shoulder. "Me first?" asked Illya, gazing down to where the steps led to a black hole.

"If you would be so kind."

Illya began to make a step toward the stairwell when he suddenly pulled up. He dug his mobile phone out of his back pocket and began pushing buttons.

"Ordering pizza now?" the girl inquired. "Hold the pineapple on mine."

Illya grinned at her and replied, "I believe we are getting very close to Stalin's hidden treasures. Sasha Petrov should be part of this. He is an important member of our team, after all."

"It is a good thought," chipped in Katya, "but where *is* he?"

"I'm not sure. He made a fresh cup of Caravan tea early this morning and said he was going to head out to the mausoleum to sit on the marble bench and watch the morning unfold. He said it clears his head."

On the other end, Illya heard Sasha's phone jingle unanswered, except for a recorded message that said Sasha was unavailable to receive the call.

Illya frowned. "I don't like this," he said. "It's not like Sasha to not answer his phone. I'm going to run out to the memorial, make sure he is okay."

"Right behind you," Katya let it be known. "I'll just throw on some shorts. I am not standing here guarding the gates of hell by myself, like some modern-day, three-headed hellhound Cerberus."

A few moments later, the two were hustling through the cabin and down the front porch steps. They jogged along the pathway lined with crocus and baby's breath around the pond where now a light morning mist had rolled out over the water.

At the end of the path, larch and spruce trees gave way to blue sky and sunlight. As the white memorial to Illya's father and mother came into view, Illya was fearing the worst.

From behind, they could see a portion of Sasha's body sitting on the marble bench. The body was stiff and unmoving. His head was bowed, chin drooping into his chest.

"Oh, no," whispered Illya to the girl, his eyes searching hers with alarm, "better stay here."

"Sasha," Illya called out, and he slowly began making his way toward the body. "Sasha," he called again, louder this time, and still no answer. Illya continued to approach the body cautiously, and as he rounded the edge of the mausoleum, Sasha's body came into full view. Nothing had prepared Illya for what he was about to see. His friend's body sat pitched forward, head bent, the sharp blade of a black-handled knife protruded from the side of his neck. Blood saturated the man's clothes and the bench on which he was perched. With his stomach tightening to near nausea, Illya slowly bent to retrieve Sasha's hat, which had fallen between his feet. Illya felt a presence beside him.

"I am so sorry, Illya," said Katya Tevoradze. "Who would do such a thing?"

"I have a pretty good idea," responded Illya, the sadness in his voice palpable. In the distance, across the field and over the river, terns swooped and called out in displeasure.

"There are only a few people who know that we are here," he spoke weakly, peering at nothingness in the distance.

"So right you are," an unseen voice said aloud from behind then. "Turn slowly. I have a gun."

Illya and the girl obeyed. The man was short in stature, his face scarred and waxy as if it seldom saw sunlight. As he trained the pistol on the couple, he carefully moved toward the dead body of Sasha Petrov. Bending, he ripped the knife from Sasha's neck. He wiped the blood from the knife blade across the jacket that Sasha was wearing and placed the knife in a scabbard he had hanging from his belt. He studied the couple in front of him.

"There are people looking for you," he said simply, a wry grin formed by his lips. "They believe you possess information that they want."

"Zaza Matrabazi," Illya said to the man.

"Very good." The man's eyebrows scuttled up on his forehead. "And his brother, Dato, from America. Don't forget about him. Apparently, you are responsible for the deaths of their three Matrabazi brothers in America. Zaza and Dato are not happy."

"So what do we do now?" Illya questioned him.

"Now," answered the man, "now, we wait. The brothers and their gang are on their way. It shouldn't be long," he added, checking his watch. "I suspect things will go badly for you. A pity. The girl is quite beautiful. It seems such a waste. Perhaps we will have some fun with her before we kill her."

"Fuck you, Rain Man," the girl spat out, "we don't need you bringin' that kind of negativity up in here. Whatever happens to me won't matter to you. You'll be dead."

"Is that so?" The man laughed arrogantly.

"A hundred percent. Van Valen's law."

"Van who?"

"Van Valen. The law of extinction."

"And how will you manage that?"

"Sometimes the Grim Reaper just appears unbidden."

"What?" The man rubbed his face in exasperation.

"Translation. It won't be me killing you. It will be Boris."

"And who is this Boris?" the man inquired, smiling smugly.

"Let me ask you something," replied Katya, crossing her arms over her chest, "and this is important, so do your best to pay attention. Do you remember the Red Queen in *Alice's Adventures in Wonderland*? Do you know what she was famous for saying?"

"What?" the man looked confused then perturbed. "I don't know what you are talking about. You are crazy, young lady. It is going to be extra fun abusing your corpse."

"I can't believe you don't remember what the Red Queen said!" Katya yelled at the man. "A child would know this."

"So tell me." He finally shook his head.

She shifted to face him fully. "The Red Queen would shout out, 'Off with their heads!'"

"Meaning?"

"Meaning," retorted Katya, "you are about to lose yours."

"Is that a fact?"

"It is an existential truth."

"And how, exactly, would this happen?"

"We talked about this," chipped in Illya Podipenko. "Boris."

"Who is this Boris character?" groused the man. "Where is he?"

"If you must know, Boris is a bear. A very large Russian brown bear. And you managed to kill the very person who was a friend of his, Sasha Petrov. Sasha who would sometimes come by in the mornings to feed Boris."

"What you did here," threw in the girl, "was some kind of special stupid. I suspect that Boris is super pissed off. Hashtag, I'd hate to be you right now. You're just going to have to trust me on this."

"You know what," the man leveled the gun in the air between them. "You are nuts, lady. Maybe I will save the Matrabazi brothers the trouble. I'll just shoot you now."

"Boris really wouldn't like that," Illya cut in, "and you don't want to make Boris angry, that I can tell you." He narrowed his focus on the man and was speaking as measured as he could.

"Shut up, old man, or I will kill you too."

"Oops," responded Illya, "too late." He shrugged his shoulders. "Sorry. We tried to warn you…"

It was then that the man holding the gun felt a hot breath on the back of his neck, and he felt the air currents around him being disturbed. When he turned to look behind him, his head cocked backward so he could peer straight up into the towering brown face and drooling, open mouth of Boris the Bear. The last thing the man ever saw was a giant bear paw veering through the air in the direction of his exposed throat. The black nails on the paw looked eight inches long and razor-sharp at the tips. The man's head came off so cleanly and with such force that it rolled like a soccer ball a bit down a hill and into the tall grasses below. The eyes remained wide open in surprise and were gawking confusingly ahead while the disconnected body, for a few moments, perplexingly remained upright and quivering as if not knowing it was dead, blood spouting from the neck, before eventually collapsing in a heap at the feet of Illya and his young companion. The body lay prone as a tranche of beef.

The two looked at one another, simultaneously shrugging their shoulders and saying, "We tried to warn him."

Minutes later, Illya stopped at the cabin's front steps. He placed a foot on the second step leading to the front porch, his other foot remaining on the ground. He threw his arm across his knee and bent his head. He was puffing like a steam engine, his lungs heaving, sucking in air in gasps. "If we make it through this alive," to the girl he managed to hack out between voluminous intakes of breath, "remind me to quit smoking."

"And ruin my childhood dreams of being a pallbearer?" Katya was breathing hard as well. After shooing Boris the bear back into the forest, they had heard vehicles approaching on the dirt road behind them and had taken off running from the family monument around the pond to the cabin.

"And what if we don't make it through this alive?" asked the girl.

"Then I will be less concerned about quitting smoking," said Illya between shallow breaths. He checked his watch then grasped the girl's hand and began surging up the steps. "Come, Katya, we need to find Stalin's hidden treasure fast. The Matrabazi brothers are somewhere behind us."

The girl could notice a narrow shift in Illya's demeanor. His tone was more serious, his eyes shining dark in commitment. Katya knew that, with the killing of his friend, Sasha Petrov, things just got a lot more personal for Illya Podipenko. Together, they dashed through the house to the marshal's study. They slid through the opening in the bookcase to where there was a dark hole leading downward to the unknown, the distinctive sound of whirling helicopter blades and heavy weapon gunfire receding behind them. Illya took a deep breath and started down the steep steps then remembered something important. He ran to the marshal's desk and rummaged the drawers for a flashlight, which he found and tested once. It emitted a strong beam. Satisfied, he then opened the middle drawer of the desk, where he knew that he would find the marshal's favorite pistol, a red-colored Glock G45P 9mm. He checked the breach for a bullet, making sure the safety was on, and tucked it into his waistband. From his pocket, he grabbed his mobile phone and punched in some numbers. He spoke quickly into the phone then hung up.

"That was Putin you called before?" asked the young girl, and Illya nodded that he had.

"Yep. It was time to sound the shofar. And to thank him. I had called him earlier, requesting he send in the troops. By the sound of things, I believe he has done just that. He had said that he would immediately send in some of his OMON Black Berets elite forces to lend us a hand. Many of them were trained in America, by the way."

"So there's that," patiently nodded Katya. "You think maybe we should get going now?"

"Good idea," he replied, stepping past the girl.

He turned on the flashlight and aimed it down into the dark hole. He found a small light switch on the wall just inside the doorway and flicked it on. The room below suddenly blinked into a dull, yellow light. Illya carefully tried out the first step to make sure it was secure. It was a bit wobbly beneath him, but sturdy enough, he decided. Illya took the steps slowly, one at a time. As he went, he could feel Katya's body adhered to his back like a limpet. The further the two descended, the stronger the odor of dank cardboard and subterranean miasma seeped into their nostrils. Suddenly, everything around them seemed damp. Above them hung a wooden sign with painted words. Illya nodded his head toward the sign for Katya to see.

She read the words aloud, "Through me you pass into the grievous city."

"I think we are entering Dante's first ring of hell," observed Illya in a whisper.

"Lucky us," Katya responded. "You had no idea this subterranean room existed?"

"No."

She joined the Moscow investigator on the concrete floor. "This is Stalin's hidden treasure?" she asked Illya with disappointed befuddlement. They stood unmoving, peering from corner to corner. The dank room was strewn with dirty cardboard boxes and discarded wooden crates.

"I don't think so," Illya responded. He flipped open the lid of the closest wooden crate. "Good grief," he said, "we've got guns."

"Guns?"

"Yeah, lots of them." Illy reached in the crate and rummaged about.

A moment later, he pulled out a revolver, turned it in his hands, and said, "A Colt Python 357 Magnum." He carefully placed it on the floor then went back to the crate. "A SIG Sauer 9-millimeter," he said, extracting another sidearm then "an old Tokarev TT-30 Soviet semiautomatic pistol," he whistled, "developed in the 1930s as a military service pistol to replace the Nagant M1895 revolver. It was then itself replaced in 1952 by the Makarov pistol. You can't even find the TT-30s anymore, they have been out of production for a long while." Illya was smiling brightly, which made his young companion frown. Finally, he fished out another weapon and clutched it to his chest.

"And here we have the darling of the Great War, the PPSh-41 Soviet open-bolt submachine gun designed by Georgi Shpagin as a cheap and simplified alternative to the PPD-40. It would later be called the 'Burp Gun' because of the sound that it made when fired. It is not much to look at, kind of ugly really, but it could spray lead quickly 900 rounds a minute. My father once told me that he relied on the PPSh-41 in Stalingrad, not as his assassin's weapon but for protection. He used the old Mosin-Nagant bolt-action rifle nicknamed 'Sveta' as his assassin's tool. The PPSh-41 was the main submachine gun of choice until the new AK-47s came along and made the PPSh-41 obsolete."

"Fascinating stuff," Katya responded. "Look, Illya, you know that I adore talking about antiquated Soviet weaponry." Her whispered words tinged with growing impatience. "And I love the smell of gun oil as much as the next girl, but perhaps another time would be better suited, rather than *right now* when we are trying to locate Stalin's cache of untold riches before the Matrabazi's thugs show up and dispatch us like yesterday's newspaper! Just sayin'."

Illya looked up into her face and offered a half-grin. "You are right, of course, my dear girl," he hurried his words, "but look, just one more piece. It's a beauty. A Mauser C96 semiautomatic pistol, manufactured in Germany. Look at this, a box magazine in front of the trigger. Note its long barrel and wooden shoulder stock for stability. And the grip is shaped like a broom handle! It was Mausers the Bolshevik revolutionaries used to execute the imperial Romanov family that shameful night in the Yekaterinburg basement in July 1918."

"And perhaps us today, if we don't get on with it."

"You are right, sorry. I have always had a fascination with guns. Must be the American bloodlines I inherited."

"Must be. Wait, what? You have American bloodlines?"

"It doesn't make me a bad person," Illya stated. "The marshal's great-grandmother was an American from San Francisco. Didn't I never mention that?"

"No, you never mentioned that!" the girl said back to him in a mocking way. "Must have slipped your mind, a little thing like that."

"I guess I thought it really wasn't important."

"Important? Maybe not. But it *is* interesting. And it is part of you, your DNA, what makes you, you. American blood in your veins!"

With his shoe, Illya absently pushed the carton of guns away and, unable to help himself, reached for another of the boxes. He opened the top flaps and stared into the contents. As he did, he told the girl about his great-great-grandfather who was a high-ranking naval officer in the Russian Baltic fleet that went to the United States' aid during the American Civil War. At the time, America was at its most vulnerable and desperately in need of a friend. Both England and France were conspiring against the United States for they feared a united America could grow into a too-powerful nation. So they wanted to keep the country divided, north against the south, and they plotted to intervene on behalf of the confederacy. Both England and France tried to enlist the Russian Empire in their surreptitious anti-American activities, but the Tsar refused and, instead, mobilized the Russian navy. The fleet began arriving in New York harbor and San Francisco in 1863. The Russian ships placed themselves under the command of President Lincoln and operated in synergy of the United States Navy.

"Does your great-great-grandfather, the Russian naval officer, enter this story soon?" the girl asked impatiently, "say before the bad guys come here to kill us?"

Illya continued, "He was part of the fleet that landed in San Francisco and confronted the Confederate cruiser Shenandoah, which then left the area and sailed elsewhere. Americans hailed the Russians as heroes. My great-great-grandfather, while in San Francisco, met a beautiful stage entertainer named Molly McIntyre. They began a torrid romance. Two years later, Molly moved to Moscow, and the couple married and began having children. My great-grandfather was one of them, and the line of American blood in my family began being passed down through the generations."

"I am a sucker for a good love story," Katya breathed out as Illya continued to fish through boxes of guns. Katya uncovered a box containing strange-looking cylinders. "What are these?" she asked Illya.

The Moscow investigator reached over and took one from the box. He turned it in his hands and smiled. "This is a fuse tube," he said at last.

"What is it for?"

"It is one of three elements for an old Soviet RGD-33 stick fragmentation grenade. Unless I miss my guess, in those two boxes over there, you'll find its counterparts. In one box, there will be the warheads and sleeves, and in the other, you'll find spring-loaded handles. The grenade was composed of these three separate pieces that were stored in different crates until use. They were assembled only before combat. The fuses were wrapped in wax paper. The fuse was timed for about four seconds, and the fragmentation kill radius was approximately 15 meters."

Katya continued rummaging through the box. "Look at this one," she said, "this one is different. Looks like an old beer can." Carefully, she handed it over to Illya, who received it with such careful gentleness that the grenade could have been a suckling infant.

"This is another type of a fragmentation grenade, an RG42. Much simpler than the complex RGD-33 stick grenade, contains about 200 grams of TNT explosive charge with a blast radius of about ten meters. These were stockpiled as reserves after the war, but, in the 1980s, there was a move to destroy them because the TNT inside of them was dangerously degrading and the grenades became unsafe."

"So you grew up with dangerous hand grenades right under your feet?" asked the girl.

"So it seems." Illya suddenly chuckled out loud, unable to help himself. "I wasn't aware of it at the time, of course," he replied. "Through all of the years, I didn't even know this cellar room existed!"

Through the dim light, the young girl regarded Illya Podipenko. "How do you know so much about these old weapons?" she asked as if she were alarmed that he did know so much about weaponry from the past.

"My father taught me," he shrugged modestly. "What can I say? He was a collector. Soviet weaponry used during the Great War was his passion."

"That's all-time bad," bellowed the girl, "these grenades are old and dangerous and yet your father stored them under your feet without ever telling you!"

"In fairness," Illya conceded the point, "they were under his feet too and Inna's. Apparently, my father wasn't too concerned about them actually exploding."

Katya glanced about the room, finally saying, "And you don't believe that these weapons are part of the Stalin hidden treasures?" A questioning frown furrowed her brow.

"No. Oh, I suppose they might be worth a little money to another collector, but this is not what we are looking for. What we are looking for is worth millions and millions, even billions, apparently."

"That's true," uttered Katya. "So where is it?"

"Good question," Illya was on his feet, peering about the small, dank room. His eyes inspected the four walls. "I am guessing we are looking for another secret room," he finally said.

He noticed a double-file cabinet against the far wall. "Come here, Katya," he said, "help me move this."

The two worked together to slide the file cabinet, lighter than Illya had anticipated, across the concrete floor, just far enough to uncover an electronic keypad on the wall behind them. They stared quietly at the red-and-green blinking lights then turned their gaze on each other.

"So you know the code for the pad?" Katya asked Illya.

"No," Illya shook his head side to side, "but I am sure my father left a clue. Search the drawers of the file cabinets."

Katya began sliding the drawers open one at a time. After a moment, she said, "Seems they are empty. Nothing in them."

Illya looked at her. "Did you try the fourth drawer?"

"Not yet, why do you say the fourth drawer?"

"Remember, the sign we read on the wall at the top of the stairwell. It said, 'Abandon all hope, you who enter here. Look for four.'"

Katya quickly complied. "Look here," she said, pulling two tan folders from the fourth drawer down and handed them to Illya.

"Empty," said Illya, flipping each open. He seemed disappointed. He was handing them back over to the girl when he noticed something. He turned the folders on their side and saw that each folder had been labeled. It was then he allowed a smile and a chuckle.

"Why are you laughing?" asked Katya.

"Because my father left us a clue about how to get into the hidden room."

"What clue?"

"These folders may be empty but they are labeled." He turned them so Katya could see. She read what the marshal had labeled them out loud. "Stalingrad," she said at first then added, "Favorite." She frowned and looked over at Illya. "This means something to you?" she asked.

"It does, *only* to me," he responded, "that is the beauty of it. Up until now, it has been possible that someone could have solved all of the clues just like we did. Difficult but possible. But these two new clues are ones that *only* I would know the answers to, no one else. And the marshal was well aware of that. The clues need to be changed to numerals that we will input on the keypad."

"So what do these clues mean to you? What does Stalingrad mean?"

"Numerically, it translates to 153. That is the number of days my father served in the rubble of Stalingrad. It was a number he would never forget. He would often tell me that even though he was the Soviet Union's most famous boy assassin, there wasn't a day that passed in war-torn Stalingrad that he didn't fear for his life amid all of the death and destruction around him. Who could blame him? Remember, he was really just a young kid at the time. He couldn't wait to get out of there and come home. He counted the days by making notches on the wooden butt of his rifle. He served in Stalingrad for 153 days before Stalin hand-selected him to join his personal staff at the Kuntsevo *dacha*."

"So 153 is our number," she said to Illya, and the militiaman nodded his head. "What about the second file folder labeled *Favorite*? Got a number for that one?"

"I certainly do."

"Care to share?" she asked, looking at him carefully.

He paused a moment to recall then stated, "Of course. The number is twelve."

"Twelve? How do you get that?"

"Simple. That was my father's favorite number. He often told me that. He would say that twelve was almost the perfect number There are twelve months in a year, twelve signs of the zodiac, twelve gods of Olympus, twelve labors of Hercules, twelve tribes of Israel, and twelve apostles of Christ, you get the idea."

The girl's face searched his. At last, she said, "So we're looking at a number to punch in the keypad as, uh, 15312?"

Illya merely nodded his head, winked at the girl, then went to work. He punched in the number and almost immediately heard the *pfffft* of a pneumatic release as the door slid open in front of them. A fluorescent tube automatically flickered to life on the ceiling of the room. Illya and the girl peered slowly around the corner of the doorway. The bright glow of the room made each of them blink and squint from the blinding, shimmering light reflecting off what seemed like a rolling hill of gold bars.

The two entered the room, their heads spooling around the environs, their eyes round, mouths agape. They were standing among five different skids of gold bars, each skid stacked about a meter high, like bricks in a building.

"Wow, do you friggin' believe this?" Katya inquired.

Illya pointed to the far wall where there were several trunks on the floor lining the wall. One by one, he threw open the lids to the trunks, which were made of lead. Each trunk's content was different than the previous one. One contained gold coins, another paper rubles, yet another thousands of diamonds. There were similar trunks filled with emeralds and rubies.

"Fuck me," whispered Katya into Illya's ear.

"Excellent point," responded the man, "well said."

"I want some."

"Help yourself."

"Stalin apparently tucked away a tidy bit for a rainy day. The number four," Illya threw out, remembering.

Katya nodded. "The fourth ring of hell. In Dante's *Inferno*. The ring of greed."

"Apparently so, it's all right here," Illya breathed out. He was about to add something when at once he thrust out an arm and with his hand squeezed the girl's arm. He put a finger to his lips. "Shh," he said. "Listen."

Cocking their heads, straining to hear, they could recognize the sound of heavy footsteps crossing the room above their heads then the creaking of the wooden steps that led down to where they were in the cellar of the *dacha*. Whoever it was, Illya realized, they were moving quickly. He and young Katya needed to seek cover immediately. His eyes rapidly cast about the room scanning the walls and possible nooks looking for hiding places, at last settling on one of the chest-high rectangular, flat-topped skids of gold right in front of them. It wasn't great, but it at least gave them a solid, three-foot-tall protective wall to crouch behind.

He was leading the girl to the edge of the skiff of gold bars when suddenly he felt a snapping sting in his left shoulder. The force sent him tumbling backward into several cardboard cartons stacked against the close by wall. He hit these with a crash, causing his knees to buckle, and his body hit the ground so unprotected that he yelped out and the air whooshed from his lungs.

"Illya!" the girl cried out. She was crouched down beside him. "Good Lord, you're hit," she said. She saw his shirt and jacket leaking blood at the shoulder.

"No, no, I'm fine, Katya, it just nicked me. It looks worse than it actually is. Just kind of stunned me." Adrenaline pumping, he used his forearms to pull himself across the floor. "Help me get behind the wall of gold for protection and we will be fine."

As Illya was pulling himself across the floor toward the skiff of gold bricks, several other shots rang out, and bullets pinged across the floor and walls around him and Katya.

"Motherfucker!" the girl screamed out.

She saw the 9 mm automatic pistol in Illya's waistband and yanked it out. She pitched herself up on an elbow and leaned against the gold protective barrier. Then she lifted her hand holding the gun above the barrier of gold and relentlessly squeezed the trigger, sending a surge of unaimed bullets randomly toward the other end of the mountain of gold bars. The roar in the small room was deafening. Carefully, Illya reached out a hand and gently grasped for the girl's hand holding the pistol.

"Easy, easy," he whispered to her. "I don't think you are hitting anything."

As if suddenly awakened, the girl said "Oh, shit, sorry, my bad, that's on me" and quickly brought the gun in close to her body. Illya smiled and gave her knee and soft pat.

"Let's find out exactly who we are dealing with," the militiaman said. "Who's there?" he yelled out. "What do you want?"

After a long moment of silence, a voice replied, "We are here for the treasure, of course. But also to kill you."

"Dato, is that you?" Illya shouted out. "You escaped the shootout in your warehouse in America. You then traveled to Russia? I'm impressed." He nodded to Katya, winked an eye, and offered a thumbs-up gesture as if to indicate so far things were going well. "Welcome to Dante's fourth ring of hell," he said, "the ring of greed."

"Of course, it is me, idiot! I am with my brother Zaza now. You would be smart to lay your weapons down and talk with us."

"Perhaps there is a way out for you," a second voice called out in horribly broken English. Illya and Katya assumed that it was the voice of the older brother Zaza. "I have brought many of my men with me. They are outside. Perhaps there is a way forward to even keeping some of the gold for yourself. After all, we are not unreasonable men even though you did kill three of our brothers in America."

"Yeah, sorry about that," Illya responded. "Things just seemed to spin out of hand. It happens." He winked once more at Katya and beckoned her closer. He whispered something in her ear. The girl thought perhaps she had misunderstood, so she said back in a whisper of her own, "You want me to shoot out the overhead lights?" she waved with the gun in the direction of the three side-by-side, long fluorescent tubes on the ceiling above the skid of gold.

He nodded, yes, then yelled out, "Your man killed a very good friend of mine this morning, Dato. I hold you and your brother personally accountable for that."

The answer came back, "You are in no position to do so, it seems to me."

"We'll see about that," Illya said, nodding toward the girl, who with Illya's automatic pistol calmly took aim at the fluorescent lights overhead. She pulled the trigger, and a second later, the lights cracked and flickered and went to darkness.

The room went to black, and the sudden change made Dato and his older brother begin firing their automatic weapons from their end of the skid of gold.

Squatting at the other end, Illya drew out an arm and through the dark pulled Katya closer to him. "Give me the pistol," he whispered to her. She complied then heard Illya say, "How are your powers of observation?"

"What?" she said questioningly.

"Which wrist does Dato wear his watch on?" he wanted to know.

"What?"

"The expensive watch he was so proud of in the warehouse in America. Left wrist or right? It's your call."

He could feel the girl staring wide-eyed at him through the dark. "Right wrist," at last she responded, unsure.

"Right wrist? Are you certain? It makes a difference where I aim."

"Aim? You are aiming your pistol at him?"

"I am. Based on where the glowing dial of his watch is on his wrist, I will calculate where to aim to hit his body. So right wrist?"

"Well, I believe so. Actually, I'm not certain. It's my best guess. We have a fifty-fifty shot, correct, right or left?"

"Yes, we do." Illya went quiet a moment.

"Then the right one."

"Right one it is," responded Illya.

Through the dark, he was honing in on the green glow in front of him. He could see the glowing radium dial of Dato Matrabazi's expensive watch jigging around as if the man on the other end of the gold was himself aiming a gun through the pitch. Illya spent another couple of seconds calculating where the man's body likely was in relation to the watch on his wrist. Then he pulled the trigger of his pistol. In the small room, it reported like a thunderclap, and it brought immediate results. A man loudly started screaming out curse words in Georgian, which meant Illya couldn't understand them.

But Katya could, and Illya asked for a rough translation.

"Well, obviously, he is quite upset," began the girl, "your shot was successful. I think you hit him in the upper arm or shoulder. He is in agony and screaming out Georgian curse words at you, quite an impressive stream of expletives. *Motherfucker*, he said, and *cocksucker*, too, for starters. Then he added *shithead*. Let's see, he challenged your mother's moral background, called you a female dog, and questioned your sexuality. Those are the highlights."

"He certainly seems angry," Illya softly observed. "I would have thought he'd have called me a bastard."

"Nope, oh, wait, yep, he just now added *bastard* to his list. He gets high marks for being thorough. Now the other one has started up screaming in Georgian, and, oh my, he called you a… I know this sounds crazy…but I swear he said…penis pincher."

"A what?"

"A penis pincher."

"Are you sure?"

"Pretty sure."

"I don't even know what that means."

"Me neither…but I *like* it. They seem pretty upset. I think they are about to charge us through the dark, guns blazing."

"Then we must act quickly," Illya responded. "Do you have your rucksack?"

"I do," Katya answered.

"Good. Be a good girl and reach in and pull out the RG-42 grenade, will you?"

"The *what*?" Katya inquired after a silence.

Illya answered matter-of-factly, "The RG-42, you know, the hand grenade from my father's collection. The one that looks like a rusty beer can. I put one in your backpack."

"You *what*? You put an old, unstable grenade in my backpack and didn't bother telling me? The very type of grenade the Red Army was gathering and destroying because the 200 grams of TNT inside it is degrading and unsafe and could explode at any time?" Through the blackness, he could feel Katya's unfathomable gaze upon him.

"That's the one, and perhaps they exaggerated," Illya quietly conceded. "I didn't think you'd mind. I figured it might become in useful at some point. Plus, I always believed the reports of the old grenades exploding was mostly a myth."

"*Mostly?*"

"Well, you can never really tell, can you? Besides, I had confidence in you. I didn't think you would let it explode. You're better than that."

"I appreciate the confidence," responded the girl dishearteningly. "Here's your grenade," she said, pushing her hand with her fingers wrapped around the cylindrical stamped-metal can through the dark.

Illya felt for it, and his finger reached through the dark when suddenly he felt the grenade slipping away.

"Wait a minute," said the girl.

"What?"

"I get to throw this."

"Pardon?"

"I've earned the right to be the one to toss the grenade. After all, it was my grandfather they killed and my uncle they attacked."

The man was quiet a moment. "Fair point," finally, conceded Illya Podipenko in a whisper. "Do you know how to remove the pin from the grenade?"

"A thousand percent. In theory."

"What about in actuality?"

"Not a clue."

Illya was thinking. "Okay, how about this. When you are ready, I will remove the pin and hand the grenade to you. You will have about three seconds to throw it after the pin is removed. Be sure not to accidentally drop the grenade at our feet when I am handing it to you or I will probably need a fresh pair of underwear."

"Yeah, awesome, it was good right up to the last part," the girl replied.

Illya chuckled. In the dark, he was rummaging through the girl's backpack. "Ah, here we are, a gun for you, you know, just in case."

"In case of what?"

"In case you feel an urge to fill the bad guys with lead before they attempt to kill us."

"I like where your head is right now," she whispered.

Illya drew his body closer to the girl. "Okay, listen," he said in a low voice, "after you throw the grenade, immediately curl up on the ground hard against this skid of gold bars. Cover your ears. I will drop on top of you to protect you."

She went quiet a moment. "*Now?* Now you will drop on top of me. I have been trying to get you to do that for a friggin' week!"

"Funny," answered Illya through the dark. "Are you ready?"

"Wait a moment," answered the girl. "Is it okay if I say something to the bad guys before I nail them with the grenade?"

"Must you?"

"Well, it seems appropriate. It's about Alice."

"Alice? Well, then, by all means."

Illya could feel the girl shift her weight, peering above the stack of gold bars. "Hey, ass clowns," she called out in the dark, "you ever read Alice?"

"What?" after a moment came the reply.

"Alice," Katya repeated demonstratively as if to a slow child, "you know, the classic books by Lewis Carroll. Ever read them?"

There was silence. Then a voice answered. "We are going to enjoy killing you and the old man."

"Listen and learn," responded the girl, her voice rising. "Alice asked the White Rabbit, 'How long is forever?' Do you know what the White Rabbit answered?"

"You are insane, young lady," one of the men yelled out.

"It is a simple question," said Katya with disappointment in her voice. "How long is forever?"

"We don't know."

Katya nudged Illya. He pulled the pin and handed the grenade to the girl.

Katya took it in her hand then called out, "When Alice asked the White Rabbit 'How long is forever?' the White Rabbit answered, 'Sometimes just one second.'"

With that, Katya, as if skipping a stone across a river, skimmed the grenade hard across the top of the skid of gold. In the dark, she could hear the grenade skittering across the top of the gold bars. It sounded like when the grenade reached the opposite end of the skid it slammed up against the wall directly behind the two Matrabazi brothers then fell to the floor at their feet. Katya immediately dropped to the concrete floor and curled up as if she were a small child. She covered her ears as Illya had instructed her then felt the full weight of his body enveloping hers from above.

The explosion was intense. The room erupted into a roar of sound and vibrations. Debris snapped through the air like buckshot. The heavy skid of gold seemed to shift a couple of inches. The air grew thick with smoke and gold dust that stung the eyes. Illya and the girl slowly clambered to their feet, coughing in spasms, waving the detritus away with their hands. They each had ringing in their ears and felt dizzy. Illya dug for the flashlight. Through the fog of the explosion, they could see a hole in the wall just on the other side of the skid of gold bars. It was still smoking.

"Are you okay?" Illya asked the girl.

"I'm fine, no worries," she answered with a cough. "I think I swallowed some gold dust."

"Not to worry," Illya tried a comforting tone. "In the middle ages, people actually drank powdered gold to relieve muscle pain."

"Yeah? What was their life expectancy back then? Twelve?" She hacked into her arm.

She pointed to an item on top of the skid of gold. "Look, Illya, what is that over there?"

"Where, next to that blown-off arm?"

"No, the arm itself! Apparently, it's from one of the bad guys. If you wrap in plastic and throw it in the back seat of your car, you'll have a matched set."

"I do like order," he nodded to the girl, "must be an age thing."

Katya was about to add something else when she and Illya each heard a sound coming from the room's new hole in the wall. Simultaneously, each spun around toward the hole, wielding pistols in their hands.

They heard a voice say "Knock, knock."

They did not respond and kept their guns leveled in front of them. Illya pulled out a flashlight and pointed it at the man, who was squinting and turning his head away from the bright light.

Illya and the girl recognized the man filling the hole in the wall and lowered their weapons.

The intruder coughed once then said, "Have I come at a bad time?"

The voice belonged to Vladimir Vladimirovich Putin.

EPILOGUE

Time passed.

Illya Podipenko thought he would not be returning to Moscow for at least two years, not until after he had finished his twenty-four-month obligation of lecturing new recruits at the FBI office in New York. His popular lecture, originally about the solving of the Rasputin case and the recovery of the Imperial Fabergé eggs, now had grown to also include the recovery of Stalin's hidden treasures, which had been since its discovery evaluated at nearly three billion US dollars.

President Putin had insisted that Illya and Katya take some of the recovered diamonds and other gemstones back to the United States with them as a "thank you" from the Russian people for a heroic job well done. But the two declined the president's generous offer although Illya did mention that he would like to take his father's chess set home with him, for sentimental reasons, as well as, puzzling, a salt-and-pepper set. He didn't think it necessary to reveal that several of the chess pieces and salt and pepper shakers had dozens and dozens of diamonds hidden within them.

Quite unexpectedly, nearly a year following the discovery of Stalin's hidden treasures in his father's secret cellar room, Illya was summoned back to Moscow by President Putin himself, who arranged a military transport for him. To Illya's surprise, and some embarrassment, a hero's welcome was awaiting him in Moscow, complete with a parade through Red Square and a special, nationally televised presentation at the unveiling of the new Stalin's Secret Treasures' Exhibit at the National Historical Museum.

The new exhibit was under the creation and direction of the ever-distressed Viktor Marchenko, who, when Illya now saw him, caused the investigator to gasp aloud. The museum curator looked to be on death's doorstep, his sweating face bleached of color and his body so skeletal that Illya thought he could see bones protruding through the skin. Viktor was sweating as if a stroke were imminent, and he was clutching to his chest a crumpled issue of *Pravda*, which declared in oversized headlines "Hero Returns to Moscow to Dedicate New Exhibit." It was clear to Illya that his friend Viktor had been under great pressure to quickly finish the new exhibit. It was actually an extension of the original Rasputin exhibit that featured the recovered Romanov jewelry and Imperial eggs. The new exhibit had examples from Stalin's personal cache of gold and jewelry. There were plenty of photographs, and a nice photo montage of both Sasha Petrov and Katya Tevoradze with written descriptions of their important roles in the recovery of the secret Stalin treasures. The written descriptions did not include the roles that Katya's grandfather and uncle played in their 1953 attempted murder of Stalin, thus causing the leader's fatal stroke, nor Illya's famous marshal father's role in planning everything and that for a short time he was actually an American spy. Putin and Viktor Marchenko readily agreed with him, thought that there was not a need to uselessly muddy the waters on Illya Podipenko's heroic accomplishments.

At the exhibit's official public unveiling, which was packed with applauding and appreciative Muscovites and media from around the world, President Putin said many nice words about those involved, especially his Moscow investigator, Illya Podipenko, who, Putin announced, upon his permanent return to Russia in little more than a year would be promoted to chief investigator of the Moscow militia's Criminal Investigations Division. Illya was, of course, quietly modest by all the attention he was receiving, but Putin gave the man a big hug, and they stood smiling for the cameras hand-in-hand, arms raised together in the air, in front of the new exhibit, broad smiles beaming for the news media. They posed in front of the statue of Investigator Podipenko, which had been moved to a more prominent location in front of the exhibit's entrance. Viktor Marchenko also informed Illya that a larger version of the statue had been commissioned for placement outside in the Alexander Gardens along the western Kremlin wall.

When the festivities had concluded, a distinguished-looking gentleman with silver hair, round spectacles, and a kind-speaking voice approached Illya Podipenko and offered his hand in friendship. He said his name was Ivan Petrov and that he was Sasha Petrov's older brother. He assured Illya that Sasha held him in highest regard and had spoken of him often, always in the fondest of terms. He spoke about how much Sasha had missed Illya when the militia investigator was away in America and how Sasha enjoyed visiting Inna out at the country *dacha* to help her out with chores, feed Boris the bear, and how he enjoyed the serenity of sitting with a cup of tea at the beautiful memorial Illya had constructed for his parents and how he would sit for hours in solitude gazing out at the field and the flowers and the river in the distance and listen to nature all around him and think about his friend so far away in New York. At the end of the conversation, the two men warmly shook hands, and Illya suddenly pulled Sasha Petrov's brother to his chest. Illya thought about his friend Sasha, and both men were brought to tears.

Katya Tevoradze had, of course, been invited to return to Moscow with Illya to take part in the ceremonies, but she kindly declined the offer. Circumstances had dramatically changed for the irrepressible, young girl upon her arrival back in the United States. Foremost, she had to attend to her uncle Grisha before he eventually passed away in his sleep in a hospital bed three months after Katya's return to the United States. He had never awoken from his coma. He passed peacefully without pain, the doctors assured her.

But there was also good news in Katya's return to the United States. She began a loving relationship with young FBI Agent Noah Carter. She sold her house on Brightwater Court in Brighton Beach, the modest house with so many memories, the home where she had grown up in Little Odessa with her grandfather Sandro and her uncle Grisha.

The happy couple moved in together in a picturesque house they bought in Stamford, Connecticut, and commuted to their jobs in the city, Noah to FBI New York headquarters and Katya to a private school on Manhattan's Upper East Side, where she taught third graders. For his part, Illya Podipenko easily slipped back into the normalcy of the solitary life he knew before ever meeting the funny, unpredictable, and intelligent girl named Katya Tevoradze.

Sadly, Katya and Illya, who had grown so close with their shared adventure of uncovering Stalin's hidden treasures, rarely saw each other upon their return to everyday life in the United States. However, they did manage one memorable meeting on the one-year anniversary of their first fateful encounter on that park bench in Central Park. It was a wonderful day, much like the day that they had first met with a blue sky and puffy clouds and a wind carrying the warmth of early summer. On that special occasion, they laughed, held hands, watched the kids' sailboats skip across the Conservatory Water, drank champagne, and wandered over to the fanciful sculpture of the famous characters from *Alice's Adventures in Wonderland*, where they stood quietly together, remembering.

It was here, on that special first anniversary day, in that setting, with Alice's crazy companions as witnesses, that Katya first told Illya that she was pregnant. She and Noah Carter were expecting the arrival, Katya excitedly told him, shortly after the first of the year. They were planning on getting married around Thanksgiving, and they wanted Illya to perform double duty, to both give away the bride and be Noah Carter's best man at the wedding.

Upon hearing this, Illya pulled her close to him, tears in his eyes. He warmly kissed her on top of the head and told her how proud he was of her and how happy he was for both she and his friend, Noah. Through her own tears, Katya informed him that, if the baby was a boy, they had already decided that they were going to name him Illya.

So it was that on Christmas Eve of that year, now husband and wife, Noah and Katya Carter, sent a limousine to Illya's flat near the university to escort him to their house out I-95 to Fairfield County on Long Island Sound in order to have a holiday dinner with the couple.

The man from Moscow sat back comfortably in the rear seat of the limo and took advantage of the chilled champagne awaiting him. He warmly peered out of the window as the city morphed into suburbs, and he noticed that the further they traveled away from the city, the more the suburban yards grew in size and the beautiful houses became grander still. Children squealed in delight as they swung from playsets while their dogs raced around them wagging their tails and yapping protectively.

Illya watched for a while before finally, sighing deeply, he lay his head back against the soft leather of the limo's rear seat and closed his eyes. In his mind's eye, as it so often happened, he saw flashing images, changing snapshots of his wonderful adventure with the girl, Katya Tevoradze, in both New York and Moscow. He thought about that first day when she surprised him on the bench in Central Park, their stroll through Little Odessa, meeting Uncle Grisha and learning his secret of Stalin's hidden treasure, their trip to the Statue of Liberty and eventually to Moscow. He thought about his friend FBI Agent Noah Carter and the bad guys, Matrabazi brothers, and President Putin and his Moscow friend, Sasha Petrov, and the kind old lady Inessa and even Boris the bear. But mostly, he thought about Katya Tevoradze and her youthful energy and her unquenchable spirit and her courage in the face of the enemy. He thought about her beautiful smile and her infectious laugh and her cold feet and her unrelenting appetite. And while these images were flashing in his head, the limo at once pulled into the driveway of a well-kept modest two-story house, painted white with green shutters, and Illya blinked open his eyes, unsure whether or not he had actually nodded off.

The limo's chauffeur immediately got out of the car and ran around to open Illya's door for him. Illya thanked the man, who looked vaguely familiar, and then he noticed the shoulder holster the man was wearing under his jacket. He realized that the driver likely was a young aspiring agent who worked for Noah Carter at the FBI.

Illya climbed the steps of the front porch, which was decorated with red poinsettia plants all around. Before ringing the doorbell, he grandly inhaled the fresh air of the country and the sweet aroma of woodsmoke drifting from the chimney above him. He paused to admire the serenity and beauty surrounding him, including several giant oak and elm trees in the front yard. The champagne from the limo brought warmth to his body, warding off the seasonal chill in the air.

Before Illya had a chance to ring the doorbell, the door flew open, and Katya let out a scream of joy, pulling the man into the house and throwing her arms around his chest.

"Illya," she bellowed out, "I have missed you! Come in, please!"

With the girl pulling him by his lapels, he stumbled into the foyer, peering around the open rooms, all so warm and inviting. He nodded toward the fireplace where logs were cracking with orange sparks.

"You don't have a fireplace poker lurking in there, do you?" he whispered fretfully.

Katya laughed. "As a matter of fact, there is a poker in there, but it is strictly for poking burning logs. No more giants to slay, thank goodness."

"Good to know." Illya smiled. From behind his back, he suddenly produced a bouquet of roses. Katya took them from him and held them to her nose.

"Illya," she said, "they are beautiful! You shouldn't have." She paused a moment, looking at them in her hand. "And there is an odd number, too, in the Russian way."

Illya nodded. "I thought it best not to bring bad luck into your house with an even number of flowers."

"Old school. I love it!" Katya shouted out.

In his other hand, the man produced a large red-and-white box.

Katya looked at the box with widened eyes. "Lee Sims Chocolates, they're the best!" she said enthusiastically. "Illya, you are going to make me fatter than I already am. Here, feel," she said, taking one of Illya's hands and laying it on top of her protruding belly.

He gave the woman's belly a few kind pats. "You are not fat, my dear Katya," he whispered. "You are beautiful as ever. You are absolutely glowing. I am so happy for you and Noah. You are going to be a great mother."

"Thank you, Illya," the woman said. She hugged him against her body and reached up to give his cheek a kiss. She remained in his arms for a couple of quiet moments until a voice called out.

"Hey, hey, what's going on in there," said Noah Carter. "Careful now, that's my lady you are holding so close. She's already pregnant, you know." Noah, in a red sweater and khakis, was carrying a silver tray with drinks on it. "Here, try this," he said, grinning, handing one to Illya. "This will get your holiday season started in the right direction."

Illya accepted a tall glass and took a sip.

"Oh, my," his eyes widened, "that is some drink! What do you call it?"

"'*Death in the Afternoon.*' Not much of a holiday-sounding drink, I'll grant you that. Supposedly invented by the author Ernest Hemingway while living on the left bank of Paris. It is part absinthe and part champagne. The lemon wedge is for garnish. Be careful, they will sneak up on you. Forewarned is forearmed."

Holding the glass in his hand, Illya followed the couple into a comfortable living room decorated for the holidays with green wreaths all around and red stockings hanging from the fireplace mantle. The room smelled wonderfully of fragrant spices and pine scents while Christmas tunes played quietly in the background.

The three sat down, on large couches around a marble square-top table. They sipped their drinks and engaged in small talk and enjoyed the warmth of the fire and companionship for a while until suddenly Illya heard the doorbell ring. At that point, Noah Carter had disappeared to freshen up his drink and Katya had hefted her wide body from the couch to announce she needed to go to the kitchen to check on how dinner was coming along. "Would you answer the front door for us?" she asked Illya.

"Of course," the man replied, easily striding across the room to the front foyer, his drink in his hand. He reached for the front doorknob, distressingly ill-prepared to welcome who was on the other side of the door.

He opened the door and stared into a pair of the most beautiful blue eyes he had ever seen. Such was the shock that it caused him to suck in his breath and stumble three steps backward, fighting to catch his balance so he would not fall down or spill his drink.

"Illya!" the girl screamed, thrusting out her arms to reel in the staggering investigator.

It was Lena Sharapova.

She reached out and grabbed onto Illya, determinedly clasping his body to her chest. She held him tight, the inspector's nose crushed up against the woman's ample cleavage. The sweet scent of perfume fluttered his eyelids to the point that he thought fainting a possibility.

"Illya, it is me, Lena! Are you surprised?"

"Very," he managed to eke out, his lips crushed against the woman's chest. "What a wonderful surprise, Lena. You are looking wonderful, beautiful as ever." He wasn't lying. She had pale skin, high cheekbones, full lips, breeding hips, and magnificently luminous eyes.

"Why, thank you, Illya, what a nice thing to say!"

The investigator attempted to wrestled out of the bear hug, but for the moment, Lena Sharapova seemed disinclined to loosen her grip on the man.

"I have missed you so, Illya. I should be upset with you," Lena stated at last, scoldingly. "You haven't called or come by in over a year. Not since our last English lesson. Are you still watching *The Simpsons* to learn the language?"

"I am," Illya confirmed, at last succeeding in escaping Lena's iron grip on him. He stepped back, cleared his throat, and attempted to speak in a voice approximating Homer Simpson's, 'Oh, Lisa, trying is just the first step toward failure.' There," he smiled, satisfied at his effort, "how was that?"

The woman put her hands to her mouth and laughed heartily. "That was excellent, Illya!" she called out. "Your English was perfect!"

"English? Who needs that? I'm never going to England." Illya offered another Homer Simpson quote, bringing another round of belly laughs from Lena Sharapova.

"Stop it, Illya, you are making me hurt!" She was bent at the waist, attempting to catch her breath.

"Lena," a voice came from behind Illya. "Welcome to our home."

It was Katya. She rushed up to the woman and embraced her.

"Thank you so much for inviting me, Katya. It is so nice meeting you at last."

"You are so beautiful, Lena. Even more beautiful than the photographs I've seen."

"And look at *you*, a gorgeous mom-to-be! How exciting!"

The two women interlocked arms as Katya guided her visitor to the living room, Illya trailing behind. They were greeted by Noah Carter dutiful carrying a tray of his special drinks. Following introductory pleasantries, Noah offered Lena a drink from his tray, saying, knotting his brow as if concerned, "As Bogart used to say, 'You are already two drinks behind.'"

Armed with fresh *Death in the Afternoon* cocktails, the four people sat around the living room table chatting and laughing and telling stories from the past, all in good fellowship. Christmas carols and the aroma of baking turkey filled the air. The vibrant conversation carried over to the dinner table, all decorated with holiday flowers and flickering candles. Illya sat directly across from Lena Sharapova and, try as he might, simply could not take his eyes off the woman. She was more beautiful than ever, he thought, with a touch of maturity adding a few sensual lines around her eyes and mouth when she smiled. He was astounded that she still managed to gather most of the light in the room to herself, and she still moved with a smooth, effortless motion like a wraith or a dancer in her youth. Her olive-colored skin was as smooth and perfect as a Lomonosov porcelain figurine.

The genial conversation continued until nearly the end of dinner when Katya inadvertently asked an innocent question that brought the room to an uneasy silence. She had asked Lena Sharapova, "What is married life like?" For some odd reason, she had an ill feeling about the question as soon as the words had left her lips.

Lena was quiet a moment, staring down at the napkin in her lap. At last, she looked up and said in a low voice, "I apologize to you, Katya, I am afraid that I did not tell you the truth when I received your invitation to dinner. I said that my husband would be out of town with diplomat duties tonight. The truth is, I am no longer married. My husband and I divorced several weeks ago. I was too embarrassed to tell you. Again, I apologize."

"Oh, my dear girl," Katya called out, rising from her chair. She skirted the table and came up from behind to give Lena a warm hug. "I am so sorry. I had no idea."

"I understand, Katya, don't fret about it. After the initial shock of it all, I am adjusting fine. I just need to find a new place to stay."

"What do you mean?" Katya returned to her chair.

"As of yesterday, I am out on the street. We sold our home in Lindenhurst. The new owners moved in yesterday. I put my things in storage, and for now, I am living in a hotel in midtown. It's not so bad, I guess. I just need to find a place."

Illya looked across the table at the young woman. His face was solemn. "I am so sorry," was all he could manage to say. His chest ached. He sighed deeply then said without first thinking things through, "You can stay with me, Lena, at least until you find your own place. My flat is three times the size that I need.

There is plenty of room for another person. You wouldn't even have to see me all that much."

"Illya, that's a brilliant idea!" Katya shouted out. Her eyes lit brightly "I've been to his flat, Lena. It's huge. It is near Columbia University. It would be perfect for you, at least temporarily."

"Well, I don't know. I don't want to be a burden…"

In an instant, the three other people at the table chimed in their opinions, all at the same time, all encouraging Lena Sharapova to take Illya up on his kind offer. And, in the end, she relented, smiling sheepishly and somehow seductively across the table at the Moscow investigator.

"I suppose we could give it a try," she said at last. "But, Illya, you must be honest with me and tell this fat cow when I become a bother to you. I insist."

"I don't think it possible that you could ever become a burden to Illya." Katya chuckled to Lena. "Besides, you will be good for him. He shouldn't be all alone like he is. He has nobody. It is not healthy for him. I once read that the absence of friends can be just as dangerous as smoking. Scientists have found a connection between loneliness and the level of protein coagulation that can cause a heart attack or a stroke. And we certainly don't want that for our Moscow friend here."

And with that, quite extraordinarily, the topic came to a close and the matter seemed settled, causing a sudden relaxation of everyone at the table, and the conversation easily drifted back to old times and shared adventures, one story easily melding into the next.

When it came time to leave, Illya and Lena gathered their things and wobbled into the foyer, feeling the effects of Hemingway's *Death in the Afternoon* cocktails. Illya helped his new roommate with her jacket then turned to embrace the hostess.

"Thank you, my darling Katya," he said in a low voice to the woman.

"Me? For what?"

"For everything. For remembering this lonely old man on Christmas, for inviting me here to your lovely home, for a wonderful dinner and great companionship. And for deviously arranging for Lena to reenter my life."

He leaned in and kissed Katya on the forehead. "You were an amazing young girl, and now you have matured into an incredible young woman. I am so proud of you."

"Thank you, my dear Illya. That is so nice of you to say. I hope I have grown up a bit since our little adventure together. It's sad sometimes, but we all must move on." She lifted her face in a sweet expression. "You remember what our friend Alice said, don't you?"

"Educate me."

She said, "It's no use going back to yesterday, I was a different person then."

ABOUT THE AUTHOR

W. H. Mefford was born in Cincinnati, Ohio, and is a journalism graduate of the University of Arizona in Tucson, Arizona.

A former news reporter for Scripps-Howard and UPI, Mr. Mefford is currently an award-winning marketing-public relations consultant specializing in the entertainment and special events fields.

Mr. Mefford is the author of six books (five international suspense thrillers) *The Rasputin Stain*, *The Sydney Access*, *Thunder Down Under*, *The President's Brother*, *Games of 80*, and *Trump: 10 Years with the Bengals* (nonfiction).

Currently living in the Cincinnati, Mr. Mefford, his wife, Marnie and three children—Allyssa, Michael, and Matthew—lived in Sydney, Australia, for four years in the mid-1980s before returning to the US.